HEART
OF THE
SUMMER
QUEEN

HOLLY ROSE

Heart
OF THE
Summer
Queen

HOLLY ROSE

ALSO BY HOLLY ROSE

Legends of Imyria
Ashes of Aether
Storm of Shadows
Tears of Twilight (2024)

Winterspell
Bride of the Winter King
Heart of the Summer Queen

Learn more at:
www.hollyrosebooks.com

Copyright © 2024 by Holly Rose

Published by Red Spark Press

The right of Holly Rose to be identified as the author of this work has been asserted in accordance with the Copyright, Designs and Patents Act 1988.

Cover illustration by Till and Dill
https://www.tillanddill.com/

ISBN (hardcover): 978-1-914503-20-7
ISBN (paperback): 978-1-914503-19-1
ISBN (eBook): 978-1-914503-18-4

To Millie.
Forever in our hearts.

Chapter 1

Last night, I tried to kill my husband.

And I failed.

Now I sit alone in these icy chambers, while my sister's death goes unavenged.

I draw my knees to my chest and pull my furs around me, shivering though I don't feel the cold. I haven't since my first night in the Crystal Palace, when the Winter King chose me as his bride. He visited my room in the dead of night and kissed me, breathing winter into me. Only through the burning hatred within did I overcome his magic.

After that, he claimed I was his Summer Queen and insisted on marrying me for a purpose. One I'll now never know.

But regardless of what he needs from me, surely a wife who tried to assassinate him can't be suitable? And if I'm no longer useful, it's only a matter of time before he comes to kill me.

I've thought about running. Of course I have. But I can't. After the king threw me onto my bed, he raised his hand and conjured a wall to seal the passage into his chambers. When he left, I stayed where I was for a long while, chained in place by the weight of my failure, until sense penetrated the numbness. I leaped to my feet and raced across to the doors on the opposite side of the room—my only other exit.

But they were locked.

I pushed down on the handles as hard as I could, and when that didn't work, I dug my nails into the gap between the doors, pulling and pulling. I even tried to dismantle the comb on my vanity, intending to use its tines as lock picks, but none came loose. And I have no weapon inside my room. Nothing I can use to defend myself. The dagger I thrust into the king's chest is in his chambers. Perhaps still on the floor, coated in his blood.

My hands tremble as they recall the weight of the blade, the way it sank into his flesh. The blood which soaked my fingers. The clink as my dagger reached his frozen heart. Unable to fracture it.

Tears flood my cheeks, as they have a thousand times this night. My eyes are raw and gritty, as if sand scrapes them.

If only my dagger worked.

If only I didn't try to kill him.

I don't know which I wish were true: whether the Winter King was dead or whether I never needed to kill him. My mind is too weary to process all the chaotic emotions of tonight.

I lift my head and look toward the window across from my bed, where moonlight pours into my room. Setting aside my furs, I tiptoe across to it, and my steps are weightless, as if I'm treading on air.

Shaking, I reach for the latches and push open the window as far as it will go. I lean out and stare at the gardens.

Usually, the palace is barren of color, but not tonight. For our wedding, the king ordered for the palace to be decorated with the colors of summer, and that extended to the gardens. Banners and flowers and ribbons are strewn everywhere, silvered by the moon.

My stomach constricts as the image of our wedding ceremony plays through my mind. Of the vows we spoke.

Of the wedding night we shared.

I grip the window ledge so hard it hurts, trying to banish that memory. It's the most painful one of all.

I push my shoulders further through the window, straining my neck to get a good look at the wall. But it's as I feared. The stones are too smooth to climb safely, and while I have previously scaled the wall at the gardens' perimeter, it's a fraction of the palace's height. Should I slip here, no soft blanket of snow lies beneath, and I'll fall to my death.

Grimacing, I tear away from the window and assess my chambers, searching for something to use as rope. My attention snags on the blankets draped across my bed. I could tie them together and hope their combined length reaches the ground, but what if a knot comes loose?

Trying to escape through the window will lead to my death. Staying here will also lead to my death. It's hard to decide which end is preferable. Dying by the Winter King's hands, or by falling?

I suppose I don't yet know what he intends to do with me. There's a chance he still needs me and will spare my life for that fact alone. If that's true, then it's best not to risk falling to my death. But I don't know how long it'll take before he decides to punish me. I could be waiting days. Weeks.

Reluctantly, I return to my bed and pull my furs back around me and stare up at the ceiling. Though I try, I can't stop those final moments from playing in my mind. The Winter King's fingers, his lips, all over my skin. My dagger plunging into his chest.

I feel hot and cold all at once. Confused yet furious. Relieved yet fearful.

Somehow, I drift to sleep. It's a restless slumber, one where I don't dream. Before any can seize me, I bolt up from my pillows, panic thrumming through my veins. But there's no immediate danger, and I can only put my reaction down to the emotional toll of today.

Finally, dawn arrives.

And he with it.

The clicking of the door's lock jolts me from the murkiness of fragmented sleep. I know it's him without having to look: the way the door opens, how it yields to his immeasurable power, the steadiness of his unforgiving footsteps.

"Adara," he says in that rich, velvety voice of his. It commands so much authority the room trembles. I hate the sound of my name on his tongue.

I lie there, facing away, eyes squeezed shut.

"Adara," he tries again, taking a step forward. Then another.

So he doesn't need to come closer, I roll onto my side and open my eyes. The sunlight radiating into my room is so fierce it blinds me, and I have to close them again at once.

Though my eyes are open for just a second, the king notices. He takes in a sharp breath.

I'm surprised he has come here this morning. I thought it would take much longer for him to punish me.

Perhaps if I examine his face, I might manage to determine his intentions, but what use is there in knowing when I'm unable to defend myself?

There's a clink of metal. As he unsheathes his sword?

No. I've never seen him wield a blade of steel. Just frost.

He continues forth—

Wait. That's wrong. His footsteps are moving away.

I can't help my eyes from snapping open, desperate to confirm whether my suspicions are true.

They are. He's by the door.

His eyes are so much colder than last night. When I struck him, they were blazing with fury, and before that, they were burning with desire.

I loathe how the memory stimulates my selfish mortal body. To my flesh, the line between lust and hate blurs, mistaking one fire for another.

How can a person feel alive but so numb?

That single moment, with our eyes burning into each other, seems to play on for years, both of us reliving a maelstrom of emotions.

Then his expression hardens, and he looks at the door rather than me. "Your maids will arrive shortly to attend to you."

He raises his hand and shatters the barrier blocking the door to his chamber. The broken shards fall to the floor, dissolving until no evidence is left.

Every muscle in my body tightens at the reminder of his incomprehensible power. I wait for him to turn his magic on me, to destroy me.

But then he shoves open the doors, not looking back as he leaves. They shudder shut, and the lock clicks.

With him gone, I force myself to sit upright, though my limbs protest. My attention trails across my room, catching on a metallic object on the floor.

A bowl.

The Winter King brought me food.

From what I can glimpse, it seems to be porridge. Perfect for a prisoner, not a queen. But it doesn't matter, since I'm not at all hungry. Quite the opposite. Even its presence makes me nauseous.

I suck in a shaky breath. The king didn't need to bring me something to eat, and it isn't at all what I expected to transpire during the first meeting after our wedding night. I thought he would bring me death, not food.

Why bother bringing me breakfast? Why not let me waste away, locked inside this room?

It seems he wishes to keep me alive. Even a murderous bride who possesses immunity to his power is useful to him.

It must be this, because I can't bear the opposite. That all his tender touches last night were no act, but came from the true depths of his heart.

That somehow, he isn't the monster who killed my sister.

If all this is true, then last night I tried to assassinate an innocent man. A man who cares for me . . .

No. It can't be true. During the nights leading up to our wedding, I considered all these thoughts countless times. Any doubt I feel is because of the way my body reacts to him. He is a villain through and through. With my own eyes, I witnessed him freezing Orlan—the captain of Father's guards, the man who trained me to wield a sword.

I must stay true to my purpose.

I knit my fingers together and lift my chin.

Even if he doesn't intend to kill me anytime soon, I can't stay here. Never again will he trust me, and if a blade through the chest won't kill him, what will?

My quest for vengeance is long over. It never stood a chance to begin with.

Sighing, I turn my thoughts to Father.

The last time I saw him, he was riding home in a carriage after nearly succumbing to the palace's dungeons. Later, I received a letter from him which contained a coded message to let me know he was fleeing home, but I don't know where he currently is. He could be anywhere in the world by now.

If word escapes that the Winter King's bride tried to assassinate him and failed, I worry Father will return to the palace and demand my release. Then the king will capture him and throw him back into those merciless dungeons, and this time he wouldn't be so lenient. He would use Father to force me to give him what he wants.

But news of my treachery may not spread that far. Perhaps no one except the king knows what happened last night, and with his great concern for his reputation, it's possible he'll want to keep it that way.

Nonetheless, I need to escape and find Father, and then the two of us must leave this kingdom.

On that last thought, I throw aside my blankets and pace over to the doors. I push and pull on the handles, doing everything I can to open them, but his entering hasn't helped the lock to loosen. It's as unyielding as ever.

I peer at the bowl of porridge on the floor. Plumes of steam swirl from it. I doubt it'll stay warm for much longer. The palace slowly turns everything in its walls to ice. Except for me and any items or people I touch.

To fight my way out of here, I need my strength. Even if I'm not hungry, I must eat. I start toward the bowl but, after three paces, stop.

Fighting out of this prison won't work. I'll never make it past the king and his guards. A more tactful approach is needed.

My best bet is to not eat a single spoonful of porridge. When my maids arrive, they'll find me in bed and think me sick from my lack of appetite. Catching them unaware will be easier than the Winter King.

But Elona and Kassia may not come alone. They may arrive with an entourage of guards, or even with the king himself. Yet I'll wait day after day for my chance, for them to believe me defeated. My claws clipped. My spirit crushed.

And then I will flee the Crystal Palace once and for all.

Chapter 2

It takes hours for Kassia and Elona to appear. During that time, I stare out at the palace gardens through my window, the events of last night playing on my mind. All day, I see fewer servants going about their business than usual. The king must have ordered most of them to stay at home. Perhaps so no gossip of what happened can spread. Nor does anyone remove the wedding decorations from the gardens, as if he wishes to convince the kingdom that the two of us are currently enjoying a blissful marriage.

Which couldn't be further from the truth.

I'm out of bed when my maids arrive. I hear their voices from down the corridor before they reach the door and dive beneath my furs.

Though my maids took so long to appear, my wait is rewarded by their coming alone. My eyes stay shut, but their footsteps indicate it's just the two of them. No guards. No Winter King.

Their strides are hesitant at first, and I wonder what he's told them. Given their caution, it seems they must know the truth.

But then their footsteps grow stronger and surer, and I can't be certain of what they know.

There's a clink of metal as one of them presumably picks up the bowl which the king left for me.

"She hasn't eaten anything," Kassia whispers.

"The queen must be as unwell as His Majesty said," Elona murmurs.

My initial suspicions were correct. He doesn't trust my maids with the truth.

I bite my tongue to stop my lips from curling into a grin. It'll be much easier to catch them off-guard if they believe me to be sick.

My maids will try to stop me, but neither has any combat experience. Yet I have little wish to fight them off, lest I hurt one of them. Throughout my time here in the palace, they've treated me with nothing but kindness.

If I escape from my room on their watch, the king will be furious. As much as I hate the possibility of them suffering his wrath in my absence, if I don't escape then I'll spend the rest of my days caged here. Besides, he can't be too enraged when he chose not to inform them of the threat I pose.

My thoughts are interrupted as Kassia clicks her tongue. "Imagine that," she mutters, "falling sick the day after your wedding. Our queen should be celebrating the joyous occasion over feasts, not cooped up in bed. It doesn't bode well for their marriage."

If only she knew the half of it.

"Kassia!" Elona scolds, though her tone is hushed. "You mustn't say such things!"

Kassia mumbles an apology, and the two of them continue through my room.

Though they pushed the door shut behind them, I didn't hear the lock click.

I pray it's still open.

One of them heads over to the corner of the room to tidy my clothes, while the other paces to the bookshelf.

I dare to open an eye.

Kassia is by the bookshelf, examining them all and retrieving the ones marred by frost. She's closer to the door and is faster than Elona, thanks to her long legs. But if I sprint hard, she won't reach me in time. And if I wait for her to collect more books, she'll have to set them down before chasing me. Between the surprise of me bolting from bed and her putting down the books, I'll gain a few extra seconds.

I wait until Kassia takes more books, and when she has five, I make my move.

I shove aside my blankets and leap from my bed, taking three steps at a time. I run as fast as I can, bare feet slapping against the floor, and I'm at the doors by the time Elona shrieks. Kassia whirls around, books tumbling from her arms.

I don't look back. My eyes stay on the doors.

My maids rush forth. I reach the doors and grab the handles and force them down, as I did hundreds of times last night, wishing that this time they will yield.

They do.

By the time my maids make it to the doors, I'm already halfway down the corridor.

They shout after me, but blood drums too loudly in my ears for me to hear.

I run so furiously that at the end of the corridor, I struggle to stop and skid across the floor. My feet burn. I ignore the pain and hurry down the next.

The Crystal Palace is a tangle of corridors and would be a maze to one unfamiliar with it, but I've traipsed these halls countless times. Without thinking, my mind maps a perfect route to the gardens.

Despite my haste, I consider whether I should slow and attempt some measure of stealth. My footsteps are so thunderous it's a wonder the king hasn't already heard me from his chambers, in the highest wing of the palace. But I'm racing against the time it takes for my maids to report my disappearance.

As I reach the lowest floor of the palace, I run into a patrol of guards. The hammering of my heart prevents me from hearing their footsteps until it's too late.

"Your Majesty!" they exclaim, frowning in greater confusion than my maids. They glance at each other, unsure how to react. Unless the king has ordered them to keep watch and ensure I don't leave the palace, they've no reason to arrest me. But if he hasn't trusted my own maids with the truth of last night, it's doubtful he'll trust a patrol of guards. Even though they likely know nothing of my assassination attempt and I'm their queen, their loyalty is to their king. And right now, I'm running through the palace in my chemise, my erratic behavior enough to raise suspicion. Then again, this isn't the first time they've seen such things.

Before they can decide what to do, I swivel around and run in the opposite direction, though it means taking a longer path to the gardens.

"Find the king!" a guard shouts.

Some chase me, while others head upstairs.

Fantastic. As soon as the guards reach the king, he'll come looking for me. If he finds me, my escape plan is sure to fail. While I might fight off or slip past a patrol of guards, the same cannot be said for the king. Not with his magic.

How long will it take for the guards to reach him? Will I have time to break into the gardens and scale the wall?

It's doubtful, but I don't let this deter me.

I must escape.

I double my pace, lungs burning in my chest. I push myself harder, though I risk pushing myself into oblivion. My vision blurs, and the corridors become a whirlwind. At this speed, it's hard to maintain my sense of direction. Have I taken all the right turnings, or am I sprinting deeper into the palace?

I collide with something and stumble.

A servant.

He's thrown off his feet from our collision, but I stay upright. He shakes his head and opens his mouth to say something, perhaps to scold me, but then his eyes scan over my red curls and recognition flashes across his expression. His irritation vanishes, remorse taking its place.

"Your Majesty!" he blurts. "Forgive me—"

Though I'm the one who should apologize to him, I don't wait to hear what he has to say. I hurry past, not looking back.

I make it to the small door leading to the gardens without running into any more guards or servants. I push it open and burst outside, almost tripping over the steps.

There are plenty of guards atop the palace's walls, but I don't bother with discretion. The guards and my maids could be informing the king this very second.

I race over the thick blanket of snow, over the fallen twigs from the bare branches. The needles pierce my feet, perhaps even breaking my skin, but I don't check to see if I'm bleeding. While I might leave a bloody trail, my footsteps are already incriminating enough.

I reach the wall marking the palace's perimeter. It's low enough to climb, and a pine tree hangs over, allowing me an easier descent on the way down. Last time, I climbed the wall in the cover of darkness, and did so with stealth, worrying the guards would spot me.

Now I scramble up as quickly as I can, shoving my fingers and toes into every crevice I find, hauling myself up the wall. My movements are frantic, and I scale it without hesitation. All that matters is reaching the top, scrambling down the pine, and diving into the forest beyond.

Weeks ago, Father sent men to rescue me, fearing what the king would do to me. We barely made it through the forest before he found us. The fact we were on horseback and had far more among us was perhaps what gave us away. Now it's just me. No horses. No guards. I'll find somewhere to hide and wait until he gives up his chase.

But how long will it take for him to surrender me to the wilderness? Will I survive that long? Little life grows in this forest, and I may find nothing to eat.

I can't think about any of that right now. I must focus on climbing the wall.

The pine's branches are so close. I reach up to grab them, to heave myself over the wall. But then they freeze. Like everything inside the palace, they become translucent all the way through. Not even a speck of green remains.

I jolt, almost tumbling from the wall. Did I do this? After living in the palace for so long, after marrying the Winter King—after lying with him—have I somehow gained his terrifying power to turn everything to frost?

The wall climbs higher, shoving the pine's branches aside. Breaking them. The wall reaches so high it blocks out the sun. From this angle, it seems to touch the sky.

I grit my teeth and look back.

It's him.

Of course it's him.

The king descends on his winged steed. He must have flown from his balcony, and I would be easily noticeable up here on the wall. Though my white chemise blends with all the terrain, my red hair is another story. The vivid hue paints a large target on my back.

I grip the wall, watching as he dismounts. He lifts his chin and stares up at me. Even from this height, his eyes glow as bright as ever.

"Adara, my queen." His tone is light but bears no humor. Only thinly restrained fury. "Will you come down from there?"

My fingers dig into the wall.

No. I will not come down. I will not surrender my freedom.

I climb higher, resolve burning fiercer. But the top moves farther from my grasp.

"Adara," he says again, this time sterner. "Come down."

"Make me," I growl, all my bitterness and hatred rolled into those two syllables.

And then I keep climbing, even though it's futile, because what else can I do? Climbing is better than admitting defeat. Than accepting that either the king will kill me or I'll spend my whole life caged in his palace.

He sighs.

Magic seizes my wrists, shackling them to the wall. My ankles too.

I writhe and hiss, but none of it forces my chains apart. While I can prevent his power from claiming any item or person, my touch does not spare that which is already frozen. I cannot melt these manacles.

The ice encases me, forming a globe, and I plummet to the ground. Snow blankets the fall, but my cage shatters.

I'm left lying on my back, staring up at the wispy clouds drifting through the sky. Seething, I grab a fistful of snow. It just annoys me more. Though I squeeze it with all my might, I cannot melt it.

The king approaches. I could spring to my feet and attack him, but what would be the point? He'll see it coming.

It's better to wait to strike. Though I can't do much damage when all I have on my body is my chemise. And sadly, I doubt it'll prove a useful weapon. Unless I tear it off and use it to strangle him.

Now there's an interesting thought . . .

He comes to a stop, his face peering down at me, all the unyielding angles of his jawline. And that damned crown.

How I long to shove my fist into the side of his cheek, hard enough his crown tumbles off.

I glare up at him. He returns my stare with a glacial expression. For a long while, neither of us say anything, flakes dancing around us.

He straightens a crease out of his tunic, breaking our stare. "You must realize how this looks?"

I exhale so hard my nostrils flare.

"Adara," he tries again, "you are making matters very difficult."

"Good," I seethe.

Damn him. Damn his reputation. I hope all the guards report home what they've seen today, how desperate I was to escape the Crystal Palace. I want evidence of the king's tyranny to push the kingdom over the edge. Already there are cracks from his cruel tradition of stealing a bride every summer.

He doesn't flinch at the venom in my voice. "If you refuse to be reasonable, I'll be forced to resort to other measures."

I bark out a hysterical laugh. "Other measures? Like what? Locking me in your dungeons like you did to my father?"

He doesn't reply. His expression grows colder. Harder.

"I thought I was your queen," I snarl, "not your prisoner."

"I thought you were my queen," he says, "not my assassin."

My lip curls. "If you wanted a docile wife, you chose the wrong woman."

He extends his hand. "Come, Adara. Let us return to the palace."

I hesitate, glancing between him and his hand. As if I'll ever accept it.

Instead, I grab his ankle and pull as hard as I can, arm straining with the effort.

It was a futile attempt, but to my surprise, he tumbles over. Unfortunately, his crown doesn't budge even when he smacks into the ground.

If I were thinking reasonably, I'd use these precious seconds to race through the gardens and find somewhere to hide but right now, I'm not thinking reasonably. My thoughts are consumed by my hatred for this man, by the fact I have lain with him and all the complicated emotions which accompany that, fanning the flames of my fury to far greater heights.

I drag myself upright and lunge toward him, fist swinging for his face.

He turns his head. The blow skims his cheek, so close his skin brushes mine, and my fist collides with the ground. The force ricochets up my arm. I bite my cheek to keep from yelping in pain, to stop him from receiving that satisfaction.

While I'm distracted, he grips my wrists and flips me over and pins me down. I struggle in his grasp, but it's no use.

I shove my knee at his groin. He evades the blow and straddles me, preventing me from kicking again.

I raise my head but he's too far away for me to head butt. With a growl, I slam my head back down, not caring that it hurts.

I've failed at everything. My assassination attempt. My escape plan. Why must he defeat me in everything I try?

I hate him, and I hate even more how close he is right now. This position brings back memories of last night. Memories I don't want to relive.

Not now. Not ever.

I force myself to meet his eyes.

I've never seen such a thunderous expression on the Winter King's usually emotionless face.

It's hard not to laugh. What does he have to be furious about? That his prisoner tried to escape?

He stands. And before I can so much as twitch a finger, he grabs my waist and hauls me over his shoulder, carrying me back toward the palace.

"I hate you!" I cry, slamming my fists against his back. But it doesn't stop him and just hurts my fists.

I drop my hands and scowl at the wall which grows smaller as he marches toward the palace.

The king descends the steps at the end of the gardens and heads through the small servants' door.

He carries me all the way to my chambers, where we find Elona and Kassia pacing around. As we enter, they drop to a deep curtsey.

"Your majesties," they say together.

He continues past them and deposits me unceremoniously at the center of my bed, as he did last night when I tried to stab him. I scowl at him, and he glares back.

Then he turns to my maids. "You are no longer required here."

Their brows furrow.

"You are unassigned from the queen for the foreseeable future," he says, "and will return to help the other servants in their duties around the palace."

"Yes, Your Majesty," they both reply.

"Leave us."

They do so without question and hurry out the room.

Then it's just the king and me.

He holds my gaze for a moment longer. "Try to rest, Adara."

With that, he too leaves, locking the doors behind him. The resulting click rumbles through my chamber, echoes through my heart. I don't bother scrambling up and trying to tear them aside. I know by now that it is a foolish endeavor.

There's no escape.

Gripping my furs, I stare at the doors. Not only has the Winter King stolen my freedom, but now my maids too.

Chapter 3

Day and night blur into one. True to the king's word, Elona and Kassia don't return to my chambers. Instead, he assigns a new maid to serve me: a stern-faced woman with gray peppering her otherwise dark hair. Merlys, I think Elona said she was called. I've never spoken to her directly, and I'm not sure I've heard her speak before, and that doesn't change even when she visits my chambers day after day. It isn't surprising the king chose her. I can't imagine Merlys gossiping to anyone about my imprisonment.

No further opportunity to escape arises. The king has learned from his previous mistake and is always present whenever Merlys enters, standing guard by the doors like a ruthless jailor.

They appear twice a day, once in the morning and once in the evening, and their visits are always in silence. When Merlys wipes my face and shoulders with a wet cloth, I long to ask her if Elona and Kassia are well, if they have suffered the king's wrath for my near escape. But I dare not ask. Not with him always within earshot. If he hears my concerns for their wellbeing, he may choose to worsen their suffering. All I can imagine is the two of them locked in the dungeons beneath the palace, clutching each other as frost consumes their flesh.

While I dearly hope the king isn't as merciless as I fear, I can't deny that was how he punished my father, whose sole crime was trying to free his daughter from a murderous tyrant.

When the king and Merlys visit, they bring with them food and water and leave both on the counter beside my bed. My throat is parched and my stomach is hollow, but I refuse to eat or drink. He needs me alive, or else he would have already driven a sword through my chest—a fitting retribution for what I did to him on our wedding night.

I have nothing left to bargain with. Except for my life. If he wishes for me to stay alive, then he will be forced to release me.

Unless he decides to replace me. To find another Summer Queen who is immune to his power.

But dying is a risk I'm willing to take. I'd much rather die in a gamble for my freedom than stay trapped in this icy cage for the rest of my life.

Soon I lose track of how many days pass.

How long can the human body withstand dehydration? A few days maybe? A week if I'm lucky?

I grow increasingly less aware of my surroundings, and then even rolling onto my side becomes impossible. My body feels chained to the bed.

Still, servants do not burst into my chambers and carry me to my freedom. The king does not order my release.

It seems I have overestimated my usefulness to him.

He's willing to let me die.

I should feel panicked by my imminent death. I should drag my body to my bedside counter and drink from the goblet Merlys left there. Not that it would save me. Though I've grown numb to the passing of time, I'm certain it was hours since they last visited. The goblet of water will be long frozen.

The greatest comfort I find in my approaching death is my absolution of guilt. All this time, the king pretended to care for me. His feelings were an act, luring me in to marry him. If he truly cared, he would release me from this prison and spare my suffering.

Driving my dagger into his chest was the right choice, and my only regret is that I failed to slay him.

Somewhere amid the haziness of my deliria, I hear Merlys's voice. I didn't notice either of them entering my chambers, and I'm unsure how long they've been present. I must have slipped out of consciousness when they arrived.

"The goblet is still untouched." Vaguely, I sense Merlys's shadow looming over me, blotting out the sunlight filtering through the window. "She will die if this continues much longer, Your Majesty."

I'm not sure whether the king responds or whether my mind slips away again. Then I feel the distant sensation of being pulled upward. My head lolls over, as if weighed down by an anchor. Gently, it's tugged up. Merlys's blurred face comes into view. My eyes struggle to see anything past her.

Something metallic presses against my mouth. The goblet.

Merlys pries apart my lips. I resist. But I lack strength, and my body betrays me. I grit my teeth, but even staying conscious is a great effort.

Merlys tips back the goblet. Cool water washes over my tongue, slides down my throat. I try to cough it up so she will fear my choking and relent, but my selfish body forgets my pledge and cares only for self-preservation.

Merlys releases me, and I collapse onto my furs, staring at the foggy ceiling.

I've failed again. Failed to win this battle of wills.

I should feel the damning weight of despair, and yet I do not. My emotions are too dulled for me to care.

I'm unsure precisely how much Merlys forced me to drink, but sense slowly returns to my mind. An overwhelming wave of bitterness slams into me.

The Winter King will never let me go. He will keep me imprisoned here forever.

At least ordering Merlys to force me to drink shows he needs me. Bargaining with my life has failed. Now I can only bargain with whatever he wants from me. Though he could very well wish to sacrifice me to further his power, and that may cost my life all the same.

Later that evening, the king arrives alone. My body instinctively tenses. Has he come without Merlys so there's no one to witness whatever he intends to do to me?

He sits beside me on my bed. I don't move. Don't let myself twitch.

"Adara," he says, and I wish deliria still consumed my mind so I'm not forced to listen to him. "You haven't eaten or drunk anything for days."

"Release me," I rasp, the words scratching the back of my throat like a serrated blade.

"If I do, you will try to kill me again. Or worse, perhaps you will lead a revolt and try to turn this kingdom against me."

I grip a fistful of the furs beneath me. A rebellion would be no less than he deserves.

There's a moment of silence. I wait for him to leave.

He does not.

"You must eat." At the periphery of my vision, I see him leaning near with the bowl of porridge at the ready. I wonder how long it will take for it to all freeze. Perhaps not more than ten minutes, maybe less if he carried it himself all the way from the kitchens.

"Why do you care?" I say to the ceiling.

"You are my wife."

I choke out a strangled laugh. "You just married me because you need me for whatever reason you need a Summer Queen."

He doesn't even try to deny it.

I roll onto my side, so I can see his expression as I ask, "Why do you need a Summer Queen? Why do you need me?"

Of course, he stays silent. Like the previous times I've asked, he refuses to tell me what he seeks. The fact he's refusing now, even after I've driven a dagger through his chest and he's holding me prisoner, means his ambitions must be dark indeed.

There goes my pitiful plan to bargain with his ambition. If he won't tell me what he wants, how can I strike a deal for my freedom?

"Whatever it is you need, I won't give it to you while I'm your prisoner."

"Eat." He digs the silver spoon into the porcelain bowl. I'm pleased to see no steam wafts up from the porridge. It must already be stone cold.

"No."

"Adara," he growls.

I turn away my head.

"I would prefer to not have to force feed you."

"You wouldn't?" I retort. "I thought tyrants got a thrill out of asserting their power over others."

He lets out a heavy sigh and sets down the porridge on the counter. "Since you arrived at the palace, I have done everything within my power to make you feel welcome. I have tried to be reasonable during these past few days, despite your shoving a dagger into my chest on our wedding night—"

"Reasonable?" I can't help from bolting upright in bed, though weariness washes through my body. "You think caging me in here is reasonable?"

"You tried to kill me!" he roars, his calm façade shattering. I want to see his rage. I want to see the monster beneath the mask. The monster I've known to be there all along. "From the moment we met, you used me!"

"Just as you used me," I snarl.

He grabs my wrist, fury blazing in his eyes. I wait for him to hit me.

The blow doesn't come.

Instead, he pulls me closer, until our faces are just inches away. "In what capacity have I used you?" His breath is hot against my cheeks.

"I am a means to an end."

His grip tightens, fingers digging into my skin. "At least I didn't try to end you."

"No," I say, lip curling. "You just ended my sister."

His shoulders tighten. "Ended her?"

It's a struggle to restrain my anger. "You murdered her. Like you murdered the three hundred Summer Brides before her."

The Winter King stares down at me. His grip doesn't relent. "Is that what you believe? That I would murder three hundred girls?"

Blood pounds in my ears. "It's the truth."

"With what evidence?"

I can't help the tears which spill from my eyes, laden with frustration and grief. He has disposed of their bodies, destroyed every trace of them. The thought of my sister suffering such torment, even in death, is too much to bear.

I pull my wrist away and draw my knees to my chest, burying my face against them. All I can see is the Winter King freezing my sister and then shattering her remains. It would be easy for him to scatter the shards across the gardens. No one would ever suspect the fragments came from a person.

"The last time I killed anyone was three centuries ago," he grinds out.

"You may have destroyed their bodies," I whisper, not lifting my head from my knees, "but you can't hide from the truth, Elaric."

He grabs my shoulders and pulls me up again so I'm forced to look at him. Too broken, I cannot resist. "I did not kill your sister."

I shake my head. Though I so desperately want to believe him, this false hope serves only to torment me. "My sister is gone. She's been gone for three years. You took her from me."

He grips my chin, steadying me. "Believe what you will, but I did not kill your sister. Nor did I kill any of the other girls."

He holds my gaze and then releases me so suddenly I stagger. He stands and whirls around, striding across the room.

I gasp, my mind struggling to process the emotions raging through me. My heart cleaves in two with the possibility that he's telling the truth. That he didn't kill my sister like I've always believed.

That she might be alive . . .

"Wait!" I blurt as he reaches the door.

He halts and looks back at me.

"If you didn't kill my sister," I say, hands trembling, "then where is she?"

The Winter King hesitates. I wait for him to shove open the doors and refuse to answer my question, as he always does. Not that I expect him to tell me anything other than that my sister's remains are scattered across the gardens. That I've trodden over the shards countless times.

She is gone, and that's the truth.

It has to be.

He exhales and pushes open the doors. "Come with me."

Chapter 4

On unsteady legs I haul myself from my bed and follow the Winter King out of my room. I wrap my furs tightly around me. Not as protection from the cold, but as protection from what I will find by following him.

The truth behind my sister's disappearance after all these years.

The king walks through the winding corridors, and the sound of his boots striking the floor rings out through the high ceilings in a macabre rhythm. In contrast, my bare feet are soundless, as if I'm an apparition gliding behind him.

The path he takes us through the palace brings us to the stairs leading to his secret chamber, the one he forbade me from entering after I tried to melt it open during my second night here. While my steps have so far been unsure, now I don't hesitate before ascending them, fearing he will change his mind. Fearing I won't learn his terrible secrets.

We reach the top of the stairs, and he walks over to the sealed double doors. Elaborate swirls are carved into their glossy surfaces. He closes his eyes and presses his palm to their center.

Blue light sparks, spreading over the doors until they're engulfed. A deafening crack rings through the silent palace. The doors split open, revealing darkness.

A part of me longs to dive through and uncover the truth, but another part fears facing what lies within. My feet stay glued to the floor as I stare beyond, and the ghost of my sister's face swirls within the shadows.

The Winter King pulls a torch from the nearest wall, a translucent rod topped by flickering light, and beckons me forth.

Step by step, I follow him into the room. The torch illuminates several yards around us. It's too dark to tell how far back the room reaches, but judging by the echo of our footsteps, it must be cavernous.

The glint of a chair's curved leg catches my eye. While frozen furniture isn't an unusual sight here in the Crystal Palace, there's something peculiar about it. Something I can't quite put my finger on . . .

Though the king continues through the room, taking his torch with him, I stumble toward the strange silhouette.

The light grows fainter as he drifts farther away. But when I reach the object, there's enough light to discern what it is.

This isn't a chair or a table or any other type of furniture at all.

It is a person.

A *frozen* person.

What I thought was the curved leg of a chair is instead the skirts of a dress, flicking out in mid motion.

The torch light disappears before I can identify her face. Before I can determine whether she is Dalia.

I stagger back.

This is what the Winter King has been hiding. A graveyard.

"Adara," he says, the light growing brighter as he starts toward me. Now I'm able to examine the statue's face clearly, and my shoulders sag in relief when I realize she isn't my sister.

The king stops a few paces behind me. Even as seconds drags into minutes, he doesn't close the distance between us. Nor does he explain why he's hiding this girl in here.

"Where is she?" My words are as hollow as I feel.

He hesitates. I wonder whether I must make my demand again, this time angrier, but then he turns and says: "This way."

The king edges into the darkness, and I hurry after him. Breath suspended.

Finally, he stops and raises his torch.

Three statues emerge. Like the first, they're all female. The only difference is these statues are lying on slabs of ice.

The Winter King offers no sign of which is Dalia. He just stays there, silent and still.

I rush forward to examine each girl, but neither the first nor second is my sister. Both appear my age and must be Summer Brides. A plaque at the head of their beds contains their names and a year—presumably the year in which they were frozen.

The first girl is called Riana, chosen in the Year 1352, while the second is called Satine, chosen in the Year 1353. Both were chosen in the two years prior to my sister . . .

My whole body trembling, I start over to the third statue. And it takes just a glimpse of her face for me to fall to my knees.

My sister. Even in death, she is as graceful as ever.

This entire time, she has been here in the palace.

I knew this forbidden chamber would contain the king's darkest secrets. I just never imagined that it would contain Dalia herself.

I grab her hand and squeeze, willing my touch to free her from this prison.

But nothing happens. I cannot thaw that which is already frozen.

She is long gone from this world, taken by this wicked king.

The man I now call my husband.

Yet he claims he did not murder my sister. I assumed that meant my sister might be alive. But the evidence lying before me now proves that was a pitiful hope.

I rise, though it's difficult with how numb my legs are. "She was here the whole time." I don't look at him as I speak. I can't. "You forbade me from entering this chamber."

The king offers no justification for his cruelty.

But it doesn't matter. Nothing can excuse what he's done.

"You feared what would happen if I learned the truth," I continue. "That after seeing my sister's body, I would refuse to marry you and you would not gain what you seek. You hid the truth out of selfishness, believing I would forget you stole my sister. But you were a fool."

I wait for his wrath for all the insults I have paid him. But he just mutters, "I do not deny that I have made many mistakes."

"Mistakes?" I exclaim, whirling to face him. White-hot anger pulses through my veins. "You call freezing my sister and lying to me a 'mistake'?"

"I did not lie to you," the king says. "You never asked me for the truth of your sister's fate."

I take a step forward, my feet digging so hard into the floor I'm sure they'll leave an imprint. "So, it's my fault?"

"Adara," he says quietly, "that isn't what I said."

I inhale. Exhale.

Then, "If I'd asked you for the truth, would you have told me?"

There's just silence.

"Get out," I snarl, though this is his palace and not mine. Though he could end me in a single breath. Now I have nothing left to lose, what use is there for fear?

When he says nothing and makes no sign of moving, I say again, "Get out!"

His eyes narrow, and I expect him to punish me. To chain my wrists, to drag me away from this room, to prevent me from ever seeing my sister again. Instead, he lowers the torch to the floor and turns away, vanishing into the darkness.

For a long while, I kneel beside my sister, my hand around her fingers. If only all my love and grief could melt her free. The torchlight flickers, and the shadows dance around us.

All these years, I have wished to see my sister's face one last time, believing it would mend the rift in my heart, but seeing her hasn't sewn a single seam between the broken halves. It has pushed them apart, breaking me though I can break no further.

After losing Dalia, I spent countless nights weeping until I had no tears left. And yet here I cry as relentlessly as I did the night the Winter King seized her, my pain as raw as ever.

Minutes pass into hours, my knees digging into the floor. All I want is to see the color return to my sister's face, to see her lifeless lips smile again.

A while later, footsteps approach. My mind vaguely registers the distant sound.

I don't turn to see whether it is the king returning, my attention remaining on my sister. Dalia is all that matters. But it isn't his shadow which looms over me. It's my maids who have arrived, though he ordered days ago for them to no longer serve me.

"Your majesty," Elona says, nudging my shoulder.

I don't move. My hand stays around Dalia's fingers.

"You can't stay here all night," Kassia adds gently. "What will not resting achieve?"

I know she speaks in good will, that she worries for my health and rightly so. I have eaten or drunk almost nothing for days. But her question triggers something deep within me. An agonizing realization of how bleak my current situation is. No matter how long I kneel here, holding my sister's hand, I cannot revive her. My determination is not enough.

Nothing is.

"You knew," I hiss, wielding my words as if they were a dagger. My maids aren't responsible for Dalia's fate—the king is—but right now, I'm hurting so much I can't suppress the urge to lash out. "All this time, you knew what happened to my sister. You knew she was here."

They lower their heads.

"You betrayed me." The pain in my chest is so intense it's as if my heart will erupt. "You knew she was in this room, and yet you refused to let me in. You told me there was nothing in here, despite knowing what lay behind these doors. And what the truth would mean to me."

"The king strictly forbade you from visiting this room," Kassia says.

"Even if you couldn't bring me into this room, you were both there when my sister was chosen three years ago. You knew she was frozen and never told me."

"We were not permitted to say," Elona says, her voice stronger now. She meets my gaze, her hazel eyes hardening.

Reasonably speaking, I know I shouldn't be too furious with my maids. They're loyal to the king. He's the one who pays them enough to keep them and their families alive. They only care for me because he ordered them to do so. Though it's a perfectly rational explanation, it doesn't lessen the ache within.

"Come now, Your Majesty," Kassia says. "Your sister would not want you to waste away like this."

The softness of her words and the truth within them somewhat abates my wrath. She's right. Dalia wouldn't want me kneeling here after starving myself for days. It would hurt her, just as much as it would if she knew I'd married her murderer to avenge her.

Regret hits me like an avalanche.

How she would hate me for treating my life so recklessly. Holding her hand, seeing her face, makes the echo of her words deafeningly loud. All she would want is for me to be safe and well and happy. Not drowning in the misery I've brought upon myself.

And maybe, just maybe, there's a way to save her. But right now, I'm in no state to think clearly.

I release my sister's hand and stand, surprising my maids. I lean over and kiss her brow, pledging a silent promise to free her.

Then I retrieve the flickering torch which the king left on the floor and follow my maids. Since Kassia also bears a torch, more of the room is illuminated as we leave, allowing me to see farther into the shadows. We pass countless statues, as many as I feared I'd find. It seems all three hundred discarded brides reside within this chamber.

We reach the exit, and my maids shut the doors behind us. I force myself not to look back. If I do, I fear I'll never be able to leave Dalia's side.

As we walk through the palace back to my room, I keep my restless thoughts to myself. Neither Kassia nor Elona say anything, but their guilt is so loud it bounces off the crystalline walls.

My shoulders sag in relief when we reach my chambers, grateful for the opportunity to be alone with my thoughts. To rest.

But my relief is short-lived.

My maids push open the doors, and there I see him—the Winter King—sitting on my bed.

Chapter 5

The Winter King looks up as we approach, his bright eyes immediately finding me.

I stop in the doorway, fists tightening. Though I thought I had no energy left to be furious, seeing his face banishes the fog of exhaustion, allowing all my anger to bubble to the surface.

Betrayal lances through me. The king ordered my maids to find me and persuade me to return to my chambers. I can forgive them for their involvement with Dalia's disappearance and hiding the truth from me, but it's hard to forgive them again. Still, with all my hatred directed at the king, I have little to spare for anyone else.

"Adara," he says.

I just stay there in the doorway, unmoving.

He reaches for the frozen bowl of stew sitting beside my bed and holds it out to my maids. Elona rushes to collect it from him. "The queen hasn't eaten in days. There was still some stew left when I collected this earlier. It will need heating and a fresh bowl to be brought up."

Elona nods. "At once, Your Majesty."

My maids leave with the bowl, maneuvering around me.

The silence that follows is suffocating, filled with so many unspoken words and emotions.

The king stares at his hands before speaking. "Adara, I'm sorry—"

"Sorry won't bring my sister back," I grind out, unwilling to hear his pitiful excuses.

He flinches at my sharp tone. "I understand you might hate me."

"Might?" I growl.

"I never intended to hurt you or Dalia or anyone—"

"You didn't mean to hurt them?" I exclaim. "What did you expect when you chose them at the Midsummer Ball?"

"I hoped they would be you," he says, looking away. "My Summer Queen."

"Until now, I'm the only bride who didn't freeze. When you chose Dalia, you knew three hundred brides before her succumbed to your magic. You knew there was little chance she would emerge unscathed. Yet you chose her anyway."

"I wish more than anything I did not bring such pain upon you."

"You only say that because I stand before you now. What about the other grieving families who've suffered because of your actions? I don't know why you seek a Summer Queen, whether it is to control your magic since you clearly have no leash for it, but your reasons don't erase the hurt."

"Adara," he says, voice brittle and broken.

There's no denying his guilt, yet I cannot help cutting through the veil of excuses, exposing all the suffering his choices have wrought.

"When you chose me, you didn't know I would be immune to your power," I say. "You chose me and risked my life like all the other girls. You can't claim that you didn't intend to hurt me as well."

"And you intended to hurt me even before you arrived at the Midsummer Ball. You wanted to be chosen, to seduce me, to drive a dagger through my chest. That was why you sang, wasn't it? To draw my attention."

"It was." The words ring in my ears even long after I've said them.

He heaves a sigh and runs a hand through his hair. "It wouldn't surprise me if you were dancing with a dagger beneath your dress that night."

"And poison."

He snaps around to face me. "Poison?"

I shrug. "It didn't work."

"When?" he demands.

"One afternoon when we were playing chess outside. We were interrupted when you were called for a meeting with the Duke of Walsworth."

"You tried to kill me twice," he says, shaking his head in disbelief.

"There were no other opportunities."

"Why must you be this cruel, Adara?"

"At least I don't deny my sins and pretend to be innocent."

"You don't understand."

"I don't understand what?"

"Do you think I *wished* to keep choosing a bride year after year, knowing they were all but certain to freeze?"

"Maybe," I say. "After all, you stow away all their bodies as if they're trophies."

His jaw hardens. "To protect them."

My heart skips a beat. "What protection do the dead require?"

"They are not dead."

"Is she alive?" I blurt. "All those girls, are they alive?"

"I do not know."

"They're either dead or alive," I snap. "Which is it?"

"Neither. They all linger between life and death."

If they are not dead, there must be a way to save them . . .

Wringing my hands together, I pace before the doors. "How can you be certain they aren't dead?"

"You do not possess magic, so you cannot feel it."

"Feel what?"

"Their life forces. Energy remains within them. It does not burn as brightly as yours, or anyone else's who is alive, and is akin to a flickering ember. Yet those who are dead do not possess this energy. Their souls are like a bed of stone-cold coals."

I keep pacing, each step more restless than the last. "Can't you revive them?"

"I have tried many times throughout the centuries. Every attempt thus far has been unsuccessful."

"Perhaps you can't free them," I say, "but maybe someone else can."

The king neither confirms nor denies my speculation.

"Is it me?" I press. "Am I the one who can save her, all of them? Is this why you have sought a Summer Queen for so long?"

Rather than answering my question, he rises and paces over to the doors. I glare at him, furious that he insists on being so cowardly.

"That's it? You're just going to leave?"

"Try to sleep, Adara," he says as he opens the doors. "You need to rest."

My lip curls. "Will you lock me up in here again tonight?"

"No," he whispers. "I will not."

With that, he leaves and the doors shut behind him. No click of the lock follows.

Elona and Kassia soon return, bearing a steaming bowl of stew. I eat faster than I can swallow, not caring that it scalds my mouth. In their effort to combat the palace's chill, they have heated it until it's molten. I eat so quickly I spare no thought for its flavors, only that it is fuel my body has gone without for days. And right now I need every ounce of strength to free Dalia from the king's spell.

When I finish, Elona takes the bowl. "Would you like another, milady?"

"No, thank you," I say. "I ate that one so quickly I fear I'll be sick if I eat any more."

She dips her head, but they both linger rather than leave.

"What has happened, milady?" Elona asks.

The question takes me by surprise. Though anyone would be curious about everything that's happened between the king and me, it's unlike Elona to ask.

"I . . . " I trail off, uncertain where to begin.

"Forgive me," she says. "It isn't my place."

"No, wait!" I call as she turns to leave. They both pause, peering at me, but the words stick in my throat.

When I don't speak, Kassia steps forward, taking my hand. "We worry for you." She squeezes tighter. "The king said you were unwell the morning after your wedding. Then you tried escaping over the walls. After that, he ordered Merlys to serve you, forbidding us from coming near. The kitchen staff noticed all your untouched, frozen meals being returned. And tonight he summoned us to escort you back here."

Elona edges closer to my bed and lowers her voice. "May I ask, milady, if he has hurt you? Is this why you tried to escape?"

"No," I choke out. "No, it was me. I tried to kill him. I drove a dagger through his chest on our wedding night."

They're silent, but the horror on their faces is clear.

"I thought he'd killed my sister," I say, the truth tumbling from my lips faster than my mind can realize. "All this time, I believed he'd murdered my sister in cold blood and disposed of her remains so no one could find any trace of her. But I was wrong. She was here all along."

Kassia clasps her hands and lowers her head. "We should have told you the truth."

"The king gave us strict orders not to allow you into that chamber or reveal its contents," Elona says. "But if we'd known at the time of your intentions to kill him, telling you the truth would have been for the best."

"Not just for the king," Kassia adds. "You deserved to know your sister's fate."

Elona hums her agreement.

"We failed you, milady," Kassia says.

I shake my head. "I shouldn't have blamed either of you. It isn't your fault."

It is mine.

I almost killed an innocent man. Well, maybe not entirely innocent. Even if he has murdered no one, it doesn't change that he stole all those girls. That they may never be revived.

But if my speculation is correct, and he needs me—his Summer Queen—to free all those girls, then it means the tradition I've always abhorred isn't just a senseless cruelty. To release them, he needs a Summer Queen but finding her meant freezing more brides. My sister was just another failed attempt to achieve that end.

Remorse slams into me, and I crumble into my pillows.

All this time, I've been so stupid. If I'd concentrated on my sister and discovering the truth behind her disappearance rather than on the king and ending his reign, I'd have learned of her fate sooner and would be closer to freeing her.

My maids sit beside me on my bed and draw me into their arms, holding me tight.

"I've made so many mistakes." My breaths are uneven as I speak. "I'm a terrible, wicked person, and I don't deserve your kindness."

"You're not wicked, milady," Elona says gently. "Just hurt."

I should have stopped to consider everything instead of fixating on killing the king. Deep down, I knew the chamber contained the answers I sought, and yet I didn't bother to pursue it again after he caught me trying to break into it, fearing another attempt would cause him to suspect my intentions. But maybe being caught again would have been for the best. Maybe if he'd known how distrustful I was of him, how I couldn't forget my sister so easily, he'd have shown me the truth rather than believing I'd forgive him in time.

This entire mess could have been averted.

"You never knew what happened to your sister," Elona says, squeezing my hand. "It's natural you assumed the worst in the absence of truth."

"Before I served here," Kassia adds, "I never understood why the king insisted on taking a bride every summer. I too believed he killed them, sacrificing them to further his power. I have a younger sister, and I feared for her when she danced at the Midsummer Ball. When he called another name, I fell to my knees in relief, even though that night someone else's sister was stolen.

"The king didn't take my sister but if he had, I too would have wished great pain upon him. Maybe I would have even dreamed of driving a dagger through his heart myself but unlike you, I would never have been brave enough to try it."

"Not brave," I mumble. "Foolish."

Foolish for so many reasons. For not exploring the truth. For believing I could kill a man whose heart is made of ice.

I swallow down hard.

It's fortunate I failed. Not only would I have become a monster, but his death may have caused my sister and the other girls to be eternally trapped in frost. Maybe their bodies would have shattered into thousands of tiny shards, never to be restored.

I've never been more grateful for failure.

"What will you do now, milady?" Kassia asks, tearing me from my thoughts.

"Free my sister," I say without hesitation. "What do you know of the spell afflicting them? Of the source of the king's magic?"

"Well, it must be a curse," Kassia says, "like in fairy tales. The king seeks his true Summer Queen, and all those who are not her—who aren't you—will be frozen by his touch."

A curse. Of course. Kassia has given a name to that which I already suspected. And now she's called it a curse, I can't believe it to be anything but that.

"Do you know how the curse can be broken?" I ask.

She presses her lips together. "True love? It must be, since he's always sought a queen, and it's usually true love's kiss in fairy tales."

"If the king really is cursed," I reply, "true love's kiss can't be the cure."

"Why not?" she says.

"We've already kissed each other." I look at the floor. "Enough times."

"Maybe it didn't work because you were plotting to kill him," Kassia says. "Maybe you need to kiss him when you aren't intending to drive a knife through his chest?"

I agree that true love can't exist when a murderous heart is involved, but her solution sounds so simplistic, and I doubt kissing the king now will break his curse.

I sigh. "What about the curse's origin? Does anyone know how it began?"

Kassia shakes her head.

"I'm not certain either," Elona admits. "The king shares little with us of his past, and few others know of the contents of that room, and I've heard no one except Kassia mention a curse. The only whispers I've heard are from those who believe the king sacrifices his brides to maintain his power."

My shoulders sink, though I didn't expect them to know. The king has reigned over three centuries, and anyone here before his curse would be long dead.

"Have you asked the king?" Kassia says.

"I've asked why he needs a Summer Queen, but he never explains, not even tonight."

"It's strange he still won't tell you." Kassia frowns. "He didn't want you to know what lay in that chamber because he believed you'd never forgive him. Now that you know, what reason does he have to keep it from you?"

"Unless he's bound by magic?" Elona suggests. "And is physically unable to tell you anything?"

"That would explain why he still keeps me in the dark," I muse. "But if I can't get the truth about his curse from him, where do I start?"

"The library," Kassia blurts. "It has books on magic. I saw some once while tidying there."

I nod slowly. I don't remember such books, but on all past visits Elona and Kassia have accompanied me. Nor was I actively searching for information on curses. Maybe now I have a specific objective and am not forced to search discreetly, it will be easier to find what I seek. "The library it is."

Chapter 6

Though I long to return to the library, my maids persuade me to rest first. After the exhaustion of tonight, I reluctantly agree. My dreams are haunted by Dalia's face, the ice shrouding her features thawing and color returning to her cheeks.

I wake at dawn and waste no time before slipping from bed, donning a fur coat, and hurrying out. I encounter no one on my way and soon reach the stone building which houses the library.

Unlike the palace, the library is free of frost, though flakes scatter across the tiles as I step inside. Shutting the heavy door against the howling wind proves a struggle.

The windows in here are few, and only faint slithers of moonlight filter through. My eyes adjust slowly to the shadows, but I know the room well enough to find matches and a candle at the old oaken desk by the door.

I take them to the nearest window to see more easily, lighting the candle and placing a glass cover over the dancing amber flame. Stepping back, I survey the rest of the library.

The shelves overflow with aged tomes, their well-worn wood having stood the test of time. I start with the nearest, scanning across it. The books are arranged by author, with no regard for content, complicating my search.

It takes half an hour to find some potentially useful volumes. I carry them to the desk and sink into the cushioned chair, turning the crusty parchment pages.

The first proves unhelpful, containing unrelated myths. Fortunately, the second book offers insight.

The title page bears the blotchy inscription 'The Lost Art of Magic.' It discusses the nature of magic and how it exists in water and air, along with every leaf and flower, person, and beast. Magic is divided into ten different aspects of nature: fire, ice, lightning, wood, wind, earth, water, light, shadow, and mind. An individual attuned to magic will possess an affinity for just one of these.

I turn the page and read as it explains how each type is used, concentrating on ice and fire. Frost magic can freeze objects, while fire burns all in its wake. The only additional detail I glean is that those who possess fire can withstand burning, while those possessing ice can endure freezing. Before this, I wondered if I had fire magic as the Summer Queen, but it's ice I am immune to. Not fire.

I rub my tired, dry eyes and reach for the next book, when a passage catches my notice.

Attunement to magic runs in bloodlines, with family members often sharing the same affinity, although not every descendant will inherit the gift. It is also rare for magic to pass down male lines, and it is for this very reason that witches are almost exclusively female.

I chew my lip as I think. Could the king be one of those rare male witches?

As I read further through the book, it talks about how witches control their given affinities. But in the king's case, magic possesses control over him.

I skim a few more pages before discarding it to rifle through the others. The next outlines two spell types: conjuration and enchantment. The former involves invoking raw magic as flames or lightning bolts, while the latter changes the state of an object, place or person.

Examples of enchantments include a man turned to stone for displeasing an earth witch, and a shadow witch casting darkness over a kingdom for countless centuries. Such enchantments are known as curses, and every enchantment must have a way to be broken. If not, the magic will harm its caster.

I tear through pages, seeking more information on breaking curses. Halfway in, I find a relevant paragraph.

The condition for breaking an enchantment is decided upon by the witch when at the time of her invoking the spell. One of the simpler conditions a witch may opt for is specifying the spell to last for a predetermined duration. The simplicity of this incantation is, however, offset by the energy required to invoke it. A duration of even a year requires far more energy than is possessed by the average witch, and as magic resides in the blood, utilizing too much energy in a spell risks draining a witch's life force and killing her. Consequently, they often tie curses to the fates using elaborate stipulations, and such enchantments may endure weeks or perhaps even eternity. The witch need only give a plausible way for her spell to be undone, but it is up to fate to decide when that condition is met. Yet if the incantation involves another besides the accursed, this person's free will may bend destiny's path. Although every enchantment possesses a way to be broken, naught guarantees it shall be broken.

I pause, my fingers lingering over the faded ink. As stated, curses can claim people, along with places and objects.

The Winter King . . .

Like Kassia suspects, he must be cursed, his magic spreading to my sister and the other girls, consuming the palace and mountain with ice. This is why he can't control his powers—they were never his to begin with. A witch cursed him and sealed it with a specific condition for it to be broken.

A condition involving a Summer Queen. Me.

I close the book, the dull thud echoing off the stone walls.

What is the condition? True love, as Kassia suggested? Has no kiss worked because we must truly love each other?

I toy with the carved wooden chair arm. I feel no love for him, never mind true love. As for the king, how can he deeply care for me when he imprisoned me?

A small voice whispers that anyone would restrain their almost-murderer, but I silence it.

It matters not what he feels. If the cure is love, I pose the greatest barrier to breaking the curse. How can I love a man I've hated for three years? Whom I dedicated my every waking moment to destroying? For my sister's sake I would force myself to love him if I could, but true love cannot be forced.

Yet I can't deny there's something between us, a desire that warms my cheeks until I'm certain they're the color of the flame flickering atop my candle. Will focusing on that attraction help overcome my bitterness and allow love to bloom?

I slump in my chair. This is ridiculous. I may never fall in love with him, and even if I do, I do not know how many years—decades—it will take. And as the book says, nothing guarantees a curse will break. My sister's freedom is too important to leave to fate.

Besides, the cure might not even be true love. It might be something else entirely. But I don't know how I will confirm this. It's possible the king and the witch who cursed him are the only people who know.

Mood grim, I resume my search for anything on curses. I read of witches trapping people in trees, cursing others to never again walk on land. Over half the cures involve true love, since witches favor it for fate's fickleness. But near the end of my current book, a passage causes me to pause.

Those subjected to a curse find their tongues bound, unable to speak a word of the sorcery which ensnares them. Nor may they inscribe anything of their affliction, for the moment pen touches page, their hands shall turn stiff. Nevertheless, this itself can prove a valuable method to discern whether one is indeed afflicted by a curse.

I frown and reread the passage. Perhaps I can employ such an approach. If I ask the king to write about his curse and he proves unable to pen a single word, it will confirm beyond all doubt that he's cursed.

Chapter 7

Clutching parchment and a pot of ink, I head out the library and back into the palace, following the winding staircases until I reach the Winter King's chambers. Eager to find him and prove the existence of his curse, I don't bother knocking on the doors and barge in sideways since my hands are full.

The king isn't in his dining room, so I press on through to his innermost bedchamber. Where we shared our wedding night.

Fortunately, I'm too focused on what I must say for my mind to wander there. I'd hate to burst in flustered.

"You're cursed," I exclaim as I step through the doors. "You're cursed and you can't tell me you are."

Only after speaking do I realize what I've caught him doing. Bathing.

Which means he's currently sitting naked in a copper tub. I try to concentrate on the ornate engravings instead of his hard chest and the bubbles scarcely covering the rest.

The ink nearly slips from my fingers.

"I—" He clears his throat. "I'll get out."

"No!" I blurt, unable to stop myself from imagining how he'll look when he climbs out. No, not imagining. Remembering. And the looming canopy bed just makes it all far worse. "Stay there. Please."

He hesitates before sinking lower into the water. Though not so low to hide his knees.

At least it's only his knees . . .

"The curse," I continue, seeking a much-needed distraction. "I searched the library and found that victims can't speak or write about their curses. So I brought these"—I hold up ink and parchment—"to prove it."

The king's fingers curl around the edge of his bathtub. I don't dare look directly at him and keep my gaze lowered. It's safer this way. If I look at him for too long, I'll lose the ability to speak.

"I also read every curse can be broken." I pause, waiting for him to add something. He doesn't. "You're certain I'm your Summer Queen?"

"Without a doubt. You alone in three hundred years are immune to my power."

"But what does any of it mean? I'm immune to frost, not fire, and I can't manipulate it like you can. Being your Summer Queen just seems to mean I can break your curse, but I don't know how."

As expected, he offers no explanation.

"And what makes everything so frustrating is that the magic prevents you from saying anything. If only there was a way you could tell me the truth."

He lowers his head. "I am sorry, Adara."

My chest constricts at the softness in his voice. It was much easier when the only emotion I possessed for him was hatred. Now I don't know how to feel.

"What about the witch who cursed you?" I ask, returning to the matter at hand. "Can you tell me who she is?"

"I cannot."

"Is she still alive?"

No answer.

I try a different question. "How long do witches live for?"

"It depends."

"On what?"

"How powerful the witch is," he says. "Some have lived for millennia."

I do not know which witch cursed him, but it's possible she's still alive. "Can you take me to her?"

He doesn't reply, of course.

I run my hand down my face. Even if he told me who the witch is and I found her, it's doubtful I'd convince her to revoke the curse.

And as much as I wish it were not the case, the cure for his curse likely involves true love. Right now, my only plan to save my sister is to wait until fate decides we're madly in love.

But sitting around and doing nothing has never suited me.

"Adara," he says, and the strained note to his voice causes me to look up. "It . . . It seems I've overstayed my welcome in here."

"What are you talking about?"

"The water."

I force myself to look at him. All the bubbles have disappeared, and in their place is a film of ice. "Don't tell me you're stuck?"

He blanches. "It's frozen around my foot."

"Can't you melt it?"

He gives me a pointed look.

"Right. I suppose you wouldn't be living in a palace of ice if you had that luxury."

He tries to pull himself out, and I have just enough time to look away before seeing every inch of his naked skin. Then there's a frustrated groan and the slosh of water, and I glimpse him sinking back into the tub.

A laugh bursts from my lips, taking me by surprise as much as the king.

"I'm glad to know my misfortune amuses you," he says with a glare.

"I'm sorry," I say, though it's a struggle to stop laughing.

He tilts his head back against the metallic rim of the tub and heaves a sigh.

"What will happen if you can't get out?" I ask.

What if he's forced to stay there for eternity, becoming one with the palace around him? At that thought, all laughter dies.

It isn't a fate I'd wish on anyone.

The Winter King casts me a withering look.

"Has it ever completely frozen?"

"Once," he says, staring at the ceiling. "Long ago, before I became accustomed to the nature of my power."

"How did you escape in the end?"

"I had to shatter it, since I could not melt it. The bathtub's exterior had frozen with it, so I had to destroy all of it."

I swallow. "Does that ability also extend to people?"

He arches a brow.

"Are you able to shatter people after freezing them?"

"I suppose."

If he can shatter people, then he could have shattered the Summer Brides, removing all evidence of them. Instead, he keeps them safely locked away in that forbidden chamber, knowing that one day his Summer Queen would come along to break his curse.

While this doesn't excuse what he's done or change the fact he took my sister, it proves not everything is as black and white as I once believed.

"Adara?" he says, pulling me from my thoughts. When I glance across at him, I notice the frost has spread. "If you are willing, I'd appreciate your help."

I blink, and pull my attention away from the water and to his face, his bright eyes meeting mine. "Of course." I place my ink and parchment on the counter by the door and start over to him. When I reach him, I focus on the end of the tub where his feet should be.

I dip my hand into his bath, and the surrounding water warms from my touch, preventing his power from freezing it completely. My fingers sink lower and luckily, they meet solid ice rather than his toes. It'd be awkward if I accidentally grabbed his feet, though even that could be worse.

I squeeze the ice wrapped around his left ankle, digging my nails in, but it doesn't relent.

After several moments of trying, I press my lips into a thin line and pull out my hand. "It seems my ability to stop your magic only works on things that aren't already frozen. I can't free your ankle."

"Then you'll have to try pulling me out. Quickly. Before the rest of the water succumbs."

"Can't you shatter the ice around your ankle?"

"It's stuck to the metal, so shattering it will also break the bathtub."

"Is that a problem? It's just a tub, and if the water leaks out everywhere, all of it will just freeze, anyway."

"I'd rather not break this bathtub," he mumbles.

Considering how similar it looks to the one my maids bring me, I'm not sure what's so special about it. Curious though I am, I don't stop to ask the question. Otherwise the frost will spread further through the water.

"All right," I say, pacing around to the other side. "I'll try to pull you out."

I loop my hands under his arms and around his chest and do my best to concentrate on the task at hand rather than the fact I'm practically hugging a naked man. When he starts to move out the water, I grit my teeth and pull, but the king is by no means light. Not with his tall, broad-shouldered stature and all those well-sculpted muscles. Muscles which I'm currently holding and trying not to think about.

Our first few attempts have no effect and his foot stays stuck, and I wonder if he'll have to shatter the water and break his beloved bathtub after all. But then, with one last heave from us both, he bursts free and tumbles out. The force is so great it knocks me off my feet.

We crash to the floor, landing in a messy heap of limbs.

Chapter 8

The surprise of the fall dazes me. I don't realize I'm lying atop him until I blink.

And he's naked.

His skin is still wet, though the water droplets glitter in the morning light from the balcony windows.

The next thing I realize is that my hand is resting on his abdomen—much lower than is safe—but I don't move it. Heat surges through my stomach.

We haven't been this close since . . .

I can't let myself think of that night. Of all the deliciously wicked things his tongue can do, of how good he felt inside me.

I know I mustn't react, but it's impossible to stop warmth from rushing across my cheeks, burning so hot I'm certain it'll melt away all my freckles.

No. None of that night was real.

I was acting. It isn't my fault my body doesn't understand the difference. It doesn't mean I feel anything for him.

And if I do, it's just lust.

I tell myself this over and over, wanting more than anything to believe it.

I don't dare to look anywhere except his face.

The only saving grace is the way I landed means I'm lying halfway across him and am not entirely straddling him.

His eyes burn into mine, and he doesn't so much as blink. Like me, he stays unnaturally rigid, not daring to move.

I'm the one to break our trance, snapping my left hand carefully up from his lower abdomen and then whirling around so my back faces him. Drawing my knees to my chest, I stare out at the bleak gardens beyond his balcony and imagine myself being repeatedly doused in a bucket of cold water.

Not that it helps.

We stay there, the tension so thick I can hardly breathe.

What would happen if I turned around and yielded to the relentless desire burning within me? What if I pressed my lips to his and kissed him as passionately as we kissed on our wedding night? Would he think me mad for desiring him and push me away?

Or would he kiss me back as frantically and drag me over to his bed where we could once more experience all those pleasures I dare not think of?

I squeeze my eyes shut.

That final question may drive me to madness.

Because, despite the heat pounding through my body, nothing can change what has happened between us. Maybe he didn't kill my sister, but he still took her, and I refuse to fall for her captor.

This is lust, and lust should extinguish if left alone for long enough. Eventually it will fade, as the flames of that night scatter into forgotten embers.

Perhaps what I feel isn't of my own making. Maybe the reason my body reacts so violently to him is because I'm his destined Summer Queen.

I cover my face with my palms. Why must everything be so damn complicated?

And yet in all this, I can't help but wonder how Elaric also feels.

The king finally moves. I keep my focus on the gardens, but I feel his presence shift as he steps forward, casting long shadows through the room. There's a whisper of fabric, more steps, and then silence.

At long last, he says from somewhere behind me, "Surely it cannot be comfortable sitting on the floor?"

"Are . . . " I begin, but then break off.

Though I fail to voice the question, he seems to know exactly what I wanted to ask.

"I am dressed," he murmurs.

Digging my nails into my palms to sober myself, I stand and turn.

True to his word, he's wrapped in dark blue silken robes and sits on one of the two armchairs near the far door. He gestures to the chair opposite him, and my mind is momentarily consumed by the memory of draping my wedding dress over it, burying my dagger deep between the heavy layers of silk.

I concentrate on my steps, keeping them steady. The king's eyes stay on me, tracking my every movement, but no matter how I try to steel myself against the barrage of emotion waging upon my heart, I fear I must be swaying with every step.

It takes too long to reach the chair, and when I finally do, I perch tentatively on the edge. The king continues to watch me, as if he wishes to say something but does not know how.

I scan across the room, searching for a distraction. My eyes stop on the copper tub now abandoned in the middle of the room. Given that the water is already frozen inside, it won't be long before the copper exterior matches the rest of the décor here.

"Shouldn't you empty the water out of the tub?" I say. "Before the rest of it freezes?"

The king leans back in his chair. "Most of it is already frozen."

"Then you might have well as shattered your way out of it."

"Doing so would have caused it to be broken beyond repair," he says. I'm not sure why we're having such a serious debate about the state of his bathtub, but it's a welcome respite from the insurmountable tension. "I'll keep it stowed away until it is no longer frozen."

"Is the bathtub important?"

"It has been in my family for a long time."

I try to identify the note of emotion in his voice but am unable to distinguish it.

"I find I have too few items of the past nowadays," he says.

I know I should avoid prying into his past—unless it involves his curse—since it risks him becoming human in my eyes.

Before I can decide whether to press him any further, he says, "You should go back to bed and try to sleep for the rest of the morning. I imagine you slept very little last night with how busy you've been in the library."

How can I sleep when I'm so close to finding a way to save my sister?

"I was wondering something," I say, not bothering to acknowledge his suggestion. "Do you remember the night my father tried to break me out of the palace?"

"I do," he says softly.

"He brought guards with him. They fought you, and you froze them."

His expression is grim, as if he dreads what I will next ask him.

"After you froze them, what happened? The last I remember, they were still there when you flew Father and me back to the palace. But I'm not sure what became of them after that. I was too concerned with rescuing Father." In a small voice, I add, "Did . . . did you shatter them?"

He quickly shakes his head. "I did not. They were already incapacitated and rendering them to tiny fragments would have been unnecessarily cruel."

"Where are they? Are they still out there in the forest?"

"After I escorted you to your chambers, I took great care in returning them to the palace. They are also in the room you visited two nights ago, along with your sister and all the previous Summer Brides."

When I break the king's curse, I'll be able to free them as well as my sister.

"You seem greatly concerned for their fate," the king says, studying me.

"They only broke into the palace because they were ordered to do so," I say, focusing on my hands so I don't have to look at him. "And one of those guards, their captain, was someone dear to me. He was the man who taught me how to wield a sword."

"I'm sorry, Adara," he whispers. "I did not intend to take away someone else dear to you."

"It's fine," I say, swallowing down the painful lump in the back of my throat. "I'll break your curse and then everything will be put right."

He says nothing but stares at me with that heavy look in his eyes, as if there are a thousand things he wishes to say but they're all too tangled together.

I stand and pace over to the counter by the door where I left the parchment and ink. Then I return to the Winter King and hold them out. I realize now that in my haste, I forgot to bring something for him to write with.

"Do you have a quill?" I ask.

He conjures a translucent pen and dips it into the pot. "Why have you brought me parchment and ink?"

"Can you write 'I am cursed?'"

The Winter King puts his pen to the parchment, and I watch intently as he begins to form the letters. He manages *I* and *am*, but as he goes to write *cursed*, his hand stops mid motion, the *c* partway formed. He turns to me and raises a brow, as if to ask what else I expected.

I inspect the abandoned sentence. In all this time I've been in the palace, I've never seen the Winter King's handwriting but it looks as elegant and regal as he does. I imagine plenty of scribes would be envious. I suppose three centuries is plenty of time to practice. "Can you really not continue?"

He turns back to the parchment and lowers his pen to the parchment again. This time the nib doesn't even touch the surface, and his hand trembles as he tries to push it down. It's as if an invisible force is fighting against him.

"Can you write the name of the witch who cursed you?"

"I cannot."

"Can't you try?"

He tries but doesn't form even a single letter. If I had the witch's first initial, it would help to narrow her down.

"Never mind," I say. While this exercise has revealed no new clues, at least it confirms the fact he's cursed and that the magic prevents him from revealing its existence. If that part of what I read is true, then every curse having a way to be broken must also be true.

Which means I can save my sister. I just need to figure out how.

I tighten my fists and start away. "I'll keep searching."

"Adara," he calls after me, "I was hoping to discuss a certain matter with you."

I stop. "What about?"

"About our marriage."

My shoulders turn rigid. "Our marriage," I say slowly.

"I have had time over the past few days to consider everything." His gaze drifts over to the balcony and stays there. "And after much consideration, I believe it would be best for our marriage to be annulled."

Annulled.

That single word hits my stomach like a lead weight.

When I don't reply, he turns back to me and scans across my face. "This is what you also wish, is it not?"

"I . . . " My mouth clamps shut. Of course having our marriage annulled is what I want. The reason I married him was to drive a dagger through his chest on our wedding night. It would be rational for us to discard our marriage.

And yet, I hesitate.

If I tell him I don't wish for our marriage to be annulled, we'll remain married forever, and forever is such a very long time, especially when I'm unsure if a life as Queen—as his wife—is what I want. Besides, he's the one who has asked this question, completely unprompted. Clearly this is what he wishes for himself. To be free of his would-be assassin. And I can't say I blame him. After what I did, I don't deserve his trust or loyalty or any part of his heart.

For us both, I force myself to say, "Yes. Yes, that is what I want. We should annul our marriage."

To erase it as if it never happened . . .

"Very well," the king says.

I do my best to read his expression, but his thoughts are masked too well, and I can't tell whether he is pleased or disappointed by my reply. But regardless of his real thoughts, he accepts my answer so readily, and the deep ache within me almost causes me to blurt out the truth: That my feelings for him are so complicated and confusing, and I do not know what I really want.

"I shall order it to be done," he declares.

Forcing out a verbal response is impossible, so I simply dip my head in acknowledgement. And then, like the coward I am, I run.

Chapter 9

Tears prick my eyes and blur my vision. I grit my teeth and force them not to fall, especially as I pass servants going about their business.

Annulling our marriage is what I should want, and yet it feels as if my heart is being cleaved in two. A part of me wants to whirl around and march back into Elaric's room and tell him I want to remain married to him, that his lips and fingers tracing across my body is all I can think about day and night, but the other part of me wishes to run as far as I can.

I'm terrified about what would happen if I told him the truth, how I wish more than anything that I hadn't been so blinded by my anger. What if he says he'll never forgive me, even if I break his curse, even if I spend every day repenting for my sins? What if I've destroyed all possibility of a future between us?

Before he brought up annulling our marriage, I intended to return to the library and resume my search for information on his curse. But now I'm in no state to concentrate, and I'm certain the paragraphs would merge together if I tried to read. That's why I return to my chambers instead of the library.

When I arrive, the doors are already ajar. Looking through, I see both Kassia and Elona rushing around, making my bed and straightening my belongings. Kind though they both are, all I want is to be alone with my messy thoughts.

I turn, but it's already too late. Kassia has spotted me.

"Milady," she calls, stepping toward me, "where are you going?"

"The library," I say quickly. Hopefully, there won't be any other servants in the library, and even if there are, I'll find a shadowy corner to sit in and hide my face with a book.

"Have you eaten anything this morning?" Elona asks, draping a blanket across my bed.

"Er, no," I say, angling away my face so Kassia can't see. But she notices anyway and catches my arm before I can flee.

"What's wrong?" Kassia asks, brows furrowing as she inspects me. "Why are you crying?"

At this, Elona leaves my bed and hurries over. She examines me as carefully as Kassia does, and then their gentle concern causes fresh tears to fall.

The two of them guide me into my chambers and sit me down on my bed, and I offer little resistance, following their movements as easily as if I were a puppet.

"What happened?" Kassia asks once we're sitting down. Perhaps for the fifth time or sixth. I've lost count.

"The king," I force out, though talking feels impossible. "I went to speak to the king."

Kassia hesitates, regarding me carefully. "What did you speak to him about? Did you ask about his curse?"

"I tried," I say. These words are easier to form. They distract me from the reason for my pain. "He couldn't tell me he's cursed, but it's as Elona said: the magic prevents him from doing so. I found a book in the library this morning which explains how those afflicted by a curse can't reveal its existence. They can't even write anything about it."

"Is this why you're upset?" Elona presses gently.

I turn away from them both, my eyes instead settling on the sealed door which leads to the king's chambers. I wonder whether he's still sitting where I left him, thinking about my answer to his question, or whether he has already gotten dressed and left to go about his business for the day.

"It's all right," Elona says, giving my hand a pat. "You needn't tell us if you do not wish to. Just know that we are both here to talk if you change your mind."

As much as I want to explain the reason for my anguish, saying it aloud proves difficult. But I should have told them of my pain when I first arrived. If I had, perhaps this entire disaster could have been avoided. It's time I learned from my past mistakes and put these painful lessons into practice.

Besides, Elona and Kassia are more than just maids. They're my friends, and I mustn't keep pushing them away.

Bracing myself, I face them both. "The king asked me if I wished to annul our marriage."

"He wants to annul it?" Kassia exclaims.

Elona's eyes narrow. "What did you say, milady?"

"I . . . I agreed."

They glance at each other, and I lower my head.

"Have you spoken to His Majesty about how you truly feel?" Kassia asks softly.

Sensing a scolding on the horizon, I decide not to respond. "Adara!"

I wait for Elona to admonish her from speaking so familiarly with me, but she does not. Apparently, even Elona is so frustrated with me she no longer cares for etiquette.

Kassia shakes her head. "Can't you see that this is what's gotten you both into this mess in the first place?"

"What is?" I mumble.

"The two of you keep avoiding talking about how you feel," Kassia says, "and all it's doing is creating one disaster after another. What if His Majesty feels similarly to you? What if his own feelings are conflicted? Maybe you'll both decide that annulling the marriage is for the best, but at least you will have discussed it together properly and laid everything out in the open."

What she says is right, and I know I should face him soon because discussing this matter will grow more difficult by the day, but Kassia wasn't there to witness the bath incident. As ridiculous as the whole thing was, it reignited confusing feelings within me.

"If it would make it any easier for you," Elona adds, "we can accompany you to the king's chambers?"

"It's all right, thank you."

At that, Kassia lets out a heavy sigh. Though her previous outburst received no stern retort from Elona, now she receives a warning glare. Kassia shrugs, and Elona doesn't press the matter beyond that and instead watches me.

"Maybe you're right that we should talk through everything properly first," I say, "but it won't change that this annulment is what the king wants. I attempted to poison him, and I drove a blade through his chest. Why would anyone wish to stay married to someone after all that?"

"But maybe if you talk about things then he'll understand you care about him and regret your choices?"

"I've already hurt him enough . . . and I don't deserve his forgiveness. It is best we go our separate ways once we break his curse."

"If that is what you believe is for the best, milady," Kassia says.

I can't help the twinge of doubt which rises, but I push it down. This situation is already so messy, and it's best Elaric is freed from it.

This *is* the right decision.

I exhale deeply and say, "Thanks for listening to me, both of you."

"A conflicted heart is a painful one," Elona says. "We're both here whenever you need us."

Since I lost Dalia, I've not had anyone to speak to. She was always the person I would turn to, and when she vanished, I had no one to talk through my grief with. Only my father, and he was broken for so long afterward. Maybe if I'd had Kassia and Elona to talk to, I'd have seen everything more clearly instead of being consumed by pain.

I know I've made many mistakes, but nothing can excuse what I have done and I can't change the past. All I can do is focus on the future and that means freeing both Elaric and my sister from the curse.

With that thought, I stand. "I'm going to head back to the library," I declare. "The sooner I can find answers about this damned curse, the better."

Chapter 10

When I return to the library, my stack of books is where I left it, and sunlight spills in through the window beside my desk. The candle I lit still burns, and the small flame flickers in its glass container. I watch it, the gentle movement captivating my mind and briefly silencing my deafening thoughts. Then I lean forward, pull off the glass container, and blow out the flame. The suffocating smell of smoke fills my nostrils, and I breathe in as much of it as I can.

Though I left Elona and Kassia just minutes ago, now that I'm alone, I feel myself breaking once more.

It's easy to rationalize that annulling our marriage is for the best, easy to say it out loud, but it's much more difficult to convince my heart. Yet since there's nothing I can do about it—the annulment is Elaric's idea. All I can do is repeat these cold, hard facts over and over.

And distract my mind with research, with finding a way to save Dalia.

The memory of her frozen face has my hands reaching for the next book in my stack. This one is bound with a crusty, dark leather cover, and the pages within are filled with various accounts on witches. Many entries are accompanied by sketches.

One drawing is features a breathtakingly beautiful woman with luscious curls. The adjacent page is entitled: *Melusine the Mad*, and I scan over the several paragraphs beneath the heading.

While the capricious nature of witches is well-documented by the countless other examples included in this tome, one of perhaps the most notable records of their volatility is through the tragic tale of Stemore Kingdom.

Unbeknownst to the court, Melusine the Mad successfully infiltrated the royal family by seducing the recently wed crown prince, Torrin. It is rumored that Torrin never once visited his wife's chambers after their wedding night, and the prince held no qualms for showing his affections publicly to his new mistress. When his wife remained without child even the following summer, it came of little surprise to anyone in the whole kingdom. Although this matter greatly distressed the king, the crown prince himself showed no concern for his lack of an heir. Perhaps the only surprise to anyone was that Torrin's new mistress stayed as barren as his wife.

By winter, the crown prince began to show greater signs of his succumbing to madness. It was reported that he rarely slept, and frequently experienced hallucinations during the day. On one occasion, he publicly defied his father before the entire court, and accused the king of conspiring with his younger brother to murder him and remove him from the line of succession.

Six months later, the king died of a sudden heart attack, and Torrin took the throne in his father's place. The new king's paranoia grew, and so did his court's concerns for his reign. Torrin was well-aware of his lords' diminishing respect for his authority, and therefore decided to make an example out of several of them. His brother wasn't spared from his suspicion, and eventually Torrin ordered his beheading during a court meeting.

Stemore Kingdom's struggles worsened with each passing month, and in the June after succeeding his father, King Torrin threw himself from the palace's highest tower and into the courtyard where many nobles were celebrating the Midsummer Festival.

Torrin's beloved mistress rushed to his side and huddled over his body. At first, she was believed to be weeping, but then her sobs turned into laughter, and she revealed her identity to the crowd as the witch Melusine, demanding their applause for the entertainment she had bestowed upon their miserable lives throughout the past two years.

Although several attempts were made to capture Melusine the Mad, she vanished from the kingdom without a trace, and as of the time of writing this account, fifty years later, no other sightings of this witch have been reported.

I tear my eyes away from the pages, lean back in my chair, and look out the window. A few servants are rushing past, carrying out their daily tasks.

I'm not sure how long ago this book was written, since there's no date at the top of the passage, and I didn't see one on the title page either. But even if this particular witch is still alive, she can't be the one responsible for Elaric's curse. While the passage didn't explicitly mention her powers, a book I read earlier this morning included 'mind' as a branch of magic, and it's possible Melusine influenced the crown prince with her powers rather than just through verbal persuasion.

Maybe Elaric's witch, whoever she is, relishes the freezing of the Crystal Palace and the disappearing girls every Midsummer Ball, much like how Melusine savored the destruction and suffering of Stemore Kingdom.

Even more so, I wonder why Elaric was cursed in the first place. Did he do something to offend her? Or did this witch have no apparent reason other than for her amusement?

One thing I can be certain of is that witches are dangerous, for both their tremendous powers and unpredictable temperaments, and the path to breaking Elaric's curse will be perilous indeed.

I flick through the next few pages, where I find plenty more passages about witches with various powers. One sketch illustrates the sinking of a kingdom, while another shows a kingdom being frozen. Eruweth, the latter was apparently called. But the book includes nothing more than that, and not the witch's name either.

I pause, my finger tracing over the castle's turrets. Could this be Elaric's witch? If there are any other books which mention the freezing of Eruweth, maybe I can find her name. But even if I succeed in identifying her, how will I know if the witch who froze Eruweth is the same one who cursed him?

Besides, by the time I finish flicking through this tome, I have encountered several more ice witches who all have a particular love of freezing and shattering their victims.

I close the book, stretch my arms, and let out a yawn. Glancing through the window, it appears to be mid-afternoon. I wonder how long it'll be before Elona and Kassia come to find me and scold me for not eating anything since breakfast. And what's the king doing right now? Is he sitting by his desk or is he staring out of his balcony windows? Is he thinking about our annulment?

Before I can ruminate any further, I head to the shelves, rummaging through them for anything on Eruweth—one of my few leads.

As Eruweth is a long-lost kingdom, I have to search the oldest tomes, many of which are missing pages. It takes an hour to gather enough books. Arms full, I return to my desk.

I make it through three more before the library door opens. Now dark beyond the windows, I lit a candle earlier to spare my eyes.

"Can you ask for my dinner to be brought here instead of my chambers—" I begin, but trail off as I turn.

It isn't my maids who stand there, but the Winter King himself.

"I will inform the servants," he says. If he notices my surprise, he makes no mention of it.

I force myself to meet his eyes, to act as if everything is fine, even though it's far from it.

All I want is to look away and bury my head in the book I was reading because maintaining this mask of neutrality is so draining. I remind myself of all the reasons why staying away from each other is for the best.

"I'm told you've spent the entire day here," he says after a moment. I'm relieved when his eyes move from mine and scan across the books piled around me.

"I have."

I brace, waiting for him to lecture me about not taking care of myself.

But none comes.

Did he really only come to find me in the library to ask if I'd been sitting here all day? Since he says nothing else, not even after several minutes pass, that seems to be the case.

"Maybe you can help me," I say, partly to break the awful silence and partly out of curiosity. While it's clear he can neither speak nor write a single word about his curse, I wonder whether he can pass me any books which might aid my search, even if indirectly.

"In what way?" he asks.

I frown, sitting back in my chair, and consider how to phrase my questions so his curse permits him to answer. "I know so little of your childhood and your life before you became the King of Avella," I say. "Is there anything in here which might shed some light upon that part of your past?"

Though I've searched extensively, I've found no mention of Elaric prior to his reign as the Winter King. While a book about his life prior to ascending the throne may not reveal anything about his curse, it could help me to find a more direct lead.

He hesitates. Then, "I suppose there might be something."

He paces over to the shelves and browses through them. As promising as his response seems, I do my best not to get my hopes up. He might not find what he's looking for, and even if he does, there's a chance it won't further my search.

Elaric returns to my desk a few minutes later, holding an old book with a dusty burgundy leather cover. He sets it down before me.

The book is unremarkable, save for its fraying, loosening stitches. Carefully, I peel back the cover and inspect the first page. I take a while to make out the sloping scrawl as saying 'Theron Tirling.' If the rest proves this messy, reading it will take all night.

I glance back at him, curious as to the book's significance.

"This is my father's journal," he says.

Whether it reveals much about his curse or not, the fact it belonged to his father piques my interest. Eagerly, I flick the page but my candle goes out.

We're cast in darkness.

The moon is fuller than last night, so more light filters in through the window, but it's still too dim to read. When my eyes adjust, I find my matches and relight my candle.

Except as soon as I try, the flame fizzles out.

I've had no problems with lighting matches in the library before, only inside the palace like on the night when I tried to melt down the doors to his forbidden chamber.

There's just one explanation . . .

I look up at him and raise a brow.

Elaric's jaw tightens. "I must go."

Before I can say anything else, he turns and leaves.

Chapter 11

Each lord of my council congratulates me with forced smiles, a few with thinly veiled pity in their eyes, and yet I have known no greater joy in this life. Perhaps I ought to be consumed by disappointment that Cerise shall never wear my crown, but from the very moment I first held her in my arms, I knew she was the most perfect thing God could bestow upon a man. It is said one cannot love any other more than their firstborn, and only now can I fathom the truth in those words. For even if Hester next bears me a boy, I fear there shall be no room left for him in my heart.

I arch a brow as I read the paragraph a second time, the amber glow of my candle dancing across the parchment. Given how stoic Elaric can be, it's surprising to discover that Theron, his father, is much more sentimental. The journal entry is dated as 24th July 1012, three-hundred-and-forty-five years ago.

I read through the following pages. At first, my pace is slow as I struggle to interpret Theron's handwriting, but then quickens as I grow accustomed to how he forms each letter. The journal's entries are dated at various intervals. Sometimes Theron writes in it the following day, other times it's weeks or even months later. What the king writes in his journal is so personal and transparent that I suspect he kept it very close to hand. While Theron has revealed nothing too damning in the portion I've read so far, his writing offers great insight to his deepest thoughts and fears, which others scheming for the throne might have sought to use to their advantage.

After the May following Cerise's birth, there's a gap of six months when the kingdom was at war with Maecia, a kingdom I've never heard of and suspect no longer exists. When he writes in his journal again, he shares his thoughts on defending his kingdom and mentions how his last battle was as a young man during his father's reign. His council implored him not to oversee the war in person, reminding him of how he has no heir, but Theron insisted battles can't be won from the comfort of a palace.

After that, he writes about the daily struggles of running a kingdom, of lords and dukes and barons scheming for their own ends, of marriage proposals being sent for his daughter despite her not even having reached her second year.

In November 1013, the queen becomes pregnant with her second child. Rumors spread throughout the kingdom: that this child might also be a daughter, that his queen might never bear him an heir, that his younger brother might inherit the throne. Theron describes his brother as a well-meaning fool more suited to parties than court, a sentiment shared by many of his council, adding further pressure to the queen's pregnancy.

His entries become infrequent once more. Then, a dozen pages later, he writes about the birth of his second child, which to the relief of his council, is a son. He names him Caltain, after his father.

While Theron doesn't write heartfelt paragraphs like he did for the birth of his daughter, he does share his relief of having an heir, and how he didn't realize the burden which was weighing on him until Caltain entered the world.

I flick through the next entries, deciding that as interesting as the workings of a king's mind are, none of what I've read so far will help me uncover the truth behind Elaric's curse.

Soon, I reach a page where Theron writes about the birth of his third child, whom he names after his wife's father: Elaric.

My gaze trails back up to the date written at the top of the entry.

6th December 1017

I can't help from my lips pulling into a smile, though a detail like the Winter King's birthday shouldn't intrigue me so much.

Here is concrete proof that he was born from a mortal mother, rather than ice and snow, like I once believed.

With how focused I am on Theron's journal, I barely notice the sound of the library door opening and am slow in turning to look.

This time, it is my maids returning and not the king.

"My goodness, it's cold in here," Kassia says, rubbing her arms.

Elona glances around the library. "Is there a window open? It's usually warmer in here than the palace."

There isn't a window open. If the library is colder than usual, I can't tell, but it must result from the king lingering here earlier. Hopefully, his magic hasn't set into any of the books. How disastrous it would be if there's one in here which contains all the answers I seek but freezes before I can find it. Maybe I should check the shelves before continuing to read Theron's journal.

"It's fine," I say with a shrug. "You know I don't feel the cold."

My maids hesitate, but the reminder seems to placate them. Elona nods. "Dinner will be ready shortly."

"Perfect," I say. "Would you be able to arrange for it to be brought here?"

"The king has already informed us of your request," Elona says. "But you've been in here all day. Surely a change in scenery would be for the best?"

She's probably right. As much as I want to, I can't stay here day and night until I find a way to break the curse. I'll end up driving myself to madness. Maybe a break from the library would be beneficial. Since I'm only a fifth of the way through Theron's journal, it'll take me the rest of the night to finish it. I can sit and read it in bed.

"All right," I say, closing the journal and standing. "Could you tell the kitchen staff that I'll have dinner in my chambers?"

Kassia's brows rise, and she eyes the book in my hands. Yet she doesn't question me.

I quickly inspect the shelves, and once I've confirmed no books are at risk of freezing, I blow out the candle and head back to my room.

There, I sit on my bed, wrapped in furs, and resume reading Theron's journal. Servants soon arrive with dinner, and I eat as quickly as I can before returning to my spot on my bed.

Two-thirds through, in the Year 1035, Theron writes of a violent plague sweeping across the kingdom. It spread from town to town, killing indiscriminately—rich and poor, young and old alike fell to the disease. Even the palace offered no refuge, first striking servants before reaching the royal family.

The first one to catch the disease was Cerise, and despite Theron's pleas, the queen insisted on staying by her daughter's bedside. A few days later, the queen also fell ill. While Elaric's sister survived, his mother was less fortunate.

But the queen's death wasn't the only tragedy to befall the royal family that year. Months later, when the kingdom was recovering from the onslaught of the plague, both Elaric and Caltain caught the disease. Much of Theron's writing during those next fateful weeks is full of grief, demanding to know what he did for God to punish him so severely.

In the end, just one son survived.

Weeks following his brother's funeral, Elaric was declared Crown Prince. Shortly after, the king's council started pressuring Theron to remarry. If anything happened to Elaric, the crown would fall into his brother's hands. Yet Theron wrote he could not bear to take a second wife and that Hester would not be so easily replaced.

Even years later, Theron was so full of grief that he didn't remarry. Knowing it was a futile endeavor, the council's focus turned to Elaric, who was now twenty-two.

But Elaric refused to entertain any prospect of marriage, regardless of how many princesses from foreign kingdoms visited Avella. Elaric insisted he didn't want to spend his life caged up in the palace and wanted to travel the world before his freedom was bound by a family and a crown. Besides, Princess

Cerise had just given birth to a son, and the king's grandson would inherit the throne before his brother.

While this child was reassurance enough for Elaric, his father still harbored great fears. The baby was so young, and it could not be certain he would survive his first year without succumbing to fever. And even if the baby remained healthy, it would take countless years for him to become of age. If another disease spread through the kingdom and claimed both Elaric and the king, his drunkard brother would have to reign in the baby's stead until he was old enough. That would be plenty of time for the kingdom to plunge into ruin.

Elaric's only argument was that it would be the same case for his children, except his sons would be even younger than his nephew. After a heated argument, with Elaric telling his father to marry again himself if the matter of producing heirs concerned him so greatly, Elaric decided to leave and pursue his desire to travel the world while he was still young.

For three years, the king heard nothing from his son. For all he knew, Elaric could have been killed in the far reaches of the world. The entries from this point forward are filled with as much anguish as when Theron lost his wife and eldest son. He writes of how he regrets pushing Elaric so hard into marriage, and that he should have known with his stubbornness it would cause him to resist harder.

A knock sounds on my door. I look up from the journal.

"Come in," I say.

The door opens to reveal Elona. "Kassia and I are heading home for the night, milady. Do you need anything else before we leave?"

I shake my head. "I'll be fine. Thank you for checking."

With that, she bids me good night and closes the door.

I lift the journal from my lap, the blue light from the candles beside my bed causing the leather edges to gleam, and I inspect its pages from the side. I have around a quarter left.

I lean back into my pillow and sigh. As enlightening as this journal is, I have little left, and I've not yet found anything to help break the curse. I'll have to begin my search anew tomorrow morning. At least I now have specific dates for the first twenty-two years of Elaric's life. And plenty of names, too. Maybe the information I've discovered tonight will point me in the right direction.

I lower the journal and keep reading.

Three years later, Elaric returned home. The king's worries were absolved, and Princess Cerise had given birth to two more sons. With three grandsons, the eldest of which was nearly four, there was less reason to fear his brother destroying the kingdom.

Throughout the following year, all was well. Elaric resumed his duties as the crown prince and visited many towns throughout the kingdom in his father's place.

And then, the flames struck.

Without warning, a town burned to ash overnight. Then another. And three more.

The enemy left few survivors, but one boy in the third town was lucky to escape with his life and ran as far as he could until he reached the nearest city. After being found by guards, he was brought before the king to report what he'd seen.

The boy spoke of a ferocious beast of scales and wings and talons, wreathed in flames.

The king sent hundreds of men to hunt the monster, and though they found its lair deep in the southwestern mountains, they were no match. Few survived, bearing horrific burns. But they'd seen its power and the truth.

The enemy was no mindless beast but also took the form of a hauntingly beautiful woman.

A witch.

I sit up straighter, fingers digging into the journal's leather case. Though this witch harnesses fire rather than ice, it's the first mention of magic I've found in Theron's journal. Could this be the clue I've been searching for?

Heart pounding in my chest, I read the next pages at double speed.

Fire rages through my kingdom, destroying more life than the plague eight years ago which took Hester and Caltain. I know not what we have done to enrage this witch, for her to begin this wicked crusade against my people, but this time our enemy has a face and a name. My son tells me he heard rumors of this villain during his travels and believes that her name is Seraphina.

While little has been heard of Seraphina in recent years, her sister Isidore, an ice witch, froze the Kingdom of Eruweth a decade ago and the island disappeared overnight. If Elaric is correct about this fire witch being related to Isidore, then I fear she seeks a kingdom of her own and has decided to seize Avella.

Elaric says he encountered another witch during his travels, one which goes by the name 'Belinda,' and he claims she is more reasonable than Seraphina and Isidore. He leaves tomorrow morning, to see if he can gain her alliance, and although I am reluctant to let him leave our kingdom again, anywhere in the world is safer than here at this moment in time.

After that entry, a month passes with no mention of Elaric's return. By then, Seraphina has destroyed countless more towns and cities and half of the kingdom has fallen. Fearing Elaric may never return, or that the kingdom will be long lost by the time he does, the king writes he plans to launch a devastating attack against the fire witch, seeking to end her reign of terror once and for all.

I turn to the next page. But it's blank. I turn to the next and the next, but every page left in this journal is empty. After declaring his intentions to fight Seraphina himself, the king never wrote another entry.

My stomach twists. I close the journal and stare into the shadows.

Elaric's father died facing Seraphina, leaving this story unfinished.

Chapter 12

Gripping the journal, I bolt up from bed and hurry out the room. I could return to the library and search for more books to determine what happened after the king died, but I'm certain I know the truth and how it all links to Elaric's curse. Asking him to finish this story will confirm my theory quicker than consulting more books.

Though my pace is frantic as I rush through the palace, I slow when I reach the innermost room of his chambers and remember to knock loudly on his doors, recalling the disaster from earlier this morning.

The doors open, and Elaric appears, wrapped in his navy robes. With how ruffled his hair is, he must have been sleeping.

"Did I wake you?"

"I wasn't asleep." He pauses, looking down at me, and then his eyes settle on the journal tucked under my arm. "Is everything all right?"

"I have questions," I blurt. "So many of them. But if you're tired, they can wait until the morning—"

"I'm not tired." Elaric holds the doors open wider for me to step through and gestures to the armchairs beside the fireplace. As I sit, he clicks his fingers and blue light sparks, dancing over the icy logs. "Shall I ask a guard to fetch us wine?"

"I'm all right, thank you," I say quickly, lowering my head as I recall the last time we drank wine together.

Why must everything remind me of our wedding night?

He sits in the opposite armchair, watching me. My mind races over every detail I've read of his past, realizing how much more human he seems to me than the last time I saw him, even though that was just hours ago. So much has changed since then, and I feel I have lived the first twenty-five years of his life with him through his father's journal.

I open my mouth to say something, but Elaric speaks before I can.

"My father was such a reserved man that I once believed he possessed no emotions," he says. "He would chastise me for any tears I shed when falling or scraping my knee in sparring, when Caltain always beat me. My brother was three years my elder and always so much taller and stronger. My father told me crying is a useless thing, serving only to sap my strength, and that my time would be better spent training to beat my brother. By the time I was eight, I had stopped crying.

"After that, the only time I cried in front of my father was during the funerals of my mother and brother—that awful year when pestilence devoured our kingdom. Yet during both funerals, my father didn't shed a single tear. I decided then that he truly had a heart made of rock."

My head snaps up, surprised by his words. "But—"

He interrupts me, a light smile playing on his lips. "But then I found his journal after his death and realized that his outward coldness only served as armor against the abundant emotion within. That is why I never truly understood my father until he passed from this world."

For so long, I've believed that Elaric's own stoicism results from his curse. But perhaps it is mostly to do with his upbringing.

"Do you keep a journal?" I ask.

"I would, if I could. Unfortunately, the journal would freeze long before I finished writing in it."

"Oh," I say softly.

"What were your questions?"

I lay the book flat on my lap and gaze down at it, mind still reeling. "Your father wrote that he intended to face the fire witch who was destroying the kingdom, but there's nothing else after that."

"Indeed," Elaric says. "I was away when he decided to strike against Seraphina. Had I returned sooner, it is possible he wouldn't have been killed."

"I'm sorry for your loss."

"It was a long time ago. But thank you."

I hesitate, unwilling to probe so soon after discussing his father's death.

Luckily, Elaric continues, "When I returned, few cities remained, crammed with refugees behind walls which offered no protection from Seraphina's flames. Those who could fled and never looked back.

"My uncle had taken over as steward, since my sister's sons were too young to rule. I expected him to cling to power given his greed, but he readily relinquished the throne. I suppose he was unwilling to bear the burden of saving a doomed kingdom."

"Your father wrote you left in search of Belinda, another witch," I say. "What happened?"

"I bargained with her for a weapon capable of withstanding magic and slaying a witch. The Sword of Veliantis."

I sit up. "Did it work? Did you kill Seraphina?"

"It was difficult to get close without being burned, even with the enchanted sword to fend off her magic, and I lost countless men battling against her, but yes. At long last, I slayed the witch and rid Avella of her terror."

"But her sister, Isidore, was maddened with rage," I continue, hairs rippling across the nape of my neck, "and sought revenge against you. Killing you wasn't enough, so she cursed you with winter for eternity, and the only way for it to be broken is through your Summer Queen, whom you've spent the past three centuries searching for."

Elaric says nothing. I know he cannot confirm this part of his past, for it directly concerns the matter of his curse. But with the way he stares so steadily at me, I know with unfathomable certainty that what I've said is the truth.

"It's true love, isn't it?" I whisper. "That's the only way to break your curse?"

"Adara . . ."

My shoulders sag. I may have unraveled the mystery of how Elaric came to be cursed, but it does not change the fact the cure still likely involves true love.

"What happened afterward?" I ask.

"After I killed Seraphina?"

I nod. "In your father's journal, it sounded like she destroyed much of the kingdom. I suppose you would have had to rebuild much of it from the ashes."

"Unfortunately, yes. Many regions had become barren wastelands and with my . . . current state, I could not travel the kingdom without freezing the land. I locked myself up in here, the Summer Palace—"

"Summer Palace?" I ask, arching a brow.

"Long ago, this part of the kingdom was remarkably sunny," he says with a laugh. "Of course, that quickly changed from the moment I made this palace my permanent home. But it is far away from any major settlements, and I gave my sister our other palace just outside of Netham."

"It's in ruins now," I say, recalling the times I've traveled to the capital with my father and seen the derelict palace in the distance.

"It is." He presses his lips together. "Though I was the first in line for my father's throne, I was unfit to inherit it. I wished for my sister to reign in my stead, but the council at the time would not accept my request. They even opposed her reign as Queen regent until the day her eldest son came of age."

"What did the council think of you remaining king?" I ask. "Did they mind, magic and all?"

"Some minded, their homes just destroyed by magic, and now their king held power too, albeit a different sort. But others took comfort in my new strength, believing I could defend against any future catastrophe. Still, those who feared me were vocal about their preference for my uncle to take the throne."

"Even though they once saw him as a useless drunkard?"

"They feared magic more than they feared my uncle's reign."

"What of your uncle himself? You said that when you returned, he was quick to yield the throne. After Seraphina's defeat, did he ever take an interest in ruling?"

"At first, the burden of a recovering kingdom was a heavy one, and my uncle detested work most of all. Yet as the years passed and Avella returned to normality, his interest in the throne became an obsession. It didn't help that I remained here, keeping my distance from the kingdom and occasionally seeing my council. Over time, my people seemed to forget that I was human and began to regard me as something other."

I don't meet his eyes. What he says echoes a belief I too have shared of him until recently.

"People blamed me for the most bitter of winters, even those who resided on the other side of the kingdom, far away. After a while, I began to wonder whether I was somehow responsible for the severe weather which seemed to worsen year by year following Seraphina's defeat. Yet even if my people's suffering was because of me, I could not abdicate my throne. My uncle's influence had grown so far that my sister's sons would not even be considered as my successors. Despite his flaws, he knew how to entertain a crowd and courted most of the lords on my council. Soon, most became enamored with him and his false promises. In reality, he would have gambled away every coin in the palace coffers within nights of being crowned king. It was not for the sake of my kingdom alone that I could not yield my crown to him, but also because of my sister."

I look up, regarding him. "Why? Because you feared he would have had both her and her children dispatched to secure his reign?"

"Partly," he says. "But it was mostly because of the way he always looked at her. I remember my father once telling me that my uncle competed with him for my mother's hand and his obsession didn't fade until long after they were wed. My sister greatly resembled my mother with her golden hair, and apparently my father once complained to my uncle about the never-ending stream of marriage proposals, and my uncle joked my father should wed her to him."

I blanch.

"I believe it was before I was even born. My sister wouldn't have even been five years old."

"That's . . . " I swallow down my nausea. "Horrifying."

"There were other disturbing accusations made against him while my father reigned, but he dismissed them all, refusing to believe his brother capable of such atrocities. My uncle never harmed my sister then, but I worried what would happen if he took the throne.

"It was during the fifth winter after Seraphina that the first assassination attempt came against me. That was when I learned I cannot die. Perhaps some would find solace in that immortality, yet to me it only confirmed I was no longer human."

The journal feels unbearably heavy in my lap. I shuffle in my armchair, still not daring to look at him directly.

"More attempts on my life were made, all of which failed, and then the kingdom plunged into civil war. Overnight, Netham was besieged by my uncle's forces, including the palace."

"Your sister . . . ?"

Elaric stares at the fireplace before us, watching the blue flames flicker. "News of the attack reached me the following morning, but by then it was already too late. When I arrived at the palace, I was greeted by the heads of my sister and her husband and their children lining the gates. I underestimated my uncle's capacity for cruelty, and I have never forgiven myself for it."

"It wasn't your fault," I whisper. "How could you have known what evil he was capable of?"

Elaric pauses and then sucks in a sharp breath. "From that day, I ensured my kingdom feared me so no one would ever again dare to incite my wrath. In a single night, I became the monster they believed me to be. I froze every man in my uncle's army, and then I shattered them all. I spared no one."

His voice trails off into the darkness. He looks at his hands before clenching them to fists. "I saved my uncle for last," he continues, voice barely a whisper. "I brought him back here, to my dungeons, freezing him slowly. The first day I shattered his fingers. I meant to drag out his agony for weeks, but failed to contain my rage. As I tortured him with frost, he returned it with words: of my nephews' screams echoing through the palace, of what he and his men did to my sister before taking her head. That was on the third day, and I obliterated him there and then."

I just sit there, staring at him as every terrible part of his story brands itself into my mind.

"His pain brought me no relief to mine," Elaric says. "And it was perhaps one of the most monstrous things I have done."

"He was the monster," I snarl. "I hope he's rotting in Hell."

"As do I," Elaric mutters. He leans back, fingers raking through his hair. "I ordered my sister and her family to be buried in Netham's palace, but it is my deepest regret I could not attend. My presence would freeze the very ground. Even now I have never visited her grave, although I have asked servants to check on her and her family over the centuries."

It's fortunate I don't sit closer, or I wouldn't be able to stop myself from embracing him, from pressing my lips to his brow. Not once did I consider he may have suffered more than me. He saved his kingdom from the monster which killed his father and was rewarded with a terrible curse. Then instead of being celebrated as the hero he was, his uncle led a civil war against him and murdered his sister and nephews.

And after three hundred years he thought he'd found his Summer Queen, only for her to drive a dagger through his chest.

It's impossibly hard to keep from crying, my chest so full of regret and grief. But what his father said is true. Crying changes nothing, neither Elaric's suffering nor my choices which have led us here. I can only shape that which lies ahead.

"I . . . " My voice breaks. "Elaric, I swear I'll do all I can to break your curse." My fierceness surprises even me. "It's cruel you could never say goodbye to your sister. Nothing is more important than family."

"You are right." He looks away from me, staring down at his hands.

"I am sorry," I say. *For everything.*

"I am sorry, too," he whispers.

And we sit there, that agonizing rift stretching between us. The two of us equally ensnared by our guilt.

In order to break his curse, I need to confirm whether true love was part of Isidore's incantation or if it's something else.

The curse allowed Elaric to pass me that book, along with his father's journal which hinted at the reason Isidore cursed him. Perhaps it'll let him take me to her.

"I would like to see Isidore," I say.

His head snaps up. "You will not." Somehow, I doubt the curse would compel him to protest so vehemently.

"Why not?"

"It's too dangerous."

"It isn't up to you to decide what's too dangerous for me." I fold my arms across my chest.

"I will not let you throw away your life so recklessly," he growls. "She will kill you the moment she lays eyes on you."

"Her magic might not even work on me. Yours doesn't, and your magic comes from hers."

His temple twitches.

"If you won't take me to see her, I'll find her myself."

"I won't allow it."

"You can't stop me."

"I will forbid you from leaving the palace."

"And keep me as your prisoner again?"

"Adara," he says, voice strained.

I don't relent. "Do you still have the sword Belinda gave you?"

"No, she came to collect it shortly after I defeated Seraphina," Elaric says. "But even if it remained in my possession, I would not give it to you."

"Why must you be so unreasonable?"

"Is it so unreasonable to insist you keep your life?"

I hold his stare for a while and then huff. "Fine. You can take me to Belinda instead."

"No."

It takes all of my restraint to keep from grabbing his father's journal and chucking it at him. "You are the most infuriating man I have ever met."

The corners of his mouth twitch up into a half smile. It just annoys me even more. "And you are the most infuriating woman I have ever met."

The way he says it causes me to flush. "Stop trying to distract me," I grumble.

His smile grows.

"If you won't take me to Isidore, my only alternative is to speak to Belinda and see if she can offer any more information."

"While Belinda may be less . . . volatile than other witches," Elaric says, smile vanishing, "it does not change the fact that she is still incredibly dangerous and is as likely to kill you as she is to help you."

"She helped you once," I point out. "Perhaps she will help you again."

"I struck a bargain with her and that was the only reason she granted me the sword to kill Seraphina."

"What bargain?"

He doesn't reply.

"I thought we were done withholding the truth? I want to break your curse and so do you, though anyone would think otherwise with how you're currently acting. How will we succeed, unless you tell me everything you can?"

He shakes his head, but he doesn't look as angry as I expect. Just frustrated. Which is fine. He can be as frustrated as he wants to be. This is for his own good.

"She asked me to retrieve poison from a wyvern," he says.

"That sounds dangerous."

"It was," he admits. "If even one drop of their poison comes into contact with your skin, it will kill you. Fortunately, Belinda provided me with an antidote, but it offered no protection against the creature's talons. I barely made it to the town nearby to find a healer."

"That's why it took you so long to return home?"

Elaric sighs. "It was."

"Couldn't Belinda collect the poison herself? Or did she lack the power to do so?"

"She's as powerful as Seraphina and Isidore," Elaric says. "Wyverns are native to the Taehan Mountains and she claimed she wasn't on friendly terms with the witch coven that resided nearby."

"I'd happily fight a wyvern in exchange for information on your curse."

He casts me a wilting look.

"If you don't tell me where she lives, I'll find her myself. And then I'll battle a wyvern alone. You can try to lock me up in your palace, but I'll eventually break free. As I nearly did a few days ago."

"I do recall," he says dryly. "I particularly enjoyed being dragged over in the snow."

I can't help my smirk. "I thought you'd enjoy that part."

He just shakes his head at me.

"So, will you take me to see Belinda?"

Elaric is silent for a moment and then says, "Very well. But if I do take you to her, you must not forget that she is a witch and will happily use you for her own gain. Be under no illusion that she can be trusted."

I nod as intently as I can.

"And you must try not to antagonize her."

"When have I ever antagonized anyone?"

Elaric arches a brow. "You are relentless when you have your heart set on something. While it doesn't bother me, Belinda may feel otherwise."

"It doesn't bother you? Then it seems I must try harder."

He gives a low chuckle. "You may antagonize me all you want, Adara."

I'm grateful for the fireplace's blue light to disguise the redness creeping across my face. "I won't antagonize the witch and I won't trust her. Do we have a deal?"

"I suppose," Elaric says.

I lift my chin. "When do we leave?"

"When would you like to leave?"

"Tomorrow morning."

With how short notice the request is, I expect him to refuse, but surprisingly he nods. "As you wish. Tomorrow morning it is."

Chapter 13

That night, I hardly sleep. Not because of grief or rage, but anticipation.

Dawn doesn't come soon enough. By the time the first rays pierce through my curtains, I've already been awake for an hour.

My attention turns to the door which leads to Elaric's chambers. Though we agreed to leave in search of Belinda this morning, we didn't specify a time. My legs itch to spring out of bed and hurry over to his door, but I force myself to stay where I am. I already disturbed him last night, and if I disturb him again this early, asking when we'll leave, he may change his mind.

Sighing, I knit my fingers together and stare up at the swirls which dance across it. My mind drifts to the events of last night. Of everything I read in Theron's journal. Of everything Elaric has suffered.

What sticks most in my mind is his inability to visit his sister's grave. Though it has been three centuries, he has yet to say his farewells.

In order to pay his respects, he needs to break his curse, and that's why he's spent so long searching for his Summer Queen. It's also why my sister was dragged into this. I can't deny that if I were in his place, I too would go to great lengths to be reunited with my sister, even if only at her resting place.

I mull over Elaric's past for a while longer before considering the prospect of meeting Belinda. Will she prove as dangerous as he claims? Will I succeed in persuading her to help us unravel the mystery of Elaric's curse?

My thoughts are interrupted as the doors shudder open and my maids burst in.

"Are you awake, milady?" Elona calls.

I push myself upright, my back supported by the well-cushioned pillows behind me. "Wide awake."

"The king ordered us to ready you for your journey," Kassia says, pulling back the curtains and allowing daylight to spill inside.

"Our journey?" Has Elaric already told them of our plans?

"To Sodryn, of course," Elona says.

I mask my surprise by fiddling with the edge of my blanket. He must have told all the servants we're traveling south to Sodryn, a pleasant seaside town. Better than them knowing he is cursed and we're leaving Avella in search of a witch.

But my maids aren't ordinary servants. They deserve the truth, and they're already aware of the forbidden chamber containing all the missing brides and his curse. What harm could come from telling them?

"We're not traveling to Sodryn," I say. Though my voice is soft, it may as well be deafeningly loud with how they swivel around and stare at me with wide eyes.

"You aren't?" Kassia exclaims. "Where in the world are you both going then?"

"It's a long story," I begin.

My response just causes them greater confusion.

I lean over, grab the journal which lies on the counter beside my bed, and hold it up. "It all started with this."

"A book?" Elona says, examining its worn cover.

"Not just any book," I say, "but the journal of the king's father."

Kassia blinks. "The king had a father? I mean, of course he must have, but it's so difficult to imagine him as being anything except the Winter King."

"It's true. There's even a passage in here which was written on the day he was born."

Kassia eyes the book with awe, and even Elona looks intrigued.

"How does the journal relate to where you're traveling, milady?" Elona asks.

I return Theron's journal to my bedside counter, and then I tell them both everything I learned last night. How Avella was threatened by Seraphina's fire magic, how Elaric slayed her and was cursed by her sister in revenge, how Belinda granted him an enchanted sword to save his kingdom.

After my maids finish helping me get dressed, we head outside to the courtyard. There, we find Elaric standing near a carriage sculpted from ice. A servant is at his side, bearing a sack so full it looks as if it will burst apart at any moment. When we reach them, the servant hands it to me, bowing his head. Unfortunately, it is as heavy as it looks.

"I ordered for it to be filled with food and other supplies," Elaric explains. Once the servant is gone and there are only the two of us and my maids, he adds in a low voice, "It is best you hold on to it for now, or else the contents will become"—he glances over at my maids—"inedible. We should be gone for two weeks at most, and unlike you, I don't require sustenance. There is also plenty of money in there to last us for several weeks, but I would rather not venture near any towns if we can help it."

I doubt other kingdoms will be pleased if Elaric accidentally plunges their lands into eternal winter, and if they discovered that the King of Avella was responsible, they would undoubtedly demand compensation.

Either as gold. Or blood.

Elaric opens the carriage door and holds it for me but before I climb inside, I drop the sack onto the ground and wrap my arms around Kassia and Elona, even though it isn't proper for a queen to hug her maidservants. While I've known them for mere months, they've become so dear to me, and if our quest to break Elaric's curse proves more dangerous than expected, I may never see them again. I wonder what would happen to them if we failed to return, and whether they'd find employment under whichever council member proclaimed himself king— after a long and bloody civil war, no doubt.

I swallow and do my best not to reveal my fear as I bid them farewell.

"You'll have to let me know what the lands beyond Avella are like," Kassia says. "I've never set foot beyond the kingdom's borders."

Elona gives her a stern look.

Only then does Kassia realize what she's loudly revealed, clamping a hand over her mouth and turning bright red.

I laugh and hug her tighter. "I'll tell you everything," I promise.

Kassia releases me, and then Elona takes my hand and squeezes it. "Be careful, milady," she says, her expression solemn.

Once I've said my farewells to my maids, I grab the sack from the floor and follow Elaric into the carriage, taking the bench opposite him. The diamond tufting etched into the benches suggests they were once cushioned, but now the ice offers little padding. We sit so close the tips of Elaric's leather boots touch mine.

"Your boots," I say, "I've been wondering why they don't freeze. And come to think of it, your rings and tunic and everything else you wear except your crown. It has crossed my mind before, but I keep forgetting to ask."

"Ah," he says. "I can only wear clothes woven with ironleaf fibers—"

"Ironleaf?"

"A plant impervious to magic," he explains.

"What about your rings? Your boots?"

"Coated with a translucent lacquer made from the plant as well."

I raise a brow. "In that case, I'm surprised you don't have more furnishings protected with ironleaf in the palace."

"It is a rare and expensive plant," Elaric says. "And the lacquer only lasts for a few years before needing to be reapplied."

I nod.

Elaric offers no warning before flicking his hand and causing the carriage to spring to life. I'm thrown forward, and barely catch myself in time to avoid landing into his lap. How embarrassing that would have been.

I'm slow to realize why the motion was so forceful.

We're flying.

I lean over to the window and look out.

The courtyard is rapidly growing smaller, and it's already difficult to see my maids waving at me. I wave back, though I doubt they'll be able to see me from this height.

I wonder what we must look like to everyone below, riding the clouds in a frozen carriage drawn by winged horses. Such a spectacle sounds like it should belong in a tale our nursemaid used to read to Dalia and me.

Through the window, I watch as we fly over the pines which sprawl down the mountain and as the ground turns from snow to grass. The only time I've seen such a view was when Elaric dragged Father and me back to the palace, and I was in no mood to enjoy the scenery.

After a while, the novelty of tiny towns and forests and lakes wears off, and I sink into the bench. Elaric's eyes drift over to me, but he doesn't speak. I wonder whether he isn't sure of what to say, or whether he's too busy concentrating on keeping us in the air. At first, I decide it's likely the latter but then both boredom and curiosity get the better of me.

"Is it difficult to keep the horses flying?" I ask.

Elaric answers immediately. "Since they're conjured from my magic, they are an extension of my consciousness and will keep flying until I command them to stop. Ordering them to change direction requires merely a single thought."

"So, you could keep flying forever?"

"Unfortunately not," he says. "Keeping the horses animated requires constant use of my magic, and my energy must be replenished after some time. But I will manage long enough for us to reach Belinda's woods."

"We can stop for the night if you need to."

"I would rather not," Elaric says. "For the same reason I would rather not enter any cities."

"What about the woods? Won't Belinda be furious if all the trees turn to ice?"

"My magic does not work there. The woods are enchanted with her power."

"I read all enchantments can be broken. That means Belinda's spell won't last forever. I wonder what she specified as the method to break the enchantment."

"It is difficult to know unless we were to ask her," he says, "but I imagine it will be linked to her life. What use is there in keeping her woods enchanted after her death? If she were to enchant it by any other means, then it would be impossible to know when the spell would break, and enchanting it to last more than a few years would require a great deal of strength. Binding it to her life makes far more sense, and many witches use such conditions for similar spells."

"Like Isidore?" I ask. "She froze a whole island to make it her home. Eruweth, it was apparently called. I wonder if she also tied its curse to her life."

Elaric doesn't reply, and just stares out the window at the world. Is the reason for his silence because he doesn't know the answer, or is it because his curse prevents him from doing so? Or maybe it is neither, and he simply has no wish to speak about the witch who has imprisoned him for centuries.

Chapter 14

We fly day and night, clouds rushing beneath us. Though the carriage is comfortable for one made of ice, flying for so long without stopping brings me great discomfort.

I've no idea how Elaric can sit there hour after hour without needing to relieve himself. Perhaps his curse provides him with superhuman levels. Yet I possess no such luxury, and my bladder remains very much mortal.

I try ignoring the urge, willing for it to pass until he stops. Surely his immortality can't make him completely immune?

But I wait and wait, and Elaric makes no mention of our stopping. In the end, I'm forced to swallow down my dignity and ask, "Would it be possible to stop the carriage tonight?"

At first, he looks ready to protest but then takes in my strained expression and his eyes soften. "It's best we avoid doing so. I know resting in the carriage won't be comfortable, but you must try to rest as much as you can."

"I don't mean stopping for the entire night," I blurt. "Or even in a city. Just a few minutes. Anywhere. Maybe in the countryside. With plenty of trees."

"Ah." He hesitates, finding this matter as awkward as me. It is, however, not one which can be ignored. "Yes. Of course. We'll be clear of Felton City in the next few minutes, and I'm sure there will be somewhere we can briefly stop. That will be soon enough?"

I give him a quick nod, though my bladder protests at the thought of having to wait even a few more minutes.

Those moments stretch on for so long, but true to his word, we begin our descent toward a field. Elaric stops us near a cluster of trees and then he opens the door, stepping out to help me down.

When I'm outside, he just stands there, shoulders rigid.

I jab my finger at the shadowy trees. "I'll be, er, back in a few minutes."

He gives a quick nod. "I'll be in the carriage."

Cringing inwardly, I dart past our winged steeds which nicker and flick their tails, like real horses.

I find a tree with plenty of bushes for cover and ensure I'm not visible from the carriage before bundling up my skirts and squatting, though I trust Elaric won't look. I'm certain the prospect alone would mortify him, and the thought draws a silent laugh from my lips.

Once I'm done, I return to the carriage where Elaric is waiting, and it seems I was quick enough since the grass hasn't yet frozen. I shut the door behind me, and we resume our flight.

An hour later, I manage to fall asleep upright but end up toppling over and hitting my head against the wall, and I immediately awaken.

"There's a blanket at the bottom of the sack," Elaric says, gesturing to it. "If you curl up on the bench, you'll be able to lie down."

I find the blanket in the sack like he promises, and though it's a squeeze, I curl up onto the bench. The softness of the blanket is a welcome comfort against the solid ice beneath.

This position allows me to sleep without accidentally knocking into the wall and waking up, but it means my legs feel cramped by the morning.

That next day continues much like the first, and I spend a good portion of it staring out at the land. The towns beyond Avella look much like our own, and I'm sure it would disappoint Kassia to learn this. But maybe they look unremarkable only because we're so high up. Maybe if we were on the ground, they'd look far more interesting.

We stop twice, once in the morning and once in the afternoon.

On that second occasion, Elaric also leaves the carriage for a few minutes, and I'm relieved to confirm he remains mortal in some ways.

And more evidence of his physical limits comes later that evening.

By nightfall, the toll of using so much magic is clear on his face. His brows pinch together with strain. But more concerningly, his usually bright eyes are glazed over with the fog of exhaustion.

"We should stop for the night," I say, regarding him carefully.

"We cannot."

"We must. What will happen if you run out of magic and can't keep the horses flying, and the carriage plummets to the ground?"

"I won't let the carriage fall," he says, frown deepening. "We have almost reached Belinda's woods, and I have enough strength to sustain the spell until then."

With his expression indicating otherwise, I'm far from convinced but don't argue with him. He's made up his mind, and I doubt I can sway him. Instead, I sit back and hope he really can keep our carriage flying until we reach the woods.

Several minutes later, I'm certain he's on the brink of collapsing. But then our carriage descends, and since it isn't a vertical plummet through the sky, it seems we have reached our destination. When I look out the window, I can make out the silhouettes of tall trees.

Yet as we near the ground, Elaric's control over the carriage weakens, resulting in us shaking either side. The land sways beneath, more like roiling waves than stable ground. And we're approaching it at an alarming velocity.

"Elaric," I gasp.

If he hears me, he shows no sign of it. His brow is creased with deep lines of concentration.

The land draws nearer. Dark trees loom over us.

Then we hit the ground. Hard.

The carriage jostles violently, throwing me against the window. Luckily, it's too small for me to tumble out. But I strike my head and temporarily lose all sense of my surroundings.

For a while, I'm trapped in a daze.

Then awareness pierces through.

I push myself upright. The carriage and horses are gone. I'm lying in long grass, blades tickling my cheek. Elaric lies a few paces away, our sack beside him.

It seems his magic reached its limit.

I rush over. His eyes are closed, and his expression is peaceful—a world apart to how it was in the carriage.

I drop to my knees and shake his shoulders.

"Elaric," I call.

Clarity bursts through the flurry of fear, and I remember to check his pulse, pressing two fingers to his neck.

I hold my breath as I wait to feel something. Anything.

It takes a few moments to feel a slow, steady beat. The rhythm of his pulse is so unlike anyone else's. But that's to be expected, given his frozen heart.

I sit back on my heels. He isn't dead. Just unconscious. Though that isn't ideal either, since we're currently sitting on the doorstep to a witch's home.

When I dare to look back at the gnarled trees, they appear even more foreboding than they did from the sky.

All I have to defend myself is the dagger strapped to my thigh. Anything could leap from those shadowy trees and ambush us. Even Belinda herself.

Minutes later, Elaric still doesn't stir. I shake his shoulders and call his name again, and to my surprise, his eyes finally drift open.

"Adara," he breathes, taking my hand. He looks up at me in puzzlement.

"You were unconscious," I explain.

Understanding dawns on his face, banishing the confusion. "Are you hurt?" he demands, though he should be more concerned about himself.

I shake my head.

"I'm sorry," he murmurs. "I thought I had enough magic left."

"You shouldn't have pushed yourself so hard."

"It seems I overestimated my abilities. When I last visited here, all those years ago, I flew on a single steed rather than in a carriage."

"We could have traveled without one," I say.

"And you would have been happy sitting behind me for two whole days?"

"We could have found somewhere in the middle of nowhere and stayed there for the night. There was no need to rush here."

Elaric pushes himself up with a groan.

Despite being unconscious only moments ago, he's much quicker on his feet than I expect and retrieves the sack, slinging it over his shoulder.

"You can't carry it," I protest. "It'll freeze."

He gestures to the dark trees up ahead. "As I mentioned yesterday, my magic will cease to work as soon as we set foot inside the woods."

With that, he trudges on.

"Elaric!" I call, though it's no use.

I hurry after him and try to grab the sack, but he angles his shoulder away. My fingers grasp empty air.

"You're injured," I say. "You should let me carry it."

"I'm not injured."

"You were unconscious."

"I'm fine."

"Liar."

He stops and turns to me, arching a silver brow. "Do I not look fine to you?"

I scan over him but aside from a small tear in the elbow of his tunic, I can't see any injury. And even if he's exhausted his magic, it doesn't seem to have affected his physical strength.

"You're so stubborn."

His lips twitch into a smirk.

Since we landed so close to the woods, it doesn't take us long to reach the trees. At first, I'm hesitant to step into their depths, fearing a strange enchantment will ensnare me. But Elaric proceeds first, and when nothing happens, I follow him.

The branches are so densely knitted together that no starlight can pass through. Cobwebs so thick they could be woven into fishing nets hang from the trees, draping them like silken curtains and glittering in the pallid light. On one of them, I notice sudden movement. A round, shadowy figure large enough to fill a dinner plate.

I try not to think about how it's by far the largest spider I've ever seen and how it may possess poisonous fangs. I clutch the hilt of my dagger beneath my skirts, though I'm not sure what use it'll be.

"Other than Belinda," I say as Elaric leads our way through the trees, "is there anything or anyone else we should be wary of meeting?"

"Not as far as I'm aware, though many beasts lurk inside these woods. Wolves and bears and manticores and creatures you've perhaps never heard of. But it isn't too late to return to the palace."

"I'm not turning back. Not when you rendered yourself unconscious to get us here."

"That doesn't matter," he says softly.

"I will not return to the palace empty-handed."

Leaving now would mean returning with no chance of freeing my sister. I need to know the truth behind breaking Elaric's curse, what I as his Summer Queen must do. Whether it really is true love and I must wait for fate to relent, or whether there is another way to end it.

"I have no magic here," he warns.

I pause, shifting aside my skirts to find the dagger secured to my thigh, and then I pull it from its sheath. Steel whispers through the leaves. I offer it to Elaric.

Frowning, he takes it.

"If we encounter any beasts in these trees," I say, "it's best you have a weapon."

"If we do, it would be wiser to run than fight them." He holds the dagger back out to me. "And you should keep this to defend yourself."

"You've had centuries more combat experience. If we are forced to fight, then our odds would be better stacked in our favor if you held a blade." Admitting all this out loud is no easy thing, but Elaric is a remarkably better fighter than I am, and I cannot argue with logic.

And it seems neither can Elaric. He just shakes his head and secures the dagger to his belt. Then we continue through the woods.

Now I'm more aware of the dangers lurking in the trees, I'm conscious of every twig snapping beneath our boots, and every whistle of wind through the dense canopy of leaves.

An owl hoots somewhere within the branches, and my skin crawls as I imagine what nightmarish creature it may prove to be. Perhaps its beak is like a vulture's, and its wings are leathery like a bat's. Maybe it even has glowing red eyes and onyx horns.

But the owl swoops down, and I glimpse it.

It's no bloodthirsty monster. Just an ordinary owl.

My attention fixed on the owl above, I'm slow to react when Elaric calls my name.

"Adara, wait—" he calls, but it's already too late.

His gaze is on the ground.

I lift my boot.

Beneath is an indigo toadstool with green spots covering its cap. A loud pop sounds.

Then the entire woods echo as a long chain of toadstools explodes.

Purple fog bursts out, devouring us both.

Chapter 15

"This way," Elaric says, voice muffled by his hand covering his mouth.

I squint, but the purple fog engulfs everything and burns my eyes. My only choice is to keep them averted down, partially closed.

Elaric's vision must be less impaired than mine, since he grabs my arm and pulls me away. Several paces later, the fog wanes and I can breathe easier. My sight returns shortly after.

"Gloomshrooms," he explains. "Their fog is poisonous."

Though we're now out of its clutches, it's too early to declare us safe. The poisonous mist seeps through the trees, chasing us.

"Can it kill us?" I ask.

"Not by itself. But it will render us unconscious for several hours."

I clench my jaw. "Long enough for something else to come and kill us."

Elaric gives a stiff nod.

We sprint through the trees, but there's no outrunning the fog. The air thickens and again, my vision distorts. Breathing becomes much harder.

Then there's another loud pop. This time it comes from beneath Elaric's boots.

Dozens follow it, far more than the first time. The resulting cloud is much greater than before, and now there is no escape.

Black spots eat at the edges of my vision. "Elaric," I call, unable to find him through the haziness. I feel my lips moving but hear no sound leaving my mouth even when I shout louder.

I find myself slipping, weightless as a cloud, teetering over the edge of a cliff, until I topple into the depths beneath.

Darkness washes over me. Consumes me.

For a long while, there's nothing.

Then I feel steel clenched in my hands. And blood. Everywhere. It coats my fingers with its nauseating stickiness.

"A-Adara."

I look down to see Elaric under me. My dagger lodged in his chest, piercing all the way through.

I scream. No sound comes out. Every part of me shakes.

"Why?" he breathes. "After everything, after all the kindness I've shown you, this is how you repay me?"

"Because I'm a monster," I choke, tears spilling down my cheeks. "A monster of the worst kind, blinded by fury and hate."

His eyes close. He does not move.

I stay there, my gaze fixed on him. My hands are glued to the dagger wedged in his broken and bloodied chest.

I beg for him to move. For his eyes to open. For his fingers to twitch.

None of that happens.

He's dead. Killed by me and my hatred.

I grip his shoulders and shake him, but he doesn't awaken. All I achieve is covering myself in blood.

His blood.

"Elaric, Elaric," I call, though I know it's useless. He's gone. Because of me. "Elaric!"

I call his name until my throat is raw. Then I collapse beside him, my limbs so heavy I can no longer move them.

But when my head meets the pillow, Elaric's chambers vanish. Along with him.

I'm alone in a dark room.

Blue light flickers, illuminating the edges of the surrounding statues.

I stagger onto my feet, legs unsteady beneath me. When I look down, my hands are still crimson. Covered in Elaric's blood, though he is nowhere to be seen.

From the corner of my eye, I notice the face of the girl lying beside me on a slab.

Dalia.

I stumble over to her, grabbing her arm. My fingers smear Elaric's blood across her translucent skin.

"Dalia," I gasp, squeezing her arm. Hoping it'll wake her up. She looks so perfectly serene in her slumber.

Her eyes flash open. They're filled with blue light—the color of Elaric's magic.

"You," she hisses.

Before I can step back, she catches my wrist. I let out a surprised yelp.

"You failed me."

While the harshness in her tone sounds nothing like my sister, there's no denying it's her voice. My knees collapse beneath me.

It has been so many years since I heard my sister's voice.

"You killed him," she snarls, her beautiful face twisting with the ugly expression. "You killed him and destroyed the only chance I had to break free."

"I . . . " I swallow, struggling to find any excuse for what I've done. It wasn't as if I didn't mean to kill Elaric. I planned it for years. I just didn't know what it would mean for my sister's fate, and that Elaric himself was innocent.

She pushes herself upright, limbs stiff like a puppet's. "Now I'm stuck like this forever. All because you were too stupid to realize what was really going on. How dare you call yourself my sister?"

"Dalia," I plead. Even though her words, her expression, are nothing like the Dalia of my memories.

I reach for her, but my fingers close around embers.

Then I'm no longer surrounded by ice, but fire.

An inferno rages around me, sweeping from roof to roof, devouring everything in its wake. The flames gnaw through wood like paper, through stone like sand.

Thick smoke fills my nostrils, suffocating me. I cough and splutter, struggling for air. Heat stings my eyes.

Steel clangs like the drums of death.

I'm standing amid a battle, though I do not know who the opponents are. Which side will see me as a friend or foe.

A horse rears. It gallops toward me, charging through ash.

I jump aside just in time and am thrown to cobblestones, grazing my hands.

When I push myself up, the horse disappears into the flames. The knight on its back swings his sword at an enemy beyond.

I stagger back, glancing around to gain my bearings.

I'm standing in a street.

My street.

The entrance to our manor lies just paces away, marked by gates which normally stand tall and proud. Now they're torn apart, sitting crooked from their hinges.

All the trees and bushes in the garden are alight, branches blackened by flame. And beyond, fire engulfs our manor.

Though I've just arrived, I know with unfathomable certainty that Father lies within our burning home.

I race through our gardens, the battle behind growing distant. I dodge falling branches and narrowly avoid being incinerated.

When I reach the steps leading to the doors, I take two at a time, almost tripping over my own feet.

I shove aside the doors. Since they're mostly worn down by flames, they offer little resistance.

There are no servants inside, but that's unsurprising. With how furiously the fire rages through our manor, only a fool would enter. Flames wreathe the curtains. Paintings are smeared from the heat radiating through the building, oil trickling down the canvases like sweat.

I charge up the staircase, not stopping until I reach Father's study on the top floor.

The fire burns fiercer up here and has already devoured most of the ceiling, leaving gaping holes. Through them lies the night sky, stars shrouded in smoke. Even the moon is obscured, and the little I can see of it is stained red.

"Father!" I cry, bursting into his study.

Smoke billows out as I open the door. I have to waft it away before I can see anything.

Shelves lie uselessly on their sides. Heaps of books blaze like bonfires.

I find Father in the corner and leap over the fallen desk as I pick my way through the ruins of his study.

"Father!" I cry again as I reach him, turning him around so I can see his face. But when I do, my attention falls on the dagger embedded into his chest.

The same dagger as the one I drove through Elaric.

"What happened?" I ask, though deep down I know the truth. "Who did this to you?"

His eyes flutter open. "You," he wheezes. "You did this. To all of us."

My fingers loosen from around his shoulder. I slump back onto my heels. "I didn't mean for this to happen."

"What did you think would happen when you murdered the king?" His voice is stronger than a dying man's should be, as if rage fuels him with these last shreds of strength. "Without a named successor, every lord of any importance wants the throne for himself. This kingdom is tearing itself apart and the people are the ones who are suffering for it. For your mistakes."

"I didn't think . . . " I trail off. Just like with my sister, I have no excuses to offer. All I can opt for is silence.

"That's the problem," he snaps. "You don't think. You just do as you wish, consequences be damned. How your actions affect others is of no concern to you, so long as you get what you want."

"That's not true," I blurt, a lump swelling in my throat. His accusations hurt so very much, peeling back a painful layer to expose a truth I've no wish to face.

I have no way to defend myself. All I can do is sit there and let his words sink in, terrifying though they are.

"I'm sorry," I whisper. "I have made so many horrible mistakes. How can I undo what I have done?"

Father's head lolls back. He falls still.

"No," I rasp. "Father, wake up! Please wake up!"

He doesn't.

Like Elaric, like Dalia, Father is gone.

I am alone in this world. Alone to watch this kingdom consume itself until it is nothing but ash.

Everything around me disappears, and I'm left in darkness.

I bring my knees to my chest and hug them, though it provides no comfort, and I cry until my eyes are dry and can't shed a single tear more.

This is no more than I deserve.

To be alone. Forgotten.

My actions have led to so much death and destruction. It is better if I stay here. At least this way, I can't cause harm—

"Adara?"

The voice echoes around me, and I can't pinpoint where it comes from. Nor do I recognize to whom it belongs.

"Adara?" the voice says again.

I'm torn from the emptiness by a pair of strong hands.

My eyes flutter open to see Elaric staring down at me.

He doesn't look angry like someone who was just murdered should be. Instead, he looks concerned.

Then I remember the purple fog. Falling into oblivion. The nightmare I just experienced was because of the poison. None of my visions were real, as much as they felt like it.

The relief I feel is so intense it hurts.

Elaric isn't dead, and neither is my father. Dalia can still be saved, and Avella isn't currently being torn apart by a civil war.

But none of that makes my guilt any less real. I *did* try to kill Elaric. And had I succeeded, everything I just witnessed could be my current reality.

"Adara," Elaric says again, frown deepening, "are you all right? Can you hear me?"

I force myself to respond. A small nod.

He helps me up into a sitting position. Everything spins around me. Pain stabs through my temples.

"Gloomshrooms," Elaric says gently. "Belinda has surrounded the woods with them. They weren't here on my previous visits. Or if they were, I did not trigger them."

When my senses return, I notice that we're sitting in a cave, and the stone floor beneath us is coarse and hard. A blanket drapes over my lap, and another is folded up behind me as a makeshift pillow.

"How are you feeling?" Elaric asks, peering at me intently.

It is then that I realize tears flood my cheeks. Hastily I wipe them away with the back of my hand, though there's no point since he's already seen them. Did I call out during my hallucinations? Did he hear me crying for him?

"I'm fine," I say quickly. "How long was I out cold for?"

"A few hours."

I wince. "Didn't the gloomshrooms affect you?"

"Only briefly."

"I didn't think poison worked on you?" As soon as I speak, I inwardly cringe at the memory of wielding poison against him myself.

"The gloomshrooms are a result of Belinda's magic," Elaric says. If the same awful thought flickers in his mind, he doesn't show it. "While neither poison nor steel can harm me, magic is a different case."

"I see."

Perhaps the reason the gloomshrooms didn't affect Elaric for as long is because Isidore's magic already floods through his veins. Did the shorter duration also cause his hallucinations to be less severe than mine? Or did he receive no such visions?

Intrigued though I am, I don't want to risk him asking me the same in return. Or else I'll have to relive all those torturous moments again.

Chapter 16

We spend the rest of the night in the cave and then continue through the woods at first light. As we trudge on through the brambles and leaves, I take great care with every step. While Elaric is convinced Belinda will have only installed her gloom-shrooms around the woods' perimeter, I don't want to take my chances. Not with the headache I woke up with this morning.

Elaric makes no comment about my slowness, however, and simply waits for me to catch up when I fall behind. If he's growing impatient, his expression doesn't at all show it.

"I've been meaning to ask you something," I say after a while. "When you sought Belinda to aid you in defeating Seraphina, weren't you at all concerned by how she would react to your request? How did you know she wouldn't instead capture you or kill you to protect a fellow witch?"

"I suppose it was a risk," Elaric admits, sweeping aside a low-hanging branch and holding it there until I pass. "But Belinda and I were already on cordial terms."

"You met her prior to asking for the sword?"

He nods. "It was while I was traveling beyond the kingdom, near a town in the far north called Midmore. I noticed an elderly woman huddled by the side of the road and called out to her, but she did not respond. When I dismounted and tapped her shoulder, she fell to the ground, unconscious. Fearing the worst, I hauled her onto my horse and rode into Midmore to find a healer."

"I wonder how she was injured."

"She never shared the reason with me."

"Perhaps she was fighting another witch?"

"Perhaps."

"So, did you find her a healer?"

"I did," he says. "By morning, she had miraculously healed, and it was as if she had never been hurt. She granted me an invisibility potion for my aid, and though I asked if she was a witch, she merely laughed and told me her name was Belinda before disappearing."

"You saved her in the past," I say, "and yet she still made you collect wyvern poison and risk your life?"

Elaric glances around at the surrounding trees, as if to check whether she is hiding within the shadows. "Indeed," he murmurs.

Given his unease, I decide it best not to slander Belinda any further. Not when offending her might mean her turning us away.

Or worse.

After another hour of walking, we reach a bridge. Though it can hardly be called that, since it's just a large, fallen tree suspended over a violent river. Hundreds of feet below, jagged rocks glint in the low light, their surfaces like polished onyx.

Elaric stops at the edge and peers at the tree trunk. "This wasn't here last time I visited."

"Then how did you cross the river?"

"As the gap was much narrower, I was able to jump across." He places his foot at the end of the trunk and pushes down. The log creaks but doesn't budge. It's wedged deep into the earth on both sides. Whoever put it here clearly intended for it to stay in place. "It should hold our weight. Although it would be wise to cross one at a time."

My eyes trail from the log down to the river rushing far beneath. I dearly hope Elaric's evaluation is correct, or else it may cost us our lives. Well, mine at least.

"I suppose there might be another way around it," Elaric says. "But it could mean wandering through the trees all day."

"It's fine," I say, lifting my chin. I don't want to alter our plans because Elaric thinks I'm too afraid to cross this bridge. "Let's do it."

Before he can change his mind, I step up onto the trunk.

"Adara!" he calls after me. It takes only three steps for his shouts to be drowned out by the rushing river.

My first few steps are strong and sure. But around a third of the way across the bridge, maintaining my balance becomes much harder.

The wind is determined to push me off, and finding grip in the smoother areas of the trunk is a challenge. I take small, slow steps as I shuffle across the bridge.

A sudden gust blows me left.

I lean right to correct it but overcompensate too much and almost lose my balance.

Arms flailing, I narrowly regain stability. My breaths come out in sharp gasps as I realize how close I was to slipping. I'm certain Elaric will have noticed my stumble, but if he's yelling my name, I can't hear him.

Maybe I should have let him cross first. If he falls, his curse should prevent him from dying, as no magic is involved.

Since I'm already halfway across, it's too late to turn around. I'll just have to trust his judgment.

Grimacing, I continue across the bridge. Though my footing is no more secure than before, I quicken, desperate to reach the other side.

The worst part about crossing the bridge is the middle. Once I'm two-thirds of the way, each step grows easier.

And then I'm on solid ground.

My legs feel strange, having held such tension. At first, I think they may give out, but I manage to stay upright.

Glancing back, I see Elaric on the other side. Even from here, his relief is evident.

I tell myself his concern is only because I'm the one who can break his curse. I cannot forget he wishes our marriage annulled.

He doesn't hesitate for long before crossing himself. Though the wind is as fierce as it was while I was on the bridge, he shows little sign of exertion and his swift, strong strides are completely unfazed.

"Are you all right?" he asks, soon stepping onto firm earth.

I give a slight nod. "Fine."

"We should reach Belinda by dusk," he says, scanning the trees ahead. "That bridge should be the last obstacle before her home. Unless anything else in these woods has changed since my last visit."

I dearly hope it hasn't.

The bridge disappears, and it isn't much longer before the river's thundering fades. An amber glow washes over the woods as the sun wanes, making the leaves look as if they're aflame.

We walk for several hours more before our path steepens, and then we begin to ascend a hill.

"We're nearly there," Elaric says. "Belinda lives atop this hill."

This knowledge fuels my weary legs, numbing the ache which consumes them.

We break through the trees, and step out beneath a darkening sky. The moon is already visible through the powdery clouds—a wispy crescent.

A sea of leaves surrounds us, all the treetops now beneath. I stop and scan around, but everywhere I look, there's no end to the trees. Nor does any other hill protrude from the woods, making this the highest point. No wonder Belinda made her home up here.

Though I thought we were near the top, it takes another half hour for the terrain to level out. By now, the stars are twinkling against the dark canvas of night.

A vile stench fills my nostrils. The closest smell I can compare it to is rotting eggs.

When we reach the apex of the hill, the smell becomes more intense, and a green glow emerges from the darkness. We stop at the edge of a chasm, and I peer down.

Bright green slime lies beneath, bubbling and frothing. A sudden explosion reaches higher than the rest, and I jolt back.

"It's corrosive enough to dissolve steel instantly," Elaric warns, pulling me farther away.

I flinch, imagining what the substance might do to flesh and bone.

Amid the green glow, a cottage-sized toadstool sits several dozen yards away. Its cap is red with black spots, rather like a ladybug, and its dark stalk has the texture of bark.

Small windows are cut into the stalk, faint light flickering through them. Between the strange cottage and corrosive swamp, there's no denying that this is the home of an immensely powerful witch.

Despite having arrived at our destination, there's one glaringly obvious problem: We have no way across. Elaric can't use his magic in Belinda's domain, so conjuring a bridge is out of the question. Nor can we swim through the deadly swamp. Since the slime is likely imbued with the witch's magic, Elaric would also be instantly dissolved.

The only other idea I can think of is chopping down a tree and dragging it here to use as a bridge. But I doubt we'd haul a large enough tree up the hill, and even if we succeeded, crossing the swamp would be far more perilous than crossing the river this morning.

I turn to Elaric. "So, what do we do now?"

To my dismay, he simply says, "We'll have to wait for Belinda to let us in."

"Will she know we're here? It isn't as if we can go to her door and knock."

Elaric nods. "She should be able to hear us from here."

"From this distance? Over that?" I point at the slime churning restlessly below.

"Her magic connects to every tree and blade of grass," Elaric says. "She will be able to hear us through them."

HEART OF THE SUMMER QUEEN

I look down at the grass. It's sparse in places, drowning in mud. With the nearest trees now a fair distance from us, I'm uncertain whether the witch will really be able to hear. "How far does her magic reach?"

"The entire woods," Elaric says.

His reply makes my skin crawl. How powerful this witch must be for her magic to reach so far. Though I've always considered Elaric's magic to be terrifying, now I realize it pales compared to a witch's. It certainly explains how Belinda's wards can neutralize his magic so easily.

"Then she's known that we are here all along?" I whisper.

"There can be little doubt of that after we triggered those gloomshrooms."

No wonder Elaric was so wary of speaking ill of her earlier. From the second we set foot inside her woods, we've surrendered ourselves to her mercy. If she attacks us, there's little we can do to defend ourselves. Considering how useless steel was against Elaric, it's unlikely my dagger would be able to even touch a witch.

My throat dries. "We just have to stand here and wait until she lets us in?"

He presses his lips into a grim line. Then drawing a breath, he addresses the cottage. "We have traveled far to meet you, Belinda, and we would be very grateful if you could spare us a few moments of your time."

Then we wait.

Even after several minutes pass, there is nothing. No sound or movement. Just the bubbling swamp.

With a sigh, Elaric drops to his knees to try again. "Belinda, if you can hear me, we very much wish to speak with you."

Still, there is only silence.

I also fall to my knees, sinking into the mud. If she can sense our kneeling, then perhaps she will believe our sincerity.

"We would be greatly in your debt," I say, projecting my voice into the night. "If there's anything we can do in exchange, we'll gladly do it."

Elaric casts me a concerned look.

Maybe telling her we're willing to do anything is a little reckless, but I'm desperate. If Belinda won't help us, what else can we do? I've already exhausted Elaric's library.

I sit and wait, staring at the cottage. I suppose we could kneel here day and night until Belinda deigns to see us. That is, as long as our presence doesn't irritate her, and she decides to use her magic against us.

And then, just as I'm about to say something else, the front door opens.

The figure which emerges is short and hunched over, her curly white hair framing her face like clouds. She clutches a knobby wooden staff, and the threadbare robes she wears seem to drown her.

"You'll wake up the entire woods shouting like that at this time of night," she chastises, shaking her head.

Elaric bows his head. "Forgive us but—"

"You wish to speak to me," she says, waving her hand dismissively. "I heard you the first time. I'm old, not deaf."

He goes to say something, but then the ground trembles.

Thick vines sprout from the side of the cliff, rushing across to where we stand. They weave tightly together, slithering like snakes, until they form a bridge long and wide enough for us to walk upon.

"Come in," Belinda calls when we don't move. "Come in."

"Careful," Elaric murmurs, turning back to me. "Should we slip, I doubt Belinda would save us."

"You're right that I wouldn't," she says with a shrill laugh. With how quietly he spoke, no ordinary person could have heard him. "Better mind your step."

Elaric steps onto the vine bridge first, his pace slow and cautious. Not wanting to be left behind or offend the witch with my hesitance, I hurry after him.

Though Belinda's vines are tightly woven together, their surface are uneven, and I take great care with my footing. The terrible smell intensifies further across the bridge, and I have to breathe through my mouth instead of my nose. Bubbles of slime charge toward me, so close the air shakes from their explosions. I don't look down as I walk, gaze pinned to the back of Elaric's silver hair, praying no drops splatter onto me. I'm mostly covered, save for my hands and face, but with how potent the slime is, even the slightest drop may penetrate my clothes and burn my skin.

We manage to reach the other side without either of us stumbling, and as we step off the vines, Belinda raises her hand and they contract at her command, returning to the earth. No traces of their existence are left.

Belinda ushers for us to follow her inside, not glancing back to check if we do. Elaric catches the door before it shudders shut, holding it open for me.

Then we step into the witch's lair.

Chapter 17

The swamp's stench is no fainter inside Belinda's cottage, and it's a wonder she can tolerate it. Maybe she's grown accustomed to it, and the benefit of having such a deadly moat outweighs the terrible smell. Or maybe she relishes it. Whichever it is, I have no wish to insult her by asking.

A second scent accompanies the swamp's. This one is more pleasant, though it's nearly suffocated by the slime's intensity. I pause and inhale deeply. Garlic and parsley, I think. She must be cooking something, though I'm not sure what.

The cottage opens to a large, circular room—as to be expected in a toadstool shaped home. At the far end, there's a fireplace with two small couches gathered around it. While the couches are worn, like the rest of the furniture, they appear to be ordinary ones. How she got all this furniture atop the hill is an interesting question, and I suspect magic must have been involved.

"Come and sit by the fire," Belinda calls, beckoning us forth.

We hesitate briefly before picking our way through the heaps of books and potion bottles.

The couch is too small to comfortably fit both Elaric and me. It's such a tight squeeze that my legs press against his. While I feel awkward sitting this close to him, I'd rather sit beside him than the witch.

"Something to eat?" Belinda asks.

"I'm not hungry, but thank you," Elaric says.

"What are you cooking?" Despite the swamp's awful smell, the faint scent of warm food is making me ravenous.

Belinda flashes me a toothy grin. "Frog spawn and dandelion soup."

"Frog spawn?" I repeat, my appetite vanishing in a bout of nausea.

"It adds a delightful tang to an otherwise bland dish," Belinda says. "Shall I fetch you a bowl?"

"No," I blurt. Noticing her sharpening expression, I quickly add, "It sounds lovely, but I'll pass thank you. I'm not too hungry."

Belinda just shrugs and heads through the door to the right.

Though I have plenty of questions to ask Elaric, whether her house has always been this way and whether he's ever tried any of her peculiar dishes on previous visits, it's best not to risk Belinda overhearing.

The two of us stare into the fireplace while we wait. Unlike the fire in the palace, conjured from Elaric's power, these flames appear to be perfectly normal ones. I wonder if they would also feel normal if I held my fingers to them, but I don't move to check.

Belinda returns a few minutes later, carrying a bowl in one hand and leaning on her wooden staff with the other. She tilts the bowl toward me. "Sure you don't fancy a bowl?"

I peer inside. The soup is thick and yellow and frothy, with a bubbly texture that's undoubtedly frog spawn. I do my best not to pull a face. As unsettling as the soup is, at least it doesn't smell too awful. "I . . . I'm sure, thank you."

"Suit yourself," Belinda says, settling down onto the couch opposite us. "All the more for me."

She sets her staff down beside her and picks up the spoon from her bowl and shovels it into her mouth, slurping noisily. When she misses her mouth, drops trickle down her chin and onto the collar of her robes. I do my best not to stare.

"So," she says after another two slurps of soup, "I already know this one." She gestures to Elaric with her spoon, and a bead of soup flies through the air, landing on the dusty rug. Then she turns to me, scanning over me from my red curls to my muddy boots. "But who are you, girl?"

"Adara," I reply. "Adara Lansford." Only after I speak do I realize my name is technically no longer Lansford. It should be Elaric's now—at least for as long as we stay married. Tirling, as was written on the front of his father's journal.

"Adara is my wife," Elaric says. My heart skips a beat. *Wife*. "The Queen of Avella."

"The Queen of Avella," Belinda muses, stirring her soup with her spoon. "Have the two of you kissed at the altar? Consummated your marriage on your wedding night?"

Warmth surges across my face. I'm grateful for the dimness of her house, or else my embarrassment would be noticeable to both of them.

At least I'm not the only who reacts. Elaric's whole body stiffens.

"Well?" the witch prompts, glancing between us.

My tongue feels too thick for my mouth. Words are impossible to form.

Luckily, Elaric answers for us both. "Yes," he says, the syllable strained.

"And here you are, still flesh and blood," Belinda says to me. She examines me for a moment longer before her eyes shift over to Elaric. "It seems you have found your true queen after all these years, and yet you sit here unchanged."

Unchanged?

I can't help my frown.

Does the witch mean she can still detect the magic flowing through Elaric's body? The frozen heart in his chest?

Or does she mean his appearance? It wouldn't be surprising if Elaric wasn't born looking as he does now. No one could naturally have skin as pale as snow, hair as silver as the moon, eyes as cold as frost.

Yet I can't imagine Elaric any other way. Did he used to have freckles like me? Were his eyes brown or green? Was his hair golden or black?

My thoughts are interrupted when Elaric lowers his head, shame branding itself across his expression.

Sitting straighter, I say, "This is why we came to speak to you. I know I'm Elaric's Summer Queen, and that he's spent three centuries searching for me. I'm supposed to break his curse but we're already married and it's still unbroken. What else must I do to end the spell?"

"True love," Belinda says, and all the hope within me shatters. "True love is required to thaw your king's heart. Until the two of you are both irrecoverably in love with one another, he will remain his frozen self."

We came all this way just for Belinda to confirm my suspicions: true love is the only remedy.

After everything between us, falling in love is ludicrous. Even more so than coming here and wishing for Belinda to name some other cure—perhaps traveling to the far reaches of the world, slaying a ferocious beast, and using its heart to melt Elaric's. That would be tangible, achievable. Not like true love.

At this rate, my sister will stay trapped forever.

Despite all this, I can't help from clinging onto denial. "Are you certain?"

"You don't believe me?" Belinda says.

"I . . . I was just wondering how you would know such a thing." It's a struggle to keep my voice steady. "Unless you were present the day Elaric was cursed?"

"I was not." Belinda lifts her bowl of soup and holds it to her lips, tilting it back. She slurps down all of it, yellow rivulets flowing down her chin.

Once the bowl is empty, she stands and potters around the room, searching her shelves for bottles before selecting one which contains a fluorescent pink substance. She pops out the cork and tips the contents into her bowl. Then she retrieves a jar of dried leaves, which are long and pointed like blades. I don't recognize what plant they belong to. She scrunches three leaves in her fist and scatters them into her bowl.

The third ingredient Belinda retrieves is much more disconcerting: tongues. Her jar contains dozens of them sitting in an oily liquid. The only relief is they look too small to be from people.

She plucks a tongue out of the jar, pinching the tip between her index finger and thumb, and deposits it at the top of her concoction. Then she returns to Elaric and me.

Belinda pauses when she reaches us, and I think she intends to show us the contents of her bowl. But her hand snaps out, and she plucks a silver hair from Elaric's head, moving faster than a woman of her age should be able to move. Elaric looks as taken aback as me. I wonder if she could best me with a sword—maybe even Elaric—though I doubt she would ever use steel rather than her magic. Not that I have any desire to fight her.

While I very much want to know what she's doing, especially now she has a lock of Elaric's hair, I fear I might enrage her if I interrupt her by asking. I watch carefully as she stirs her ingredients, though the severed tongue is impossible to blend with everything else. After several stirs, she holds a palm over the bowl and closes her eyes. When she moves her hand, the goo is no longer pink but green.

All the ingredients are thoroughly blended, with no leaves or hair or tongue in sight.

Belinda lifts the bowl to her lips, and for a terrible moment, I expect she will drink the mixture. Instead, she blows across its surface.

Emerald smoke billows out, filling the entire room. It's so thick it engulfs the fireplace.

My stomach flips, fearing Belinda is poisoning us. That like with her gloomshrooms, I'll be rendered unconscious and forced to endure more nightmares.

But then a voice rumbles through the cottage:

"Wherever you go shall forever snow,
"And all you hold will grow cold.
"For eternity this spell will be,
"'Less your Summer Queen thaws you free."

The voice has an unearthly quality yet is undeniably female, though it belongs neither to Belinda nor anyone else I know.

It has to be Isidore's.

The green smoke vanishes as quickly as it appeared. When it clears, my gaze trails across to Elaric.

His face is blood-stricken, as if he has heard a ghost, and his skin is at least several shades paler—if that's at all possible. He swallows down hard.

My mind replays each line several times, especially the last:

'Less your Summer Queen thaws you free.

"This is the exact incantation Isidore used to cast Elaric's curse?" I ask.

The witch sets down her bowl onto the nearest table. "It is."

"Only Elaric's Summer Queen is mentioned. There's nothing explicitly related to true love."

"You still doubt that the curse requires true love to be broken?" Belinda asks with a laugh. "If it does not refer to true love, what else can it be? Unless Isidore intended for the curse to be broken by him cutting out your heart and eating it."

I recoil. Belinda cackles.

Elaric's fists tighten, knuckles straining. Though he says nothing to Belinda's comment, his reaction doesn't go unnoticed.

"Not fond of that suggestion, are we?" she taunts.

While Elaric's expression is thunderous, he holds his tongue. Offending her here would be foolish.

"If the cure is true love," I say, breaking the silence, "is there any way to bypass it?"

"Worried about finding it?" Belinda asks, head tilting as she regards me.

My shoulders tense. Everything between Elaric and me is so complicated, and I'm not prepared to explain to her how I believed he murdered my sister, how I tried twice to assassinate him—including on our wedding night.

Fortunately, Belinda continues, sparing us from having to answer.

"You're right to worry," she says. "True love is a fickle beast. Some attain it immediately, while for others it never develops, even after decades."

I swallow. What she says voices my greatest fear. That no matter how long we spend together, that even on my deathbed, Elaric's curse will endure.

Dalia's face flashes through my mind. My chest grows heavy.

"I read that not all curses are broken," I say, voice quiet compared to the crackling fire. "And that a witch must simply provide a possibility for a curse to be broken."

"Indeed. While your immunity to his power proves you are his fated Summer Queen, this does not guarantee you'll ever end the curse. For instance, if you died tomorrow, there'd be no one left to break it and it would last forever. Or perhaps you'll live long, yet never cultivate true love."

My nails bite my palms. All we've gained is confirmation of my suspicions. The only thing we can do now is return home and hope love one day blooms between us. But it seems so foolish. How can such true love thrive in soil so toxic?

"What if I killed Isidore?" My bold question reverberates through the room. "Would that break his curse?"

My suggestion is terrifying—I don't know if Belinda has any ties to Isidore. At least she aided in killing Seraphina, her sister. But three hundred years have passed, and perhaps the two have long reconciled.

"Adara . . . " Elaric says before Belinda can reply. His voice is low, a warning.

I ignore him. My eyes stay on Belinda.

"Well?" I press.

Belinda is quiet, stroking her chin. "You would never defeat her. It would be a pitiful fight, a mouse battling a lion."

Elaric bolts up. "Three hundred years ago I came here with that same intention, and you said it would not work."

"It would not," she says, unbothered by the sharpness in his words. "As I explained then, you're bound by her curse and cannot kill her. Your sword would never pierce her heart, never draw blood. Nor could you tell anyone to aid you. Even if they puzzled out the curse as your queen has, they could never reach Isidore without succumbing to her magic."

Elaric's magic is the same as Isidore's—an extension of hers. I too likely won't succumb to it. But that doesn't mean she won't be able to kill me. Elaric has used his power to bind me with chains, and I couldn't break free. In the same way, I won't be immune to Isidore driving a blade through my chest. My only advantage over any other mortal is she can't freeze my whole body with a mere thought.

With a reluctant sigh, Elaric settles back beside me on the couch.

I turn back to Belinda. "Three centuries ago, you gave Elaric an enchanted sword to kill Seraphina."

"I did," she says. "The Sword of Veliantis, capable of absorbing any magic. Allowing you to get close enough to a witch to kill her."

"Is this sword still in your possession?" I ask.

Belinda's eyes glint. "It is."

"And might you be willing to lend us this sword in order to kill Isidore?"

"For the right price."

Elaric swivels around to me, grabbing my shoulder. "Adara, this plan means placing yourself in great danger. I cannot stand by and watch you be harmed because of me—"

I brush his hand from my shoulder. "It isn't because of you," I say, looking at Belinda rather than him. "I'm doing this for Dalia alone."

It's a lie. A horrible lie. And yet it's one I must make. I'm doing this for him, as well as Dalia. He deserves to visit his sister's grave without fear of freezing all of Netham. He deserves to be freed from Isidore's chains and to live a normal, happy life. To marry a beautiful princess from a faraway land. To marry her because he wishes to, and not because a curse forced him to.

But if he knew any of this, he'd never let me go ahead with this plan. He'd haul me over his shoulder, march me out of Belinda's woods, and fly me back to the Crystal Palace, binding me with his power. That's why it's best he believes I'm willing to fulfill whatever bargain Belinda demands of me—to face the Isidore's wrath—because of Dalia alone.

I don't need to look at him to feel the pain emanating from him. Even Belinda likely notices, despite Elaric normally keeping such tight rein over his emotions. The fact he can't restrain his reaction shows how deeply I've wounded him, and it makes me feel awful.

But I don't retract my words. Nor do I make any attempt to soften their blow.

I will repay him for everything I've ever done by breaking his curse, this I swear. I will not ask for his forgiveness, but I promise I will end the nightmare he has endured for these past three centuries.

I lift my chin and look Belinda in the eye. "Name your price."

A smile stretches across the witch's lips, and she is quiet for a moment, savoring the satisfaction of the bargain she has wrought. Then she knits her fingers together, resting them upon her lap and starts, "Deep within the kingdom of Dastrya lies a forest in the valley between the two mountains known as Valgus and Roswin."

So far beyond our kingdom, the names of these mountains are not ones I recognize. Maybe Elaric does. Perhaps he visited that region during his time traveling as a young prince. Judging from the lack of confusion upon his face, it seems he's likely heard of them. But convincing him to take me there will be another matter entirely.

"This forest is known as Brimlore," the witch says, "and inside it, one can find a lake."

"A lake?" I repeat.

Belinda sent Elaric to retrieve wyvern poison in exchange for the sword, so what will she name as her price this time? A magical pearl, or perhaps rare seaweed?

No, it's more likely that a powerful, ancient beast dwells inside that lake, and Belinda is sending me to collect its gills. Or fangs.

"That is what I said." Belinda's mouth pulls into a tight smile, one which makes me wary of interrupting her again. "Now, within this lake, lies the entrance to a cave where an elusive herb grows. It is known as brambleweed."

While I'm not surprised by Belinda's interest in an herb, given the countless leaves and roots and flowers which fill the jars and pots on her shelves, I wasn't expecting her request to be so straightforward. But I very much doubt her words convey the entire truth.

I wait for her to continue, but she does not.

Warily, I ask, "You would lend me the Sword of Veliantis for a mere herb?" Maybe I shouldn't ask this, in case she changes her mind and alters her request to be far more dangerous.

"Brambleweed is no mere herb, my dear. It's a vital ingredient for many powerful healing potions. But more importantly, this herb is not one which can be commonly found. It is a finicky plant, refusing to grow anywhere which isn't dark and damp enough for its liking. Even the faintest glimmer of sunlight causes the plant to wither and die. Like many others, I have tried to cultivate it in my own garden, but never have seedlings survived beyond sprouts. Due to its usefulness and scarcity, this valuable plant has been harvested to near extinction."

"Then this cave is one of the few places left where it can be found?"

"It is," Belinda says, "and is known to few, its location well hidden from the rest of the world."

I frown, thinking it all over. "Will the lake itself be easy to find? Or if the forest has several lakes, how can we be certain that we'll have found the correct one?"

"It is located just a short walk from the Ruins of Festyn."

I turn to Elaric at that. "Do you know where that is?"

Elaric hesitates before saying, "I do."

"Three leaves are all I require," the witch says. "Picking any more than this risks the plant shriveling and dying. Given that

I know no other locations in which it grows, killing this one would be a great inconvenience."

I nod. "I'll be careful to take no more than three leaves."

Satisfied with my response, the witch rises and returns to her shelves, rummaging through them until she locates a small vial of a pale-yellow liquid. "I'd imagine you will want this."

I peer at it curiously as she approaches. "What is it?"

"Setarrel Stalk," she says, passing it over to me, "the antidote to brambleweed."

"An antidote?" I exclaim.

"For the poison, of course."

Well, that's the danger I was expecting.

Grimacing, I glance across at Elaric. He looks even less pleased by this whole matter than he did to begin with. Except he looks far from surprised by the mention of poison.

"Beware the thorns," Belinda says. "One prick can paralyze even a grizzly."

Chapter 18

"Are you sure about this, Adara?" Elaric asks once we're back in the carriage. Belinda's woods whir beneath us, leaves rippling like emerald waves.

I keep my gaze fixed on the window, staring out of it rather than at him.

I can't blame him for questioning this plan. It comes with substantial risk. I'll have to trust that the antidote Belinda has given me will ward off the brambleweed's poison and count on her wanting the leaves urgently enough to ensure I return with them. At least the antidote she gave to Elaric years ago for the wyvern venom worked.

But the danger of retrieving the leaves pales compared to what will come after: Slaying Isidore.

Our only alternative is to return to the Crystal Palace together and pray true love can somehow find us. It would be far safer than battling a witch. Yet as Belinda said, there's no guarantee fate will ever deem us to be truly in love.

I smother every doubt in my heart as I say, "Nothing will change my mind. One way or another, I will save my sister."

"I understand," he says. I don't miss the glimmer of pain in his eyes.

And you.

I close my eyes gripping the window ledge.

I'm doing this for you, too.

Having spent all day trekking through Belinda's woods, sleep comes easily, cramped though it is on the bench. Elaric doesn't again raise any concerns over my plan to slay Isidore, not even throughout the rest of the following morning.

We reach Brimlore Forest the next afternoon. The dense fog shrouds the trees, making it difficult to see much of the world below. Drops pitter-patter overhead on the carriage roof like the clinking of bells. We circle the forest thrice before halting.

"I can't see the lake anywhere," Elaric says.

"I doubt we'll see through the fog," I say, leaning over and looking through the window, "and it'll be dark soon. Maybe it would be best to find somewhere to take shelter for the night? Hopefully by morning, the fog will have lifted enough for us to find the lake."

Eager though I am to retrieve the brambleweed and return to Belinda, I have little desire to wander around the entire forest all night, especially in the rain.

Elaric frowns. "Stopping for the night may prove problematic."

"Why?" I ask.

"In Belinda's woods, her protective wards suppressed my magic. Here, that will not be the case." Elaric gestures out the window. "See? Already my presence is causing the raindrops to freeze, and we've yet to reach the ground."

As I look out, I see that what he says is true. The raindrops transform into hailstones as they fall, not even requiring his direct touch.

"How long would the magic last?" I ask, turning back to Elaric. "Would the forest stay frozen forever or one day melt?"

"It depends," he says. "If my magic completely seizes an object, its effect cannot be reversed."

No wonder he so rarely leaves his palace.

All this poses a problem for our plan to search the forest. We'll have to set foot inside it and likely spend considerable time looking around before we find the lake. Waiting until morning means stopping to make camp, and any cave or shelter would freeze over almost immediately.

"You could leave me to search alone on foot," I say.

"I will not."

"What alternative do we have? Flying aimlessly all night? Surely that would just exhaust your magic?"

After a long pause, Elaric sighs and shakes his head. Without another word, he turns around our carriage to begin our descent into the misty forest.

The view through the window becomes a blur streaked with the green of rushing treetops. Then, amid the foggy rush, the remains of stone walls and collapsed arches catch my notice.

"Wait!" I blurt.

Elaric stops, the carriage suspended in midair.

"There, look!" I point out the window at the crumbling towers of a castle, faintly visible through the fog.

"The Ruins of Festyn," Elaric murmurs, peering out.

"Belinda said the lake lies near here," I say. "We should land and look around. Or at least find shelter for the night."

Elaric guides the carriage down through the misty canopy until we reach the center of Festyn's courtyard.

Once landed, he rises and pushes open the door, offering his hand to assist my descent. Though undeserving of such consideration, I accept, ignoring the tingle rushing from my fingertips as he helps me down.

With both of us grounded, Elaric raises his hand and dissolves the carriage into thousands of glittering shards.

Upon closer inspection, the ruins are even more damaged than they first appeared. Several towers tilt at precarious angles, ready to collapse entirely. The stone lion statues standing guard along the walls are all decapitated or otherwise broken into pieces. Thick moss creeps up the cracked exterior walls, and cobwebs trail across the arched walkways like ragged ribbons. Countless years with no upkeep have weathered the castle into decay.

After surveying the surrounding ruins, I turn back to Elaric, intending to discuss which direction to begin our search. But the question dies in my throat as I take in his pained expression.

Deep lines are carved into his brow, and I can't help but wonder what grievous thoughts weigh so heavily on his mind. I wouldn't expect him to have any connection to this remote castle, so far from home. Perhaps a dear friend once dwelled at this court, or perhaps he visited here himself during those years he spent traveling beyond Avella.

"Have you been here before?" I ask gently.

Elaric pauses, eyes roaming across the ruins. "Once. Long ago for my cousin's wedding. He was the Crown Prince of Festyn."

"You had relatives from here?"

Elaric nods but offers nothing more than that, and I don't pry further into such personal matters.

Is the sorrow in his eyes for his cousin? Or is it perhaps less for any one person, and more for the stark reminder of his own immortality? Three hundred years ago, these grand halls would have thrived in vibrant splendor rather than desolation.

The wind whips through the trees as rain pelts down in relentless sheets. My hair is soon soaked, clinging to my neck in wet tendrils. My gray cloak darkens and grows heavier with the moisture. Though raindrops hit Elaric, each freezes mere inches from touching him, transforming into pebble-size hailstones which clink across the courtyard like glass.

We stand in the downpour for several minutes before Elaric speaks again. "We should begin our search," he says, attention locked on the weathered lion statue across the courtyard. I follow his gaze to see frost already weaving up the beast's hindquarters, spiraling toward its back.

Glancing around, I realize the spread of his magic is not limited to the statue alone. The moss climbing the wall beside us is paling into wispy white tendrils. Within minutes, his magic will devour everything.

I turn back to Elaric and see even deeper pain shining in his eyes, the burden of his curse laid bare.

My heart aches to comfort him, to wrap him in a fierce embrace until all his grief fades. But that is no longer my place. Now my touch would just inflict more suffering.

I vow to break his curse, to liberate him from this prison of misery, even if it takes my last breath.

"Adara?" Elaric prompts.

I tear myself from my thoughts, pushing away my impossible longing. "You're right," I reply steadily. "We should press on."

We start out the courtyard, and when we reach the crumbling arch marking its exit, Elaric pauses, glancing into the shadowy forest. Our path forks ahead. Both directions are as overgrown and identical to each other.

"Which way shall we try first?" he asks.

Though Belinda claimed the lake would be near to the castle's ruins, it could still be many miles away. If we lose our way, we risk wandering in circles through the darkness all night.

I set my mouth in a determined line. Neither path looks preferable, so we'll just have to choose one at random. "Let's try right first?"

With a nod, Elaric steps into the trees. I follow close behind.

We venture deeper into the forest, forging past soaked branches as rain drips through the canopy. Behind us lies a trail of Elaric's magic, hailstones glittering among the frost-covered needles. The tension across his face reveals his anguish, though he says nothing as his curse continues its rampage.

As we walk, I melt what I can reach, my fingers running over branches, trying to slow the spread. But before long, his magic consumes whole trees, bark and branches locked helplessly in wintry shackles. If this continues, soon even the lake we seek will freeze completely. And then we'll be unable to find the cave within and retrieve the brambleweed.

Should we return empty-handed, I doubt Belinda will be merciful enough to offer us a second chance. Or if she did, her next demand might prove far more dangerous. Taking the sword by force won't be an option, not with the wards blocking Elaric's magic. Attempting to do so would be suicide.

I stop.

After a few paces, Elaric looks back at me. "What's the matter?"

I chew on my lip, struggling to find the right words. Ones which won't cast any blame on him. Besides, I'm not even sure what to propose we do instead. Returning to the castle's ruins will cause them to freeze overnight. And by morning, winter may entirely engulf Brimlore Forest.

"Your magic . . ." I start. "How long will it take to spread to the lake?"

Elaric surveys the trees, wincing at the undeniable devastation. I flinch as well, hating the additional pain I've inflicted through asking the question.

"A few hours likely," he says grimly, "though it depends on the its size. A larger body of water will take more time to freeze entirely."

I nod. Hopefully, our destination will prove vast enough to withstand his magic long enough for us to reach it. Though a greater size will make it more difficult to search for the cave amid its waters.

Elaric summons an orb of glowing light in his hand, casting it forward. The ghostly blue illumination drifts ahead, revealing our surroundings in intermittent fragments. Though gnarled limbs writhe all around us as we walk, I'm thankful at least one burden has eased: the rain stopped a short while ago and no longer drenches us.

After an hour more, Elaric slows to a stop. The dark shadows beneath his eyes are illuminated by the orb's light. "It's growing late. We ought to head back to the ruins before we lose our way."

Weary though I am, I have little desire to return there. Not just because I'm eager to find the lake but also because I dread what will happen if we spend the night in the ruins. Elaric would wake to see the chaos of his curse and so much shame would fill his expression.

"Soon," I say, mulling over the decision. "Why don't we search for another hour before calling it a night?" Having said that, we have little means of keeping track of the time with how deep we are inside the forest.

Elaric nods. "Very well. Another hour then."

We continue through the trees, and with every step, I see the uncertainty growing in his expression. Yet he does not suggest for us to stop. He isn't the one who requires sleep. Given his immortality, I suspect he could easily keep walking day and night until he reached the end of the world. But as for me, my strides are slowing, even when I try to fuel them with as much energy as I can. Exhaustion is sinking its claws ever deeper, and taking each step becomes much harder.

And then my clumsy feet trip over a protruding root, and I stumble. Elaric catches my arm, steadying me.

"Adara," Elaric says firmly.

I sigh, too tired to argue against the truth. I've pushed my limits to their brink.

He surveys my sagging posture with concern. "The ruins are too far to walk in your current state. I'll conjure a carriage to fly us back."

"Using your magic will quicken its spread. Which will be disastrous if the lake lies nearby."

His expression grows sterner.

I decide to offer a compromise. "Why don't we make camp here for the night? The ground will be dry from your frost."

"It's unlikely you'll sleep well amid hail, even wrapped in your cloak."

"I'll manage fine."

Elaric looks unconvinced but says, "If you are certain."

I don't give him the chance to protest any further before leading the way, scouring the misty forest for somewhere to make camp. It'll be best if we can find a cave, but if not then somewhere flat enough to lie down will have to do.

Yet as we walk, the ground remains lumpy, thick tree roots writhing through it. Nor do I spot any caves lurking nearby.

Just as I'm about to admit defeat and suggest returning to the ruins, a glint amid the trees catches my eye.

I quicken toward it, pushing past clawing branches. My heart races. Maybe it's only glittering ice, or a trickling stream.

Or maybe . . .

"Adara, wait!" Elaric calls after me.

I plunge through the bushes, skidding to a stop upon a pebbled shore.

Chapter 19

A vast lake stretches before us, its surface glimmering in the dim light.

Elaric halts beside me on the bank. I'm relieved to see it's large enough that his magic hasn't yet consumed it, but not too large that searching its waters will take all night.

"This is it," Elaric murmurs.

Reeds tickle my calves as I scan across the rippling water. From here, there's no way to tell where the cave lies. But I suppose it's more likely to lie along the lake's edges than in the middle, and so my best bet will be swimming around the perimeter until I find it.

I shrug the sack off my shoulder and set it several paces away, though I suspect even at this distance our belongings might freeze beyond repair if I take too long with my search.

"Wait here," I say to Elaric. "I'll be as quick as I can."

His eyes narrow, assessing the waters. "I hope your swimming is strong enough."

"As strong as my climbing," I assure him, forcing a grin. Though in truth, looking out at these dark waters causes my stomach to knot.

When I glance back at him, reluctance is written across his face. "I'll be right here, if you need me."

I give him a nod, though I'm not sure what help he can offer. If I'm drowning, any attempt he makes to save me will cause the whole lake to freeze. Then we won't be able to reach the cave. It's best I do nothing to alarm him.

The last time I swam was in the lake behind our manor, and it was years ago, before Dalia disappeared. I can only hope my muscles will recall the motions once immersed in the water.

I step toward the lake but then halt, glancing down at my clothes. Swimming in them will cause them to be soaked through, and with Elaric here, I'll be unable to light a fire to dry them. I only have a spare dress with me, so I can't afford to dispose of my breeches. And carrying around soaked clothes will be cumbersome.

My only choice is to take them off, stripping fully. Under-garments included . . .

I hesitate, glancing back at Elaric.

"Is everything all right?" His brow furrows in puzzlement.

I open my mouth but speech fails me, throat tightening. He just eyes me curiously, unaware of the heat crawling up my neck.

I shouldn't let this fluster me. It's not as if he's never seen me naked before.

And just like that, traitorous memories ignite—his hands and lips trailing across my skin. I extinguish the thought before it burns out of control.

I swallow down hard, concentrating on the task at hand. The lake. The cave. The herb.

It matters not if Elaric sees me naked. We share no intimacy now. This is a necessity, nothing more.

"It's nothing," I state as firmly as I can. Then I turn back to the lake and unclasp my cloak. Fabric rustles as it hits the ground, bundling around my feet. Next, I shuffle out of my breeches and leave them discarded with my cloak. And when I remove my tunic and am left in my undergarments, I hear the sharp intake of breath behind me.

Air kisses my bare skin. I make my mind as numb as the chilling breeze, doing my best to forget Elaric's presence behind me.

Steeling myself, I peel off my undergarments. And then I'm left standing there, naked to the night.

I refuse to turn to see if Elaric is watching. I don't need to know. I don't *want* to know.

Edging closer to the water, I dip my toes into the depths.

Crimson flashes beneath.

I pause, crouching down to peer into the lake. The surface is still, and whatever I thought I saw is nowhere to be seen. Maybe I imagined it.

I dip my fingers in and stir the water.

Red whirs toward me.

I pull back my hand. Just in time.

Fangs snap up, narrowly missing my fingers. I glimpse serpentine eyes and ruby scales before the creature vanishes.

Gasping, I stagger backward and miss my footing, hitting the ground. Pebbles graze my bare legs.

"Adara!" Elaric calls, hurrying beside me.

His arm wraps around my waist, and he helps me onto my feet. Then my back is pressed against his chest, and thanks to the danger lurking in the depths, my nakedness is entirely forgotten by us both.

"What happened?" he demands. "Are you hurt?"

With a shaking hand, I point toward the now deceptively still water. "Something's in there. Didn't you see it?"

"I wasn't looking," he says tightly. "What was it?"

"Something long and red, with fangs that nearly bit my fingers off. It vanished into the water before I could see it properly."

He tenses. "It must have been a Zaroy Eel."

I just shake my head. "Maybe? I don't know. I've never heard of them before."

"You are not going in there," he growls, grabbing my shoulders and spinning me around to face him. "We're heading back to the palace right now and forgetting all of this nonsense about Belinda and the sword."

I glare up at him. "I'm not leaving." Maybe it's not sensible to jump into a lake full of monstrous eels, but I hate him ordering me around like this. Besides, there could be a way to reach the cave without being torn to shreds.

"Adara . . . " His voice rumbles in a warning. I refuse to heed it.

"I struck this bargain with Belinda, and I intend to uphold it."

"This proves she cannot be trusted."

"She gave you the sword when you returned with the wyvern poison."

"She failed to mention that this lake is infested with Zaroy Eels," he seethes. "I will not stand here and watch you be torn apart."

"I'll out-swim them," I say with as much confidence as I can feign. "Surely they have a weakness?"

"Why must you be so stubborn?"

I just stare at him, refusing to yield.

He runs a hand down his face. "You will not change your mind?"

"I will not."

Heaving a sigh, he releases my shoulders. "Very well," he says reluctantly. "Zaroy Eels have poor vision and rely on detecting vibrations to hunt prey."

"So, the slower I move through the water, the less likely it is they'll detect my presence?"

Elaric nods. "They also possess the ability to smell blood. A single drop will send them into a frenzy."

I glance down at my limbs, searching for any open wounds. Thankfully, the branches left no cuts.

"I'm in half a mind to haul you over my shoulder and drag you back to the palace," he grumbles.

"Then you'd have to make me your prisoner again, or else I'd simply leave and come back here myself."

"I know," he admits. "And that's the only reason I'm not dragging you back home."

Home.

Warmth blooms through my whole being. Even though he asked for our marriage to be dissolved, he still regards the Crystal Palace as my home.

I quickly smother the spark of hope, lest it distract me from the task ahead. Inhaling sharply, I step closer to the water again.

"At the first sight of you in danger," Elaric warns, "I will freeze them. The whole damned lake if I must."

I dare not argue with the fierceness in his words.

Cautiously, I peer into the lake, searching for any sign of the creatures. I linger over the edge for a minute and then another, but no flash of scales appears.

Then I tentatively dip my fingers into the water, ready to retract them. Only liquid meets my skin.

Growing bolder, I stir the surface, disturbing it. No frenzied fangs emerge.

Heart racing, I next immerse my toes. The water remains still.

And then, as slowly as I can, I slip into the lake.

Chapter 20

Cold water rushes over me, and I shiver. Despite my immunity as the Summer Queen protecting me from Elaric's magic, it does nothing to prevent the natural chill of the lake from seeping into my body. Having grown unaccustomed to the sensation of coldness, the icy temperature permeates deep into my bones.

I hold as still as I can, kicking ever so gently to stay afloat. Elaric's gaze burns into the back of my head. Without needing to turn around, I know he's watching my every move.

Several yards ahead, the surface ripples. I tense, readying myself in case a Zaroy Eel emerges and charges in my direction. But if one does, I have little hope of defending myself. My only weapon is the small dagger strapped to my thigh. And it's doubtful I could swim to safety in time.

I can only rely on stealth.

Luckily, the rippling proves to be the wind, and the water stills.

"Adara," Elaric calls from the bank, his voice quiet compared to my thundering pulse. "Please be careful."

What reassurances can I offer him? If I were being careful, I wouldn't be swimming naked in a lake full of man-eating eels.

With a deep breath, I lower myself under the surface.

It takes my eyes a few moments to adapt to the murky light of the depths before I'm able to scan my surroundings.

Once certain there are no eels nearby, I gently propel myself left, gliding along the lake's edge and disturbing the water as little as I can.

The lake is deeper than I expect, and so it takes me a while to reach the bottom, my palms scraping across the rock in search of any opening. I manage mere yards before I'm forced to return to the surface. I do so carefully to avoid stirring the water.

Over and over I repeat this, my slow pace becoming an increasing concern. Scouring the lake may take all night, and by then Elaric's magic will have frozen all the water.

But I dare not quicken. Doing so may cause a flurry of eels to rush toward me.

I'm not sure how much longer it takes before I reach halfway around the lake, but my body is quickly waning from the exertion. Despite my slow pace, pushing through the water requires significant strength.

As I resume my search, I begin to question whether Belinda was being truthful about the lake or whether she has sent us on a fool's errand. Perhaps the error lies with Elaric and me for choosing the incorrect lake, though it's only a short distance from the castle ruins. I suppose there was no definitive marker to verify this spot, and we just assumed this was the right location based on its proximity to Festyn.

Though it seems probable this is the lake we're searching for, Belinda mentioned nothing about Zaroy Eels standing between me and the cave, and there's a chance I'm currently risking my life for nothing.

I don't allow myself to dwell on these thoughts for long.

As I resurface for air, I glimpse a flash of crimson. Heart plummeting, I turn rigid, barely daring to breathe.

An eel glides toward me, and for one horrifying moment I believe it's found me. But then it changes its trajectory, drifting to a cluster of rocks nearby.

I nearly sigh in relief, but it remains far too close and offers no indication of leaving. My already strained lungs scream for oxygen as the eel continues to hover by the rocks.

I'm trapped.

Moving now will draw it toward me. But if I stay here much longer, I'll drown.

Holding my breath is quickly growing impossible. My chest burns, and my vision blurs. The water seems to spin as dizziness sets in.

What if the eel doesn't leave? What if I lose consciousness before it does?

Right as my lungs are nearly bursting, the eel darts away. I watch until it vanishes entirely, only then daring to kick up.

I swim carefully, fighting against every instinct urging me to bolt for air. Lungs screaming, I force my movements to remain steady.

Then I break the surface and suck in all the air I can, coughing and spluttering.

"Adara!" Elaric shouts.

I long to answer, to reassure him of my safety, but speech proves impossible. Each heaving breath incites more coughing.

"Adara!" he calls again, fear elevating the pitch of his voice.

I worry his panic may prompt him to freeze the whole lake.

"I-I'm fine," I rasp. While my voice is shaky, hopefully it offers enough reassurance that he won't resort to any drastic measures.

Ignoring burning lungs, I gulp a breath and submerge again—both to avoid Elaric's worried questioning, and to keep watch for potential threats below. If he knew how near that last eel came, I doubt he would permit me to continue my search.

Once more, my hands skim across the rough perimeter of the lake, searching for the opening. After such a close encounter with that eel, my chest feels badly bruised, and I can't hold my breath for as long, slowing my search.

Just as frustration peaks, I spot an opening—a narrow cleft near the lake's bed.

Relief washes through me, but I don't hesitate before shifting closer toward the cave.

The gap is slender but I'm able to slide through. Yet if I were any broader, it would be impossible. I doubt Elaric would manage at all.

I carefully maneuver my body to avoid the jagged edges, not letting my skin graze the coarse surface. Even the smallest nick will doom me.

But I've underestimated the length of the tunnel. As I drift farther into its depths, the passage shows no sign of ending. My lungs are already strained from before and begin tiring too soon.

Just as faintness sets in from air deprivation, the tunnel widens.

I burst through the surface and emerge into a cavern, half-choking as I gasp for air. Treading water gently, I examine the cave, my frantic breaths echoing around me.

Wet rocky walls gleam everywhere, sparkling like a tapestry of black diamonds.

I wade up the slope, leaving the water and stepping onto solid ground. As well as a prickly plant sprouting in the center, scattered bones occupy the cave.

My mouth dries as I peer at the closest heap of remains.

A human skull lies there . . .

Swallowing down the bile rising in my throat, my eyes drift over to the brambleweed ahead. Whoever lies at my feet came here to harvest its leaves but were poisoned and trapped, imprisoned by their own body until they perished from dehydration or starvation.

My fingers wrap around the small vial hanging around my neck, reassuring myself it's still there. If I accidentally prick my finger on a thorn, I need to be quick in swallowing the antidote or I'll join the skeletons which decorate this dank cave.

I approach warily, half expecting the brambles to suddenly rush forth with grasping, thorny tendrils. But the plant remains lifeless.

Unsheathing my dagger, I crouch before its twisted vines and gently tug a leaf upward. I slide my blade beneath it and saw its stem, severing it from the central mass.

Once the leaf is freed from the plant, I inspect its underside, which is covered in tiny bumps. Only the vines themselves bear sharp thorns. While touching the leaves seems safe enough, I must still take great care.

Gritting my teeth, I shift my attention from the leaf and return to the rest of the plant.

Three leaves is what Belinda specified. Harvesting more than that risks the herb withering and dying.

I place the first leaf beside me on the floor and set to work severing a second. This one cuts free with even less effort.

Then I move to a third leaf, but its stem refuses to give way. My blade scrapes in vain against the wood-like base.

Growing impatient, I throw more force into the sawing motion. The stem snaps unexpectedly, causing my dagger to fly from my hand.

Instinctively, I reach for the hilt.

My hand collides with a barbed vine. Pain spears through me.

I recoil sharply and cradle my hand. A deep red bead swells on the back.

A thorn has pierced my skin.

Chapter 21

Dropping the leaf, I grab the vial from my neck. I need to drink it fast, before the poison seizes my muscles. If my body locks up, I won't be able to swallow the antidote.

With my teeth, I pry out the wooden stopper, nipping my lip in my haste. As the cork falls from my fingers, I drink every bitter drop of the antidote, refusing to let even a trace escape.

Then I just stand there rigid, waiting for some sign of the antidote taking effect. Surely if it reaches my blood quickly enough, the paralysis will still be stopped?

But what if Belinda didn't supply me with enough? What if the antidote has somehow been tainted and rendered useless since she gave it to me?

The creeping numbness provides my answer.

My fingers first succumb, morphing into stone and ignoring every demand to move. The impossible weight drags me to the ground.

I scream soundless cries, pleading for some small scrap of movement from my limbs. But no matter how fiercely I battle against the poison, my body continues to defy me.

The last time I felt like this was on my first night in the Crystal Palace, when Elaric visited my chambers and kissed me, his frost surging through my body.

I pray that like that night, these chains will suddenly spring free. But the paralysis consumes my legs, spreading across all of me.

What if it reaches my heart and stops it?

All I can do is lie there, staring up at the dark stone ceiling. I can close my eyes and breathe but aside from that, I can't move a single muscle. I'm trapped inside my own body.

I picture Elaric pacing the beside the lake, his unrest spurring his magic to spread. Unless I break free, the whole lake will soon share my fate.

After vanishing beneath the waves, Elaric won't know what has happened to me. There will be only two possibilities in his mind—either that I successfully found the cave and swam inside, or was torn apart by the eels. Perhaps I should have called over to let him know before diving in. At least then he'd know where I am.

But even if he was aware of my location, I doubt he could reach me. His presence would render the water solid around him, just like in his bathtub. Maybe he could freeze the water into a tunnel, but that's assuming he'll even find the cave beneath all the ice.

Each moment blurs into the next as I lose grasp on the passage of time. Reality slips away, sensations muted against the panic screaming inside my skull.

I can't tell if minutes have crawled by, or hours.

Did I fail to drink every drop? Or is this entire quest some trick orchestrated by Belinda? But why bother with such an elaborate ruse? While in her woods Elaric possessed no magic, and it would have been easy for her to defeat us.

Yet there's no other explanation. The cure has proven useless.

This is it then. My final resting place.

Even terror and despair grow dull, my emotions numbing along with physical sensation. There's only a timeless calm, as if I've already detached from the world around me.

And then, as the last shred of hope flickers out, my little toe twitches.

Suddenly, I can feel it, as well as the moist air surrounding it. That feeling extends to the rest of my foot, and then I can wiggle all my toes.

Slowly, sensation returns to my limbs, the poison's effects retreating.

Gasping, I force myself upright. I hold out my hand, marveling at the ability to move my fingers, when only seconds ago such a feat was impossible.

I sit there, staring at the brambleweed ahead, its pointed leaves glinting. Though the poison has left my body, it takes longer to leave my mind. The feeling of being locked in your own body is not an easy thing to forget.

When my mind finishes processing what has happened, I push myself onto my feet. I'm not sure precisely how long the paralysis imprisoned me, but standing is strenuous, as if I've spent countless weeks lying ill in bed and am now walking again for the first time.

My steps are unsteady at first, but I manage to find the leaves I dropped. One is somewhat crumpled, but Belinda may not mind if she can still use it in her potions.

My dagger lies before the brambleweed, and I carefully retrieve it, keeping away from all the deadly thorns. While the antidote still flows in my veins, I don't know whether it will neutralize another dose of the poison, and it isn't something I'm keen to test.

I sheathe my blade and then consider the leaves in my hand. Aside from my dagger's holster, I don't have any way of storing the leaves on my body. I can't even tuck them into the top of my breeches, since I'm wearing nothing at all.

It seems my only option is to stuff the leaves into the empty antidote vial, but I'll need to roll them up to fit them inside. And while I took great pain in drinking every drop of antidote, it's possible traces remain inside the vial. The drops may react with the brambleweed leaves, rendering them useless. Then Belinda may decide I haven't fulfilled my end of our deal and will send me on yet another quest to risk my life.

But there's nothing else I can do, so I take the leaves and put them inside the vial as gently as I can, securing them in place with the stopper.

The next problem to consider is my wounded hand. Though the scratch has dried, it hasn't scabbed over completely, and water may cause it to bleed again. If even a drop seeps into the lake, every Zaroy Eel will charge for me before I can swim out the cave.

I pace forward to the water and splash some onto the back of my injured hand, waiting to see if any blood trickles out.

None does, even when I splash it again, so I dare to hold it underwater. Though it stings considerably, no blood leaks out.

Entering the lake with an open wound isn't wise, but I can't sit and wait in this cave for it to heal. That could take several days, and by then, Elaric will have certainly frozen the lake. And the entire forest.

Swallowing down fear, I step into the pool, following the slope downward until I'm fully immersed.

Water laps over me. Pushing myself under the surface, I scan for the exit. When I find it, I squeeze my shoulders through the gap, minding the coarse sides, and swim through the narrow tunnel. I reach the other side without drawing any more blood.

I'm just about to return to the surface for air when I notice an eel several yards ahead.

Heart seizing, I cease all motion, praying my movements so far were controlled enough to avoid catching its notice. That it won't be able to smell the blood from my wound.

I stay still, watching.

It too doesn't move.

And just as I think it's about to turn away, it charges for me.

I dart left, trying to reach the shore and pull myself out before it nears me. Now I make no attempt at stealth, splashing furiously with all the haste I can muster. Even if it means drawing the other eels toward me.

As I break the surface, my hopes sink. On this side of the lake, towering rocks form the perimeter. Their faces are smooth and slippery, offering no handholds to climb.

I'm trapped.

And out of time. The eel is almost upon me, with doubtless more close behind.

"Adara!" comes Elaric's distant cry from across the lake. But he's too far to reach me. To stop all the fangs from tearing through me.

Still, I thrash on with my dwindling strength, frantically splashing through the water. I don't know where I'm swimming toward. I don't have time to consider it. Nor do I dare waste precious seconds by diving under water and gauging how close the eel is.

"Adara!" he shouts again.

I can spare no breath on replies. I can only swim for my life.

And then everything stops.

One minute I'm swimming, and then I'm not. Everything around me stills, the restless currents banished.

Chapter 22

It takes my frenzied mind a moment to realize exactly what just happened.

Elaric froze the lake with a single thought, even though he's standing so far away on the other side.

The water is suspended around me, forming an indentation. The surface is a few feet above, close enough I should be able to reach up and drag myself out.

Rising to my feet is a struggle on the smooth surface. The clear ice reveals the dark waters as if encased in glass.

Just an arm's length away lies the eel, fangs bared wide in preparation of a lethal strike. Its next surge through water would have shredded me into ribbons.

Dread shivers through me.

If Elaric delayed in freezing the lake, I'd be dead right now.

When I look behind, I see the shadowy figures of more trapped eels. Though they're several yards away, they would have reached me soon after the first.

"Adara!" Elaric's cry rings out, no longer muffled by the splashing of water. Footsteps echo, growing nearer as he crosses the lake.

I grip the icy ledge and drag my body up with gritted teeth. It proves a great effort after all of tonight's trials.

Elaric grabs my arms, inspecting me carefully. Alarm flares across his face as he notices the swollen puncture marring the back of my hand.

"It's nothing," I insist, pulling away my hand. But his grip is unyielding.

"The paralysis . . . " Fear laces his voice.

"I'm fine," I say quickly.

Elaric's eyes drop to the antidote vial at my neck, now containing the crumpled brambleweed leaves stuffed inside. A muscle feathers in his jaw. "I should have never let you do this."

I straighten as much as my weary body permits. "You know you could never have stopped me." I do my best to steel my voice but cannot prevent the slight waver. Now adrenaline is wearing off, I'm left swaying on my feet.

"Those things nearly had you," he grinds out.

I avert my gaze, unable to meet his piercing eyes. "Thank you. For saving me."

He grips my other hand. "You needn't thank me for saving your life, Adara. I would never let anything hurt you."

I keep my eyes lowered, unprepared to confront the emotion burning behind those words.

"You're shivering," he says, scanning over me. "And so pale."

I only now realize that I am indeed shivering. In fact, I'm freezing, though not from Elaric's magic. The lake's water drenching my hair and skin is untouched by frost. With the biting wind rolling over us, I can't seem to stop from trembling.

"I'm f-fine," I force out, but my teeth betray me by chattering.

Elaric pins me with an incredulous look before sweeping me up into his arms. A vague notion of protest crosses my mind, but we both know my exhausted body would collapse long before making it across the lake alone.

I relax into his sturdy embrace. Though his touch would freeze anyone else, the chill within me is already receding from his warmth.

Elaric crosses the lake swiftly. I savor his closeness as he carries me to shore. There, he sets me on the grass beneath the trees overlooking the lake. Frost crisps the blades, but soon thaws at my touch. His magic has yet to reach all the way through to the soil.

The grass tickles my bare legs, and I abruptly remember my nakedness. Elaric looks away.

"I'll get our belongings," he says, already heading over to the sack and my bundle of discarded clothes.

I huddle against the bitter wind, knees gathered to my chest in a pitiful attempt at modesty. I occupy my hands by wringing out my soaked curls, though it has little effect.

Elaric returns shortly, placing my clothes beside me and offering a blanket. "Here," he says, keeping his eyes away from me.

Heat floods my cheeks as I hastily accept the blanket. I can't decide which is worse: his staring or his awkwardness.

I wrap the coarse fabric around myself as a shield, and the blanket skims my thighs like a makeshift dress. I tuck the corner beneath my arm to secure it in place.

Once the blanket is covering me, the tension somewhat lessens. Elaric settles opposite me on the grass. It takes mere seconds before the blades beneath him turn to solid ice. His magic spreads until it climbs the nearby trees, and just a small circle of grass around me is spared.

Elaric surveys the creeping ice, eyes catching on a discarded branch consumed by glittering frost. Pain shadows his expression.

Heaving a sigh, he turns back to me. "I'm sorry, Adara."

"What for?"

"It's my fault you're forced to endure this chill."

"It isn't your fault," I reply. "I'm the one who jumped into the lake. The reason I'm cold has nothing to do with you. Your magic doesn't affect me."

"But it is preventing you from warming up. If we could light a fire, you could sit beside it and would soon dry off."

I bow my head, words failing. I can't deny the truth in what he says, yet I hate the self-loathing buried within every syllable. If only there was something I could say to dampen the blame he is currently placing on himself.

All I can do is to try to reduce my shivering, so that he has less to feel guilty about. My skin is fairly dry, but my hair still drips beneath the blanket. Wringing out my curls before did little to help that.

I dig through the sack for a comb and a ribbon. Then I brush through my hair slowly, worried that reaching up too suddenly may cause my blanket to slip.

All the strands are so knotted that combing it is a great effort, and my arms are weary from swimming.

"Let me help," Elaric says.

Before I can reply, he's already beside me.

Hesitantly, I pass the comb to him and my body tenses as he sits down next to me.

With him sitting so near, I am reminded of the fact I wear nothing beneath the blanket and am overly aware of all the places the coarse fabric touches my skin.

Though Elaric combs through my hair with great care, snags are inevitable. I wince as the tines catch a strand.

He stills. "Have I hurt you?"

"It's fine."

He pauses before continuing, now slower and gentler. The sensation of his fingers brushing over the curve of my shoulder and the nape of my neck is so delightful that I close my eyes, almost drifting to sleep despite sitting upright.

"Have I ever told you how lovely your hair is, Adara?" His hushed voice jolts me back.

"No," I say, "I don't believe you have."

His fingers trail over a lock. "Never have I seen hair so bright, as if spun from flame."

I flush at the compliment. "I . . . thank you."

We lapse into silence once more as Elaric resumes combing my hair. When he finishes, I pass him the ribbon but his attempt to tie my locks fails miserably.

"I fear my skills are limited to combing," he admits sheepishly, handing back the comb and the ribbon.

"It's fine," I say with a laugh, taking them both.

Neither the comb nor ribbon shows any sign of frost despite being in his hands. Staying in contact with my hair must have prevented the spread of his magic.

I gesture to his hair which trails past his broad shoulders. "Don't you ever tie yours back? Even while fighting?"

"Fighting?" he repeats. "I have fought no wars over these past centuries. Nowadays, there is no need for such practicalities."

I suppose no mortal can pose much of a threat against his power. When he fought Orlan and his men, the skirmish lasted for mere minutes, even though Elaric was terribly outnumbered.

I take a section of my hair and run the comb through it, scraping it upward. "What was your hair like before the curse? Was it still long then, or short?"

"It skimmed my shoulders."

As I examine him, I imagine him with hair several inches shorter. I decide the longer length makes him look more regal. "Has it always been white?"

He shakes his head. "Golden."

Like his sister then, according to what we told me before we left the palace.

I brush out another section thoughtfully. "And what about your eyes? Were they still blue?"

"Green," he says. "There's an old portrait of me somewhere in the palace's storehouses. When we return home, I'll find it so you can look."

I smile at that. "Then I look forward to seeing it." Except if we return home, I hope we will do so having slain Isidore and broken Elaric's curse. With the frost gone from around his heart, his appearance would have already returned to how it once was.

When I finish securing the rest of my hair, I turn to find Elaric already watching me, his expression unreadable.

"Are you still cold?" he asks.

"Not really." At least no chatter undermines me now.

He grabs my hands, frowning at their slight trembling. "I don't believe you."

"Fine, maybe a little." I sigh, relenting. "But I'm already feeling much better."

His arms sweep around me, enveloping me in warmth. My pulse thrums feverishly. "How about now?" His murmur caresses my hair.

I lean deeper into him, my own arms wrapping tentatively around him. "Yes," I whisper. "Thank you."

"You must rest," he tells me, "especially after enduring so much today."

I nod against his shoulder, though I make no attempt to unwind my arms.

After a pause, his grip loosens. I worry he will withdraw, taking away all his warmth. But then he guides us both down onto the grass, keeping me tucked against him.

"Will you manage to rest like this?" he asks, his breath tickling my ear.

The uncertainty is obvious behind those words: Do I mind lying with him like this, wrapped only in a blanket and his arms, when all I've ever done is push him away?

I inch back, closing that last bit of distance between us. "I will."

With that, any lingering doubt is dissolved, and Elaric's arms wrap around me even tighter. Eyes fluttering shut, I focus on his chest rising and falling behind me, his heartbeat a soothing rhythm.

Before long, I drift to sleep, sheltered in his arms.

Chapter 23

I'm not sure how long passes before I stir, but Elaric still cradles me fiercely even in his sleep. The weight of slumber shrouds my mind, and for a while I simply lie there, watching the shadows flicker across the trees. Everywhere I look is chained by ice, not a single leaf or bush spared.

Given how far Elaric's magic has spread, it seems I was asleep for several hours.

I sigh, knowing how much he will hate to see its effects on the surrounding area. But nothing can be done about it right now.

Elaric is lying so motionlessly behind me I'm certain he must be asleep. Having no wish to disturb his rest, I carefully shuffle around in his arms until I'm facing him.

My gaze drifts over his features: the sharpness of his jaw, the gentle curve of his lip, the stubble powdering his face. In the low light his hair appears silver and looks so soft and silken, much unlike mine.

It's rare I've had the opportunity to examine him closely, but now he's asleep, I can admire him at my leisure, without him knowing.

Yet the more I study him, the more difficult it becomes to stop myself from reaching out and touching his face. All the while, my heart aches with the realization that this is what we could have shared, had I not been so blinded by my revenge. Had I stopped to consider there might be more to my sister's disappearance than I first believed.

But now everything is shattered between us. I blink back tears to stop them from falling. Regret surges through me.

And guilt. So much guilt.

If only I could take back what I did. If only I could glue back together the fragments of what we once had. But I fear in trying to do so, I would inflict more damage to the fragile remains.

All I can do is lie here and savor the way it feels to lie in his arms, mourning the ghost of what we once shared.

So deep in my own thoughts, I'm slow to notice that Elaric's eyes have opened. That he is staring back at me just as intently.

The breath catches in the back of my throat. It's loud enough I'm sure he hears it. But his eyes don't leave mine.

"Adara," he murmurs, reaching out and brushing away the damp curl which has fallen from the ribbon and into my face.

My heart pounds in my chest. I should say it now. Everything. Even if he never forgives me.

But it's so silent, and this moment feels so delicate. I have no wish to trample over it with my messy emotions.

And most of all, I'm terrified.

"You were gone for so long under the water," he says gently. "Even after you emerged unharmed, I thought you would freeze to death before my very eyes." His fingers trail across my cheek, and he tips my chin up to meet his gaze. "The thought of losing you was unbearable."

"Elaric," I whisper, not knowing what else to say. I should tell him I don't want our marriage to be annulled, but then I'll be making a promise I don't know if I can keep. I've already hurt him so much. I can't let him down again.

So, I say nothing.

The intensity, the longing, in his eyes is too much to bear. I break our stare, instead looking down at the coarse blanket wrapped around my chest.

"Have you warmed up?" Elaric asks.

"Yes, I have," I say, glancing up to meet his eyes briefly. "Thank you."

He pauses, noticing our entwined limbs. "Would you like me to let you go?"

Simple words, yet laden with deeper meaning. His gaze spears me, searching for the truth in mine.

My voice is breathless as I say, "No. Don't let me go."

And then the suffocating tension shatters as his mouth claims mine. Or perhaps it is I who first closes that final distance. Not that it matters. My mind is lost to all but the fervor between us.

Our kiss is frenzied, as if the other will slip through our fingers. His lips burn against mine, and he pulls me closer, until there's no line to where I end and he begins.

His teeth graze my lip, and the furnace within me ignites into an untamable inferno, fueled by all the thoughts I've had of him since our wedding night, all those painfully tense moments where the two of us have wanted each other so desperately. Though it has been only two weeks since that night, now we kiss as if we have been starved of each other for eternity.

"Adara," he says. I feel my name against my lips. A question.

"I want you," I murmur. "I want you so much."

Whatever control he has left is frayed by that. His tongue demands entry, swirling around, exploring my mouth. I allow him to claim me, as I wish so dearly for him to claim the rest of me.

His hands run down my bare shoulders, my skin burning at his touch, and the solidness of his muscles bears down into me.

"I need you," he rasps. Evidence of his desire digs into my leg, and a fresh wave of yearning crashes into me, my core slickening with restless need.

I arch into him, but it's not enough. Not until he's inside me. But there's little time to protest.

His fingers wander across my chest, finding the corner of the blanket I tucked under my arm.

My breath hitches as he plucks out the folded fabric. And then, before I can blink, he tears the blanket from around me, leaving me exposed beneath him.

Cool night air rolls over me I as Elaric scans over every inch of my naked flesh. His burning gaze renders my nipples into hardened peaks.

"You're perfect." His fingers glide across my collarbone, and I shiver. "Every part of you is perfect."

"Please," I moan.

He tilts his head, regarding me, and a smirk dances upon his lips. I roll my hips, but I can hardly move with him straddling me.

"Please," I say again.

His fingers return to my face, tracing my lips. "Tell me what you want, Adara."

"You," I gasp. "All of you."

His hand brushes up the inside of my thigh, the calluses on his palm grazing my skin. Higher he climbs, though his hand slows. Until it comes to a stop.

And then, just as I'm convinced he'll advance no further, his fingers sink into me, parting my wet folds.

The movement is so sudden I can't stop from crying out. I clench around his fingers, aching for more. Yet he pulls them out, torturously slow. I open my mouth to object, to beg, but then he slides his fingers back in.

Pleasure sparks through me like lightning.

"Like this?" he asks, eyes gleaming as he lowers his lips to my breast.

I try to speak, but my attempt fails as his tongue flicks over my nipple. His smirk only grows.

Though I relish what he's currently doing to me, this wasn't what I had in mind.

"More," I force out between rasping breaths.

"More of what?" he asks, raising a brow.

"You, inside me."

He pushes his fingers even deeper inside me, giving me a wicked grin. "I am inside you."

"No," I say. "Not like this."

He pulls his fingers out, suddenly. And I'm left feeling woefully empty.

Elaric reaches for the stays of his breeches, untying them and slipping out of them. My core tightens at the realization of how hard he is, as desperate for me as I am for him.

Wanting him as bare as I am, I pull off his tunic, lifting it over his head. The moonlight glistens across his skin, highlighting every edge of his toned body.

I chart the solidness of his chest, the defined lines of his abdomen. Then I delve lower, until my fingers reach him. My hand closes around his hard length.

Growling, he grabs my hand and pins it to the grass. His other hand roams across my thighs, spreading them apart, and presses himself against my swollen entrance. Heat lances through my stomach at the feel of him.

I buck against him, needing him deeper than just the tip.

He obliges my wishes in a single, swift thrust that buries him to the hilt. I gasp, my body stretching to accommodate him. Then he shifts back, hand on my hip, withdrawing inch by inch.

It feels like an age passes as he pauses, until he slides all the way back in. A groan rumbles in the back of his throat, trembling across my skin. The decadent fullness turns my blood into molten pleasure.

He releases my wrist, fingers brushing over my breasts as he pushes into me. I reach up, hands sliding around his neck and tugging him closer. Our lips meet and his tongue tangles with mine, dancing to the same rhythm as our bodies.

Our kiss breaks, his arm encircling my waist. He pulls me up into his lap, remaining deep inside me as we shift positions. He lowers his head, lips finding my breast, and draws my nipple into his mouth. A jolt shudders through me as his teeth graze the sensitive spot.

Then we're tumbling together onto the grass, his hips driving up to meet mine. I place both hands on his chest as I straddle him.

Yet the second my palms meet his chest, his whole body turns so rigid. As if he's turned into stone.

I wonder if he's already reached his peak, but then he's pushing me off, sliding out. Emptiness weighs on me.

I wait for his arms to close around me, for him to drag me back into his warm embrace.

Except he grabs his clothes and stands, looking anywhere but at me.

"Elaric?" My voice breaks around his name.

He says nothing as he pulls back on his breeches and turns away, tunic bunched in his fist.

I bolt up, legs unsteady beneath me.

"Elaric?" I try again, panic flooding through my veins.

"I can't," he says, his voice so hollow and cold. "Adara, I can't."

And with that, he steps into the trees. Leaving me alone in the shadows.

Chapter 24

Elaric does not return that night.

Though I huddle in my blanket, I can't dispel the chill set deep in my bones.

One moment his arms were around me, and I was living a blissful dream.

In the next, he was gone. The illusion shattered, shards piercing my heart.

I can still taste his lips on mine. I can still feel him inside me.

The ghost of our passion just makes me feel hollower.

But I can't blame him for it. This is my fault. I knew things would never again be the same between us. I should have clung to my senses and ended our kiss before it spiraled out of control. It was selfish and foolish of me to believe we could go back to what we were, even if just for one night.

Things went too far. *I* pushed him too far. And now I've broken the fragile remnants of our relationship. I'm not sure we'll ever return to the tentative friendship we've formed over the past week.

I clutch my blanket, though it does nothing to soothe the ache within.

Part of me yearns to chase him down through the trees, to confess how I've spent every waking moment since our wedding night regretting it all, how he means so very much to me.

But such a confession would be for my sake alone, to earn his forgiveness and regain what I've lost.

Maybe the reason he feels drawn to me is because of the magic binding me to him as his fated Summer Queen. With the curse broken, he might wake up and realize he would have never chosen me otherwise.

Cutting ties between us is what I must do for his sake, even if my heart feels like it's bleeding.

For now, we must be nothing more than allies focused on our quest. After we return to Belinda, slay Isidore, and break his curse, we will go our separate ways, leaving all this behind us.

Eventually dreamless sleep finds me. But when I wake, the pit in my stomach is just as deep.

To my surprise, as I sit up and rub my eyes, I spot Elaric leaning against a nearby tree. He faces away from me, but must sense my stirring since he turns in my direction. He's careful to avoid my gaze.

"You should eat," he says to the lake, voice clipped. "We will leave shortly."

I say nothing, pretending to be fascinated with rummaging through the provisions in our sack. I find a loaf of bread and attempt to eat a slice, but it tastes like chalk.

Still naked beneath the coarse blanket, I find a tree to dress behind. Elaric turns away as I do, body tense. Though the wind bites at me as I unwrap my blanket and pull on my breeches and tunic, my skin burns with shame.

Stepping back into our frozen campsite, I force steadiness into my voice. "I'm ready."

Silently Elaric rises, conjuring the carriage and winged steeds once more. He approaches the door then pauses, partly turning toward me. My eyes drop to the ground, unable to meet his. Even slight glances cut too deeply.

Elaric pulls open the door. An agonized moment drags by while he waits, holding it open for me to climb in.

I half wish he would storm inside the carriage, punctuating his unspoken fury by slamming the door behind him. Rage would at least clarify our current positions. This ambiguity only serves to twist the knife in my chest deeper.

We should speak about last night, lay bare all our regrets and questions before the stifling tension suffocates us both.

But no matter how I try, I can't form the words. All the desire and hurt and pain are too big to voice aloud.

I hurry past, not looking at him. Every nerve in my body tingles from his nearness as I step into the carriage. My pulse is so deafeningly loud, especially compared to the silent forest surrounding us.

Elaric enters quietly and shuts the door. I glue my eyes to the window as he sits on the bench opposite mine. The translucent trees beyond fail to distract me. But I cling to the attempt, regardless.

He directs the carriage over the forest. Neither of us speaks. The view blurs outside my window as I fixate on anything besides him and the memory of last night.

It takes several miles before the trees turn green again, showing just how far Elaric's power has spread overnight. Only the outskirts are intact. How long will it take for people of the nearby towns to notice the unnatural state of Brimlore Forest? Is Elaric's power well known beyond our kingdom? Will the local people blame him for the unnatural winter, or will they suspect it to be the work of a powerful ice witch?

Before long, the forest is far behind us, and we're soaring through the powdery clouds. Golden sunlight pierces through the windows.

Serene though the view may be, it does little to dampen the heaviness weighing on my heart.

Elaric says nothing throughout the entire morning. The flight back to Belinda's woods will take a whole day and then we'll have to trek through the woods to reach her cottage. If he maintains this silence for that long, I'll be driven to madness.

With a deep breath, I tear away from the window and force myself to look at him for the first time since leaving the forest.

Everything within me constricts as his bright eyes meet mine.

"Elaric," I mutter.

The haziness in his eyes vanishes at the sound of his name. How I wish I could read his thoughts, now more than ever. If I knew what he was feeling then I could be confident in saying the right thing. As it stands, I fear the wrong words will only worsen matters.

"Last night . . . " I start.

"Last night was a mistake." His voice is firm. How I wish it was a broken whisper.

It takes everything in me not to flinch. I don't know why it catches me by surprise, why it hurts. His actions last night made his feelings transparent.

"A moment of weakness," he adds, driving guilt deeper into me.

Tears sting my eyes. I turn and face the window so he doesn't see them.

My fingers curl around the window ledge. I ground myself in the present by focusing on the way the harsh edges dig into my palm.

Yet my frantic thoughts aren't so easily extinguished. All I want is to stand up and demand to know whether wrapping his arms around me was also a weakness, whether his attentiveness toward me was also a mistake. But I don't. That would be selfish.

He deserves better than me.

When Elaric next speaks, his voice is as frigid as winter. "It will not happen again."

Chapter 25

I avoid meeting Elaric's gaze for the rest of that afternoon, dreading the cold scorn I'll find there. Though deserved, his words cleave my heart. It takes all my strength not to collapse and release the tears clamoring for escape.

The tension within me coils ever tighter, surging into a pounding headache which threatens to crush my skull. My thoughts cycle between our ruinous wedding night and the disaster of last night, each recollection a fresh stab of anguish.

I know this self-torture serves no good use, yet I cannot stop it. I should slam my eyes shut, force order on my chaotic emotions before they shatter what little composure remains.

But I cannot escape the knife I drove through my own heart. His words were not unfair, only the truth. I orchestrated this tragedy through my pride and fear, and now I have no choice but to endure it.

Merciful exhaustion drags me into dreamless sleep, sparing me the nightmares which would leave me weeping. I never want him to see such fragility in me again.

I'm unsure how much time passes before Elaric's voice wakes me.

"We're here," he says. It's a slight relief that no disgust lingers in his tone.

All reassurances vanish when I dare to lift my head and meet his cold eyes. Air flees my lungs as his bitter words echo in my mind.

Last night was a mistake.
A moment of weakness.
It won't happen again.

Thirteen words, I count. Thirteen words were all he spoke, and yet they were enough to destroy me.

I focus on the trees ahead of us, on the wind rustling through their leaves and try to steady my frantic pulse.

Elaric rises and grabs the sack from beside me on the bench. Before I can offer to carry it, he whirls around and marches out the carriage.

As I swing my rigid legs off the bench, I visualize my sister: the frost fading from her delicate features, her voice rousing at long last. Her memory offers momentum to my hesitant steps until I'm standing out the carriage and beneath the cloud-streaked sky.

Inhaling fresh air, I follow Elaric as he cuts across the field toward the looming trees, not looking back. With a snap of his fingers, the carriage dissolves behind us.

Though he maintains his swift pace, he waits at the shadowy verge for me to catch up, and for that I'm thankful. While we may have formed a tentative agreement with Belinda, there may be plenty more dangers lurking in the shadows. Dangers I wouldn't want to face alone, especially not when all I have is a dagger to defend myself.

As I step alongside him, I notice ice spreading across the sack. Standing on my tiptoes, I press both palms flat to the fabric until his magic recedes.

Elaric turns to me.

My breath snags painfully as our gazes lock together. "The sack. It was freezing over." Each syllable clings to my throat.

He just stares at me. For a strained beat, I think he may respond. But then he spins on his heel and starts into the trees. I keep enough distance between us as I trail after him.

Several strides pass before Elaric finally speaks. "Mind your step. The gloomshrooms will be as volatile as they were last time." By now, the dense canopy plunges us in murky dimness, the bright meadows long gone.

My gut clenches as memories of the gloomshrooms flood back.

The knife burying deep in Elaric's chest. My sister's curses for ensuring her eternal imprisonment. My father's disappointment at me for my selfish, thoughtless actions.

It's hard to suppress the shudder which ripples through me.

We soon reach the first cluster of gloomshrooms and carefully pick our way around them. The long grass makes it a challenge to spot them, and so our progress slows to a crawl, neither of us wishing to experience those nightmares again.

Just as I think we've safely cleared the rings of gloomshrooms, the ground rumbles. I brace for the telltale hiss and purple haze. But neither sound nor smoke emerges.

I glance down, fearing I'll find a squashed gloomshroom beneath my boot. But there's only emerald grass.

Unless Elaric is the one who activated them this time . . .

When I look up, I don't see hazy plumes but instead green light emanating from the broad tree trunk ahead. As we watch, the vivid glow fades. Bark fractures open in the shape of a doorway.

Then Belinda hobbles out, her wooden staff supporting each unsteady step. Her wild hair overflows with leaves and twigs sticking out at all angles.

Her sharp eyes fix on us both, brilliant green glinting beneath her craggy brows. As her thin lips crease into a humorless smile, I fight the urge to step toward Elaric.

"So you return," she drawls, "and not empty-handed, I hope?"

I unsling the cord from my neck, retrieving the vial into which I stuffed the brambleweed. The leaves are more scrunched up than I like, and I cringe.

I raise the vial but don't take another step. What if she breaks her end of the bargain? What if, after everything, we leave these woods empty-handed?

Before I can utter a single word about requiring the sword in exchange for the vial, a vine rushes forward and coils around my arm. I try to pull away, but the vine tightens until I'm sure blood ceases to flow through my veins.

The vine creeps higher, winding up to my hand. Elaric starts toward me. But before he can reach me, the vine snags around the vial and tears it from my grasp.

I'm released suddenly and stagger, narrowly catching myself before tumbling to the grass.

Seething in rage and pain, I double over. My arm throbs as blood flows back through, accompanied by a smattering of needles, and though the vial's surface was smooth, the force at which it left my hand has burned my palm.

The vine slithers across to Belinda, depositing the vial into her hand. Dread trickles through me.

I had no illusions about her power the last time we visited, but all this just proves how easily she could end us if she wishes to.

The witch pulls the stopper from the vial, and her spindly fingers reach inside, plucking out the squashed brambleweed leaves. She lifts them to her hooked nose and sniffs briefly before returning them to the vial. Then she starts toward the hollow tree trunk, clutching her staff.

"Wait," I blurt. "You promised us the Sword of Veliantis!"

Wind rustles through the trees, a stark contrast to my deafeningly loud heartbeat.

She stops. "I did."

Elaric's expression darkens. If Belinda refuses to hand over the sword, there's nothing we can do.

"And you're going to break your word?" I ask, consequences be damned. All I can see is my sister's face, frozen forever.

Holding my breath, I wait for more vines to race toward me. To tear through me.

But the woods are unnervingly still.

"You dare to accuse me of such a thing, girl?" Her eyes gleam as she speaks, hinting at the deadly power she holds.

My throat dries. Knowing how precariously I'm currently playing with my life, I opt to stay silent, hoping her rage will pass.

"You should be grateful I don't take your tongue for such careless words," she hisses.

I flinch inwardly.

Belinda's gaze pierces mine before she turns back to the hollow tree. "Follow me," she says and then vanishes through the strange door.

I glance at Elaric, and he nods to where Belinda is disappearing into the tree. Though he protested about allying with her last time, now he seems willing to follow her into the unknown. His previous concerns were for my safety, but maybe he now thinks the prize is worth the risk. With the sword within reach, ending this may outweigh all else.

I stop before the tree trunk and reach out to the emerald light pouring from the dark opening. As my fingertips brush the magic, my skin tingles, the sensation spreading up my arm. It feels like bubbles fizzing and bursting around me.

I dare to take another step into the light until it envelops me.

Then wind blasts into me, and the tingling stops.

Once my eyes adjust, I realize I'm on the other side of the portal. Below, trees stretch all around me, and I'm standing upon the hill which Belinda makes her home.

The rustling of leaves is accompanied by the bubbling of the swamp ahead. The stench is even more terrible than I remember, and it takes all of my willpower not to pinch my nose.

Elaric steps out from the tree, the grim look on his face indicating that he finds Belinda's strange magic as unsettling as I do.

Sudden movement to the left catches my eye. I turn to see Belinda weaving vines into a bridge, extending it across the swamp to reach her toadstool hut. Barely has it formed before she walks across it.

Not wanting her to change her mind, I start across it tentatively. When she doesn't retract the vines to throw me into the deadly swamp, I quicken my pace, Elaric close behind.

Belinda doesn't hold the door for us as we enter. She has already disappeared into the back room. While it's mid-afternoon, there are few windows in here and so her dim cottage relies on the central hearth for light.

As Belinda doesn't invite us to sit, we stay standing while awaiting her return. Fortunately, she reappears swiftly.

She stops before us and holds out a bundle, wrapped in cloth and secured by a coarse thread. As I take it from her, I can feel its rigid edges beneath the cover. Though there's little doubt that the object is a sword, whether it's the Sword of Veliantis is another matter entirely.

Elaric reaches over and pulls on a thread, unraveling it and tearing aside the cloth.

Firelight glints across the exposed metal, blinding in its brilliance. Rubies encrust the golden hilt, sparkling like droplets of fresh blood.

Taking the sword from my arms, Elaric makes for the door. I hesitate, fearing an abrupt exit may further antagonize Belinda. Making an enemy of her seems unwise. We may require her assistance again in the near future.

"Leaving so soon?" Belinda calls after him.

Elaric stops in the doorway but doesn't turn back. "We have fulfilled our end of the bargain, as have you. Our dealings here have reached their end."

"You wish to kill Isidore, do you not?" Belinda presses. The lilt to her voice ripples across my skin.

"Yes," I say steadily, burying any traces of distrust, "we do."

HEART OF THE SUMMER QUEEN

"And do you know where to find her?"

I meet Elaric's eyes. He gives a slight shake of his head.

Belinda's grin spreads. I shudder at the glee in her expression.

It's clear our business here is far from finished. She intends to strike another bargain, likely demanding a steeper payment. Without knowing Isidore's location, this weapon is meaningless.

Reluctantly, I ask, "Do you know where she is?"

"Of course I do."

With that, she starts over to the surrounding shelves, rummaging through her collection of jars and vials. I glance at Elaric. Though I want to talk to him about all of this, it's impossible to have such a conversation from facial expressions alone. And I dare not breathe a single word of it while standing in her home.

"Ah, just what we need," she declares, lifting a jar filled with orange jelly. Then she continues on, rifling along a back shelf until she retrieves a small metallic object.

"Hold this," Belinda says, returning to us and holding out a silver necklace to me. Embedded into its pendant is a cloudy stone resembling quartz, and it glows a creamy hue in the hearth's light. With her talon-like nails, she fishes out a long strand of white hair from the jar of jelly.

"A lock from Isidore's head," she declares.

Belinda takes the necklace from me and winds Isidore's hair tightly around the pendant, pulling it so taut I expect it to snap. But then her magic flows from her fingertips, dissolving the hair into an oozing liquid which coats the stone with murky green.

"There," she says, offering the enchanted pendant back to me.

I inspect it, but the stone appears ordinary except for its change in color. "How will this help us locate Isidore?"

"Dangle it by the chain," Belinda tells me.

I do as she says, pinching the thin silver links between two fingers. Abruptly the pendant jerks and twists to point toward the kitchen.

"It will act as a compass to lead you to Isidore, wherever she goes," she explains.

"How long will the spell last?"

"Long enough to suit your needs," she says.

I press my lips together, wanting more certainty but not daring to push Belinda too far. I don't want her to snatch back the pendant, infuriated by our relentless requests.

"Thank you," I say carefully. "And what do you require from us in return?" My fingers tighten around the pendant as I await her response, worrying what she will want in exchange.

"Consider it a gift, along with these." Belinda returns to the shelves and, after sifting through them, produces two vividly colored vials. One red, one blue.

"They are for you," she says, handing them both to Elaric, "and you alone. Your wife shall have no use for them."

The reminder of the marriage Elaric will soon annul steals all the air from my lungs.

I do my best to steady my subsequent breaths, lest Belinda or Elaric notice my reaction.

"What is their purpose?" Elaric asks, inspecting the vials.

"The blue one contains Irremisa. One mouthful will suppress all the magic in your veins. Even your aura will be hidden, preventing Isidore from sensing your power as you approach."

He frowns. "Years ago I came to you, asking if you possessed such a medicine. You claimed none exists."

"Medicine?" Belinda laughs. "This is no medicine. It is a poison, used primarily to subdue enemy witches. Suppressing magic comes at a significant cost, and your body will resist its effects, blood boiling in your veins. A wonderful side effect for torture, might I add."

"The pain would have been of no consequence," Elaric states. "I would have endured it every day for the last three centuries to be rid of this damned magic."

"I do not have centuries' worth of this potion to waste," Belinda retorts, "and even if I did, no matter how determined you may be, you would have succumbed to madness after suffering its effects for so long."

Elaric says nothing to that, and though the witch might think him pacified by her answer, I know otherwise. If she'd offered this potion sooner, he would've endured any torment for a just one day free from magic—long enough to visit his sister's grave.

"What about the red one?" I ask, pointing to it.

"That is Ruposley," Belinda says, "the antidote to Irremisa. It will neutralize the effects, restoring the flow of magic through your veins."

"And how soon do they take effect after ingesting?" Elaric asks.

"Both potions act immediately," Belinda says with a smile, the wrinkles around her eyes deepening. She shifts her weight, leaning on her staff. "Now, before you both leave, perhaps I can interest you in some bat wings? They just started cooking before you arrived . . . "

Chapter 26

We leave shortly after I finish sampling Belinda's fried bat wings. While I'm initially hesitant, the crispy meat looks far more appetizing than her previous frogspawn stew, with a flavor somewhere between beef and pork despite the tiny bones. I offer some to Elaric but he refuses. I suppose my appreciation of the witch's food may be due to the lack of a proper meal since leaving the palace.

The witch's hospitality even extends to inviting us to stay the night, but her hut has just one spare room and the thought of sharing a bed with Elaric fills me with dread, especially after last night. Besides, the swamp's stench singes my nostrils, and sleeping under a witch's roof is far from a wise idea. Though she's been welcoming tonight, there's no telling how her mood might change in the morning.

Thankfully, Elaric appears equally reluctant to stay overnight. Belinda shrugs as we take our leave, claiming she cares little either way, but ushers us out the door with clear annoyance. At least she doesn't decide to drive us out with her vines, so we can't have offended her too much.

Now far from Belinda's woods, we sit inside Elaric's carriage once more, gliding over countless towns and cities. Each hour I check our direction with the enchanted pendant, and Elaric adjusts our course accordingly.

Though the atmosphere remains tense, it's a little less strained now since finding Isidore acts as distraction from our own affairs. Yet when I close my eyes, I still feel his lips on mine—hear his bitter words. The pain within has dulled from a piercing wound to a numb ache, but meeting his eyes causes a fresh stab. I avoid his gaze as much as I can.

Many hours later, we reach the sea.

I've visited the coast very few times in my life, and though the night shrouds much of the horizon, it remains a sight to behold. The steady sway of the waves is mesmerizing, dancing to a melody I can hardly hear from all the way up here in the carriage, and seeing no grass or trees or buildings for miles on end makes it appear like a world of its own.

Through the window, I see a small fishing town lying behind us, serving as the last trace of humanity before the unending waves beyond.

"Does the pendant still point ahead?" Elaric asks, slowing the carriage to a stop.

I pull the necklace over my head, untangling the curl which has snagged around it. Once freed, I pinch the chain between my thumb and index finger.

The pendant snaps up, pointing in almost the same direction as it did half an hour ago. Except now it veers ever so slightly right.

Elaric frowns at both it and the waves. "Isidore must dwell somewhere upon the sea."

I nod, the scraps of lore I uncovered in the library returning to me. "When I was searching the library, I found a book which mentioned Eruweth. It said long ago, she froze the kingdom, and it disappeared without a trace."

"I was a boy when it happened. I suppose it must now drift the oceans like an iceberg, hidden somewhere upon the waves, and that is why no one has found it since."

"Until us," I say, pinching the necklace's chain harder in my fingers.

"Until us," Elaric repeats, tone firm with resolve. Meeting his eyes now causes no unbearable ache, just invigorating purpose.

Together, we will break this damned curse at long last.

"The question now is," Elaric says, pulling me from my thoughts, "how we continue from here."

I tilt my head, not following his implication. "What do you mean?"

"We could press on in the carriage," he explains, "but relying on magic risks alerting Isidore before we even reach Eruweth's shores."

I hesitate. "Do you think she can already detect you from this distance?"

Elaric leans closer to the window, gazing into the dark horizon. "The kingdom is still beyond our sight, so it seems unlikely."

I chew my lip, considering our options. "If we keep flying, it's doubtful we'll have anywhere to land except Eruweth. But then she would sense us even before you can suppress your magic. And we can't swim all the way there." I flick my eyes across his broad shoulders. "Though I suppose you might manage such a feat."

A wry smile plays on his lips. "Not against the tide."

"Ice floats," I say. "Maybe you'd simply drift along."

His amusement fades. "While it's possible, I have no intention of testing such a theory now. Even if I did float, there is no way to predict where I may end up."

I purse my lips. "Maybe the tide will be in our favor."

"And if not?"

"You could restore your magic instantly with Belinda's antidote and fly us back to shore."

Elaric's jaw tightens. "Swimming us to Eruweth will be too perilous."

"Why not at least try? At worst, you may have to freeze the sea or fly us back."

"At worst, you could slip from my arms and drown."

Hope flutters in my chest before I snuff it out. Elaric worries for my safety only because I alone can slay Isidore and break his curse. It isn't because he harbors any feelings for me. His blunt words this morning made that abundantly clear.

I try to sound casual, to hide all the emotion swelling within. "I doubt that very much. I have great faith in your ability to keep ahold of me."

"Regardless of that, if we're swept out to sea and I have to fly us back, you'll be soaked through. We'll be unable to light a fire until we return to shore, and depending on the distance, you may die of hypothermia before then."

I suppose the frigid lake water did almost kill me, never mind the open ocean. "Perhaps you are right," I admit, "but that is a risk—"

"I am not willing to take," Elaric interjects, with a stern look.

I glare at him. But his resolute expression makes it clear he won't be swayed.

"Fine," I huff, leaning back against the solid cushions. "Suggest an alternative then."

"A boat," he states.

I glance back at the fishing village behind us. Perhaps we can buy or hire a boat from someone there, provided Elaric brought enough gold. We've spent nothing so far and our coin pouch seems heavy. Then again, I'm unsure how much fishing boats usually cost.

"A rowboat won't work," I say, looking through the window at the unruly waves far below. They'd swiftly claim such a small vessel. "We'll need a proper fishing boat at the very least. Maybe something larger still."

"Hiring a crew would be best," Elaric says, "but we lack the funds for that right now. If Eruweth lies too far away, we must return to Avella and procure a brig."

I fiddle with the enchanted pendant in my hands, looking down at that instead of his face. "I don't know how to sail."

"You can navigate instead. If we find a small fishing boat, I can manage it alone."

I cast him an exasperated look. "Holding up a pendant is hardly taxing."

His eyes gleam with amusement. "But necessary all the same."

The thought of standing around idly while Elaric is left doing all the work irks me. But hopefully sailing will be easy to learn, and the waves and wind will co-operate with us.

Chapter 27

With our plan decided, Elaric redirects the carriage toward the fishing village. We soar over it before landing near the surrounding woods. The settlement now appears to be a sparkling of fireflies peeking through the dense trees.

After dismissing the carriage, Elaric retrieves the blue vial of Irremisa potion from our sack. Grimly, he pops the cork free and tips back the vial to drink what I estimate to be roughly a fifth.

"Do you think that was enough to suppress your magic?" I ask.

Elaric holds up the vial toward the dim moonlight filtering through the canopy, inspecting its remaining contents. "Let's hope so. There are few doses left inside it."

I glance down, noticing the frost already fringing the fallen leaves beneath his boots. His power hasn't yet reached farther than that, but maybe it's my immunity preventing its spread.

There's only one way to tell.

"Wait!" I take a deliberate step back.

He frowns. "What for?"

"To see if your magic spreads even after drinking the potion," I say, pointing toward the ice lacing through the grass. "I can't stand too close, or else it'll be difficult to tell if it's the potion or my presence suppressing your magic."

We watch the ground for several tense moments. But then Elaric lurches forward with a gasp, bracing one hand against a nearby tree trunk.

I rush over without sparing a single thought for our test and grab his arm. "Elaric? Are you hurt?"

"The Irremisa potion," he says through uneven breaths. "It must be taking effect."

He straightens with apparent effort, muscles tensing against what must be agony blazing through his veins. He tries to mask it, but involuntary winces disrupt his usual stoicism.

"Will you be all right?" I ask, studying his strained expression. If even Elaric is struggling to hide the pain, it must be unimaginable. In this state, will he manage the walk into the town? What about sailing to Eruweth?

"I'm fine," he forces out, though I don't believe him for one second. I bite back the protest bubbling on my lips. Despite my worries, further arguments won't help matters at all.

If only Belinda offered him another potion for the pain. But perhaps combining several potions is risky, or perhaps she simply didn't care to provide it.

He takes a step forward and then another, each becoming a little steadier. A few more and he's marching on toward the trees. If not for what I witnessed minutes ago, I wouldn't believe him to be in pain at all. As I hurry after him, I spot no frost trailing his strides.

It seems the Irremisa potion is working precisely as intended.

It takes around half an hour to reach the village. Perhaps Elaric could have flown us much closer, but we would have risked the villagers spotting the carriage during our descent. While the cover of night may have helped to obscure it, a gleam of ice amid the stars would have aroused suspicions of magic.

Though Elaric does not wear his crown and the ground no longer freezes beneath his feet, his white hair and bright eyes will make him an obvious target for such suspicions. I'm unsure how this part of the world views magic, but I've heard in some regions, witches are feared and hunted. Even if these people don't inherently fear magic, they may have heard of Avella's Winter King and may immediately suspect Elaric's true identity. While he may not be currently wearing his finery, his posture provides more evidence of his regality than any crown could. And a foreign king visiting these lands uninvited will surely incite a great deal of political turmoil.

Luckily, the late hour keeps curious gazes to a minimum as we walk along the narrow dirt lanes. Most villagers we pass are too glassy-eyed from ale to do more than glance briefly at Elaric's unusual features before we turn down the next bend.

"We need fresh supplies," Elaric says a few streets later.

I pause, considering the dark buildings. "That'll have to wait until the morning. Along with our boat. It's unlikely we'll find one at this hour."

Elaric nods. "Then we ought to find somewhere to stay the night, preferably a place still serving food this late. You haven't had a warm meal since we left the palace."

"I had bat wings before," I say.

"They don't count."

"They were warm."

"They weren't a meal," he retorts. "And there were more bones than meat on those things."

"You can't judge them until you've tried them."

He just shakes his head at me and continues through the streets.

Further into the village, just a street away from the harbor, we come to an inn called 'The Rusty Anchor.' While the doors and windows are shut, raucous laughter escapes into the otherwise quiet night. I squint through the window, but the glass is too cloudy from the contrast to the cool air.

"It sounds rather busy," I say.

"With drunkards," Elaric replies. "If we're fortunate, most will be locals and there will still be rooms left for tonight."

If they don't have any rooms, we'll have to wander around the village until we find an inn which does. And failing that, we'll have to find somewhere outside the village to make camp. But after several nights of sleeping on the grass, my back yearns for a bed. Especially since we'll be spending the next few nights cramped on a fishing boat.

Pushing open the door, Elaric steps inside. He strides past the tables filled with large groups of men, all banging their ale mugs onto the table and singing old sea shanties at the top of their lungs, and heads over to the counter at the far end where the barkeep is pouring pints. I keep my head lowered as I follow, not wanting to draw any attention. There are few other women in here, and I don't miss the hungry leers the drunkards flash at the serving girls passing them ale.

While both Elaric and I can handle ourselves in a fight, getting drawn into any confrontation here would be perilous given how vastly outnumbered we are. Elaric would have to drink Ruposley to regain his magic, resulting in a spectacle no generation of this village would ever forget.

The bartender finishes serving the patron next to us and then turns our way. "What'll it be then? Ale or whiskey for you folks?"

"We're not here to drink," Elaric says, though I wouldn't mind a drink myself. "We only require a room for the night."

The man scratches his beard. "We're down to just one empty room, I'm afraid."

"There's only one left?" I blurt.

The barkeep's eyes shift to me. "That a problem, lass?"

"Of course not," Elaric interjects smoothly, "don't mind my wife."

I struggle not to flinch at that word.

Elaric barters for the room, but I'm unsure whether we're being overcharged. Having never stayed overnight in an inn before, I've little way to gauge if the rate is reasonable. They aren't the sort of place young ladies are supposed to frequent. My only visit to one ended with Orlan dragging me away from the gambling table and Father confining me to my chambers for three whole days.

"Is the kitchen still serving food tonight?" Elaric asks, passing several coins across the worn countertop.

"For another hour at least," the barkeep says, taking our deposit and giving us a tarnished brass key in exchange. "We can have meals brought up to your room if you'd prefer?"

Elaric turns, eyeing the crowded tables behind us. "We'll eat down here." His gaze settles on two empty seats tucked near the fireplace. "We'll take that table."

"One of the girls will bring your meals over shortly," the barkeep says.

As we start over to the table, Elaric says to me, "It is quite peculiar being amid such a large crowd."

I suppose the few times he's ever been in a room with so many people were during the Midsummer Balls and even then, he sat at a great distance from everyone else. Having lived in solitude in for so long, perhaps the laughter of all the drunkards around us sounds even louder to his ears than it does to mine.

"Is that why you wanted to eat down here instead of in our room?" I ask, noticing how his eyes sweep across our lively surroundings.

"Partly," he admits, pulling out a chair for me as we reach our table beside the hearth. "But mostly for the fireplace."

I glance at the blazing flames, watching as the amber plumes dance, stirring the surrounding shadows. With his presence usually extinguishing all heat, it must be so long since Elaric has ever stood this close to a fire.

"Can you feel its warmth?" I ask, settling onto my chair. The legs squeak beneath me as I shuffle closer to the table.

"I cannot," he says. "My skin recognizes neither cold nor warmth." He raises his hand and edges nearer to the fire, watching as the light washes over his pale skin. "Yet there is still comfort in sitting so close to it. Perhaps it is only a figment of my imagination, formed from my memories of what warmth used to feel like."

"You've felt no warmth for three whole centuries?"

"No, except . . . " He pauses. "Except for yours."

I look down at the table and fiddle with a crack running across the wood, recalling how warm I too felt in his arms.

A moment passes. The silence is unbearable. Fearing everything will turn more awkward if we dwell in it for too long, I say, "Would your skin burn if you put your hand in the fire?"

Maybe that isn't the most artful of conversation changes, but I don't know what else to say.

At least it brings a small smile to Elaric's lips. "It shouldn't. Or at least, I don't think it should."

"Maybe you should try."

"It would be an interesting experiment," Elaric says with a chuckle, "but I wonder what everyone else would think if I stuck my hand in the fire. And even more so, what they would think if I did not burn."

"Half of these men are too drunk to remember their own names," I point out, "much less take note."

"Perhaps, but the staff are very much sober. Most of them, that is."

"I suppose so."

The barkeep's words prove true, and two heaping plates arrive shortly. I turn ravenous at the smell of warm food and can't eat quickly enough. Perhaps Elaric was right that bat wings don't qualify as an adequate meal, especially not when one has had little else all day.

The pork served on my plate is also much more succulent and less bony than Belinda's bat wings. The potatoes are fluffy, and while the carrots are a little harder than I usually prefer, I eat every single one of them, along with everything else on my plate.

By the time I finish, Elaric has barely touched his food. He's left half his meat and three potatoes.

"Are you still hungry?" he asks, noticing my staring at his plate.

I quickly shake my head. "No, not at all."

"Liar," he says. "You're drooling over my food."

"I'm not."

"Are you certain? There's a spot right here." He traces one finger down from the corner of his mouth.

The gesture is so unlike him I can't help from bursting into laughter. I wonder at the reason for his light mood. Is it because of being here, in this warm tavern, surrounded by so many others? Or is it because of the Irremisa suppressing his magic, alleviating the weight of his curse from his shoulders?

He lowers his cutlery and pushes his plate across the table. "Here, you finish it."

I nudge the plate toward him. "I can't."

"Why not?" he asks, pushing it back to me.

"It's your food," I say.

"I have no need for food."

"I'm already full."

He casts me an incredulous look. "Very well. I shall ask someone to collect both of our plates."

"Wait," I exclaim as he goes to stand. "If you really don't want it, I'll finish it."

He casts me a triumphant smirk, but I'm too busy tucking into the rest of his food to care.

Chapter 28

Once I've cleared Elaric's plate, we start up the narrow creaking staircase to find our room for the night. The inn contains at least a dozen rooms, judging by the row of doors we pass. We soon spot one with a tarnished '7' nailed to its center.

Elaric unlocks it with the key the barkeep gave us and then stands aside, holding open the wooden door for me.

As I enter the dimly-lit room, my stomach swoops.

There's only one bed. . .

I press my lips together. Of course there's only one bed, not twin beds like a foolish part of my mind imagined. Elaric and I will have to share it. All this wouldn't be as awkward if we hadn't shared a bed before, if we didn't know what it feels like to lie in each other's arms.

Before I can gather my thoughts, Elaric closes the door behind us and says, "I'll sleep on the floor."

I stare at him, trying to decipher the emotion upon his face. But his expression is as stoic as ever. "Surely the floor won't be comfortable?"

Elaric looks as surprised by my question as I am. For a long moment, he says nothing and we both just stand there.

"It'll be far too hard, and you won't catch even a second of sleep." As I speak, I draw my face into the blankest expression I can manage. I can't tell if I succeed beneath his sharp gaze.

"You know I don't require sleep," he says.

"I know," I say quickly. "But if you lie there all night long, you'll wake with a terrible pain in your back. And your neck. Then sailing in the morning will be difficult if you can hardly move. I don't know the first thing about sailing, so—"

He takes a step closer, lips twitching in what appears to be thinly veiled mirth. "I am not so weak that sleeping on the floor will incapacitate me. You have nothing to worry about Adara."

I swallow hard, struggling to regain composure in the wake of my careless words. What is wrong with me? I should simply let him take the floor if that's what he prefers.

"What if we reach Eruweth and you—" My rambling dies as Elaric catches my chin, tilting my gaze up. I didn't even realize he was pacing toward me.

My breath hitches as I brace for the worst. As I wait for him to tell me how he will never sleep beside me again. That I'm a fool for dreaming that anything might ever happen between us—

"Adara," he says.

"Yes?" It comes out more of a squeak than I like.

"Do you want me to join you on the bed?"

The blood drains from my face. "I . . . er . . . "

All words fail me, though I couldn't seem to rein them in just seconds ago.

I can't tell him the truth. That I want him to join me on the bed, that I want us to return to what we were before I drove a knife into his chest.

He has already made it clear what happened last night was a terrible mistake.

Lying is impossible beneath his searing gaze. But neither is my heart willing to deny his offer, dangerous though hope may be.

"Adara?" he prompts.

My fragile resolve cracks. Unbearable pain swells within, and I can't meet his eyes any longer.

I pull away, and his lack of resistance slices deeper than any rejection. It confirms he doesn't want this.

Doesn't want me.

If he'd held me longer, if he'd needled me further, perhaps I could have blamed saying yes on his persistence rather than the longing in my heart. Now I've pulled away, I realize how much I wish I'd said yes and faced the consequences. Even if he never spoke to me again.

I face the door, focusing on all the imperfections running across the wood. On the way the brass handle is worn in places, countless different hands having pulled it open over the years. I try to imagine all those people and what they might have looked like. Anything to distract my mind from him.

"We'll put pillows between us," I say to the door, wishing for the sentence to come out stronger than I feel.

Elaric doesn't reply, though I don't doubt he heard me. I don't dare glance back and see whether disappointment or relief is currently flickering across his expression.

How seeing relief would break me.

Casting aside my thoughts, I concentrate on my steps as I march over to the bed and tear aside the sheets. I shove a large pillow down the bed's center and then sink into the blankets. Closing my eyes, I lie still, pretending to be asleep to escape the awfulness of this entire situation.

It would be so much easier if the lumpy mattress swallowed me whole.

"Do you intend to sleep with your boots on?" Elaric says, ruining any chance of a hasty retreat.

Damn it. I should swing my legs out of bed and pull them off since I hate sleeping with my boots on. But I can't bear the thought of moving. It risks glimpsing him and lengthening this painful conversation.

The boots will have to stay on. All night.

I don't so much as twitch in response, and Elaric doesn't push the matter any further.

There's a brief pause and then shadows wash over my face as Elaric blows out the candles, casting us in darkness. The mattress dips as he climbs in.

Only a pillow separates us. Yet it feels like a hundred-mile-long wall.

There's the rustling of sheets, the groan of springs as he turns, and then nothing. No more movement.

The laughter of the drunkards echoes through the creaky floorboards. As well as the banging of ale mugs. Someone shouting as they lose at cards. Persistent though the noise is, I'm glad for it. Silence would be far worse. I doubt I'd be brave enough to even breathe.

I'm unsure how long I lie there before I realize that while my body might be exhausted, my mind is wide awake.

Blearily, I trace the dancing shadows and the sliver of light cutting beneath the door. The dim rays paint a sprawling rectangle across the beam ceiling.

But staring into the darkness does nothing to dull my mind. Sleep remains elusive. And now I'm becoming increasingly aware of my feet swelling in my boots. The leather pinching my toes.

I know I should lie here until sleep finds me, but words bubble on my tongue. I hold them in as long as I can, but then they're boiling over and—

"Are you awake?" I whisper into the void, immediately regretting speaking. I should have stayed quiet. Should have pretended to be asleep. This incident of sharing a bed would have passed, and everything would have been fine in the morning. While sailing to Eruweth, we'd be focused on our quest to slay Isidore.

No response immediately follows. I dearly hope he's asleep. But that wish is dashed as he says, "I am."

I force myself to think of something to say. Anything.

"Does it still hurt?" I manage.

"Hmm?" comes his reply, the sound rumbling across my pillow.

"The Irremisa potion," I say.

"A little."

"Oh." I pull my blanket to my chest. "Well, I hope it hurts less in the morning."

Then silence. Again.

Embarrassment courses through me, and I consider pulling my blanket even further over me until it covers my face. It's an inviting thought, but then Elaric will know how much sharing a bed is bothering me.

I close my eyes and try again to sleep, to banish all worries from my mind. But my thoughts are so invasive and won't leave me alone. Minutes later, I end up saying, "Elaric?"

"Yes, Adara?"

My throat tightens. What I want to ask is on the very tip of my tongue, but it's as if my vocal cords have ceased to work.

If I ask my question, it might make it true.

"What is it?" The bed shifts as he rolls onto his side. I don't turn to look. If I do, I'll find myself face to face with him, just a flimsy pillow between us.

"Do . . . " I start but my voice breaks. I grit my teeth and force it to come out steady. If I don't ask my question now, I never will. "Do you hate me?"

He's quiet. My heart beats so loudly I'd be surprised if he doesn't hear it.

"Why do you ask?"

Bile rises to my throat. Him asking me that is as good as him saying yes, he hates me. And why shouldn't he? Everything I've done deserves his hatred, not his forgiveness. I know this, and yet I've allowed myself to hope for otherwise.

Though the truth hurts, I'm glad I asked. Maybe with enough time, my foolish heart will discard the feelings it still clings to.

"No reason," I say, as nonchalantly as I can.

"Adara." The pillow behind me disappears, and he's grabbing my shoulder, pulling me toward him.

I'm hurting so much I yield without thought, and then I'm lying on my back, staring up at him.

"Why do you think I hate you?" His voice is a growl.

"Because you should," I begin, "after everything I've done. Any sane person would."

"Then I mustn't be sane," he murmurs, playing with a lock of my hair in his fingers.

I blink, confused. "You don't hate me?"

"No."

"But this morning . . . "

He sighs, releasing my hair. "There are many things I should not have said, and I am sorry for it."

"Last night," I say, slowly. Carefully. "Was that a mistake?"

He looks away. "Yes."

My heart sinks. I try to pull away, but he holds me fast.

"And no." He swallows. "Adara, I don't know."

"If that's how you feel, maybe you're right."

He takes my hand and squeezes it. "I am sorry."

"I'm sorry, too."

Hard though it is to face the truth, we've both ignored our feelings for too long and now wounds fester between us. If we don't have this conversation tonight, we never will.

"Why did you pull away?" I dare to ask. "Aren't you furious with me?"

"No, not furious." He exhales deeply, releasing my hand to lie beside me. "You must understand, this is difficult for me. Even now, being this close."

"I'll understand if you can never forgive me," I say. "Anyone could understand that."

"I forgive you, Adara. I forgave you the moment I understood the reason for your hatred. I know how much you loved your sister, and I am the one who took her from you."

"Not out of cruelty."

"No," he says softly. "Not out of cruelty."

I roll to face him. "But I don't understand. If you aren't furious at me, if you don't hate me, why did you pull away?"

"I never meant to hurt you, and I am deeply sorry if I have." He runs a hand through his hair, staring at the ceiling.

I study his strained expression until it becomes clear he has no intention of answering my question.

Deciding not to press him further, I turn away. At least he no longer hates me. Even if things will never again be the same between us, his forgiveness is more than I deserve.

This time, when I close my eyes, the peace of knowing he has forgiven me allows sleep to find me more easily.

I'm just drifting off as Elaric says, "I don't want you to feel forced to be with me."

My eyes snap open at once. "What do you mean?"

"I will honor what I said before we left the palace about annulling our marriage," he says. "You needn't stay married to me if you—"

I whirl around to face him. "I don't want to annul our marriage." The statement is bold, vowing to spend a lifetime with this man, but right now, I do not care. All I know is that I want him, that I wish so much for everything to be as it was.

"But you married me because you hated me," he whispers. "To kill me."

The air empties from my lungs. And then all I can do is cry. I have no way of translating my feelings into words.

He pulls me into his arms, holding me close to his chest. "Adara . . . "

"I'm so sorry, Elaric," I mutter, my face buried into the fabric of his tunic.

"I know," he says quietly. Then he hesitates, choosing his next words carefully. "I understand your feelings are not the same as mine, and I do not wish for you to feel obliged to stay with me merely because we are married."

"Is that why you pulled away?"

"Yes."

"But I do want you."

His hands wrap around my waist as he slides me higher up the bed, our noses almost touching. "You don't understand. I don't just want you—I need you." With a feather-light touch, his fingertips brush along my jawline. "I want your happiness, and I know you would never have chosen me had you not sought to kill me. I would rather annul our marriage, even if it risks losing you, and spend every day trying to win your heart. Then I would know you chose me for the same reason I chose you."

"What reason?" I ask, my voice so slight and fragile.

"Because I love you."

Chapter 29

My lower lip trembles at his confession.

"Elaric . . . " I trail off, uncertain of what to say. I can't tell him I love him too, since that carries with it an impossible promise. And yet there's no denying the intensity of my feelings.

"I love you," he says again, eyes so full of emotion. Once I thought him cold and detached. Now passion spills from him as he lays his devotion bare before me. "And I will spend years—decades—trying to win your heart."

While the tears I shed before have dried, now my eyes swell with a fresh wave. But these result from another emotion entirely. One far stronger.

"Just give me time," I breathe. A promise, even if he does not realize it. Because the truth is that he already owns a substantial part of my heart, and it's inevitable he'll soon claim the rest.

"As long as you need," he says, his fingers lacing through my hair.

I lean into his solid embrace, savoring the warmth his touch sparks through me.

Yet the bliss is interrupted as Elaric says, "But I would still prefer to annul our marriage and start over."

I grip his shoulders, my fingers digging into them. "No."

"Why not?" he asks.

"I don't want to."

The corner of his lip twitches. "You need to give me a better reason."

"Isn't desiring not to reason enough?"

"I would prefer it to be because of your burning desire for me," he counters, smirk growing.

Heat floods my cheeks. What audacity this man has, using threats of annulment to force me to admit my desire for him.

"Perhaps you are right," he says, his fingers tracing my neck and leaving a path of lightning in their wake. "Maybe we ought not to annul it. For if we did, it would be most improper to do this . . . "

I open my mouth to ask him what he means but before I can, his lips are on mine and he's kissing me with wild abandon.

I moan into him, the sound reverberating through us both. I arch into him, wanting—needing—more. The way my body reacts so readily to him provides undeniable evidence of my longing.

His hand slips beneath my tunic, palm scorching across my stomach. My breath snags as he glides even higher. "And especially this . . . "

He brushes over my nipple, which peaks at his touch. As he rolls it between his fingers, a gasp shudders through me. Pleasure rises, smoldering like fire beneath my skin.

"Tell me, Adara," he says, his voice ragged against my mouth. "Tell me you refuse the annulment because you want this."

I mutter something incomprehensible, even to my own ears. Rational thought becomes even more impossible as his lips trail down my neck, as he tugs down the fabric of my tunic and continues across my collarbone.

Need washes through my lower belly, thighs slickening with anticipation.

"Tell me," he demands.

"Yes," I whisper.

He tilts his head, a brow arching as he regards me. "Yes, what?"

"I want this. I want you."

"Then perhaps I ought to grant my queen her wish," he says, eyes glinting with a devious light, "and banish all thought of annulment."

In the next instant, he's yanking my tunic up, over my head. It's a wonder the threads don't rip from his impatience.

Tunic now gone, my chest is left bare to his hungry gaze. Unbearable tension coils within me as he rakes over my naked skin.

"Touch me," I plead, when he makes no sign of moving. "Elaric, please."

His perusal only continues, so I reach up and wrap my hands around his neck, dragging him toward me. As our lips crash together, I feel the corners of his mouth turning up into a silent laugh.

Our tongues writhe together in a tantalizing dance, but my rhythm falters as Elaric's hand drifts to the waistband of my breeches. His fingers skim across my hip bone. I jerk up toward him.

But I've no need to beg now. So swift are his movements that by the time I realize he's sliding down my breeches, they're already off.

Then I'm wholly naked beneath him.

Instinctively, my legs wrap around him, closing that last bit of distance between us. The hardness of his arousal presses against my throbbing center, the fabric of his breeches offering blissful friction as I roll against him.

With a groan, he grabs my wrists and pulls them over my head, pinning me to the mattress. "I have half a mind to take a dose of the Ruposley potion," he says, "so I can use my magic to shackle you to the bed and do with you as I please."

A fresh wave of need pulses through me as I imagine such a scene, icy chains glinting in the dim light as Elaric renders me a slave to my desire.

I swallow thickly, steadying myself. "A pity it would mean freezing the entire village."

"A pity indeed," he says with a chuckle. "Though it would be certainly worth it."

At first, I think he intends to release my wrists and make good on his suggestion. But then his hand roams up my thigh, stopping mere inches short of my aching core. "Alas," he says, tracing back down my thigh—much to my dismay, "I doubt I could peel myself from you long enough to retrieve the potion."

"Elaric," I gasp.

"Yes, Adara?" he asks, as casually as if I were inquiring about the weather.

"Stop teasing me and get on with it," I hiss.

His eyes narrow as he holds my stare, refusing to yield. "Have you forgotten that I am your king, and it is within my right to do with you as I please?"

"Elaric—"

My protest dies in my mouth. Without warning, his finger slips inside me.

He holds it there still, neither delving deeper nor withdrawing. I arch up, yearning for more, but he keeps me firmly pinned under him. Beneath his weight, I can't shift even an inch.

"You are the most stubborn woman I have ever met," he says, though I hardly hear over the desire pounding through me like a drum, "and you have no idea how much satisfaction it brings me to know I can reduce you to a desperate mess."

Then his mouth is hot on my breast, tongue swirling over my painfully hard nipple, and all objection melts away. In this moment, there's nothing but the barrage of sheer pleasure he is waging upon my body.

"Elaric," I whimper, straining against his grasp. The calluses on his palms graze the soft flesh of my wrists.

Elaric's eyes flick up to my face for a fleeting moment, mouth still on me. He smiles against my skin, and then his undivided attention returns to my breast, savoring and nipping.

His fingers press into me, harder, as if to punish me for testing the strength of his grip. Then he curls them until he reaches a delightful spot deep within me, and my thighs tense, clenching together. He edges them back out with his knees, forcing me open wider than before, and I decide I may as well be chained to the mattress with how I'm so helpless against his might.

And just when the tension is rising to a crescendo, he releases me.

My wrists are freed, and his lips leave my breast. Even my legs are granted a second's respite.

Suddenly, I fear the same will happen as last night. That he'll pull away and storm off, door shuddering shut behind him as he finds a table downstairs to spend the night rather than our bed.

But as I exhale, I notice the heady desire in his eyes and realize my fears are mistaken. He has no intention of pulling away tonight. No, his expression makes it abundantly clear he's barely begun with me.

A cry escapes me as his head lowers to my thighs. As his tongue slides down my swollen core in a forceful movement which leaves me trembling for more.

He repeats the motion—slower and crueler. My cry turns to a whimper, legs quivering. His hand bears down on them, preventing me from rising, but this time, I don't struggle against him. The whirlwind coursing through me tangles all my thoughts.

Then his fingers return inside me, the gesture so unexpected that I shudder.

"Do you remember," he says, his breath brushing over my wet folds, "a few days ago, when you tried to pull me out of that bathtub?"

I nod. How could I ever forget that incident?

"It took every ounce of self-control not to claim you there and then on the icy floor."

A moan tears through me.

"Would you have let me, Adara?" He finishes his question with a teasing lick to that taut bundle of nerves, and I can hardly remember what he asked me. Then his teeth nip that same, deliciously sensitive spot. I buck uncontrollably against him, realizing now how utterly at his mercy I am.

"If I had just slid my hand up your skirts and touched you like this"—his fingers bear deeper into me, emphasizing his point—"would you have said yes?"

I don't know how my mind is functioning well enough to say, "It sounds like that incident has been on your mind."

"For so many nights," he says, "it has plagued me."

"How inconvenient."

He lets out a sigh and now seems so serious I'm no longer certain he's jesting. "You don't understand what torture it is to dream such feverish dreams night after night, only to wake in a lonely bed."

I pause, thinking of my own incessant longing for him, and decide that I likely understand much more than he realizes.

"I wanted you so badly that it almost drove me to madness. Twice, I nearly lost all reason and scarcely stopped myself from barging into your chambers and taking you as a husband should."

"Perhaps you should have," I whisper, despite knowing from his expression how dangerous that is.

A growl rumbles in the back of his throat, and then his mouth is back on me, hot and demanding. His teeth grazing, his tongue alternating between caressing and punishing. And while his mouth works to a frenzied rhythm, all I can think about is him storming into my room in the middle of night, uninvited. The surprise as he grabs me, unapologetic and unyielding.

I imagine it to be like that first night, when he stole into my room to grant me that frozen kiss. Except there would be no frost. Just insatiable heat. And he would tear away the thin silk of my nightgown as ferociously as he tore off my tunic before.

The fabric would be thinner and flimsier and would likely rip. And he would claim me there and then, surrounded by the remnants of my nightgown, with the same hungry, possessive look in his eyes right now—

"Elaric," I cry out, not caring who might hear.

Everything within me tenses, like a spring drawn too painfully tight. And then his eyes glint with such triumph that all the tension comes undone. I might say his name. Quietly or loudly—I'm not sure. Pleasure washes over me in such violent waves I lose my entire being to it.

I'm vaguely aware of him grabbing my waist, flipping me over, and pushing me down so that my cheek is pressed into the flimsy pillow that was supposed to be a barrier between us. Between *this*.

His fingers run down my backside, tracing my curves, and then he squeezes so hard the air rushes from my lungs.

He offers no warning before pushing himself inside me, burying himself so suddenly and so deeply I can't help from calling out. And yet the fullness of him feels so delightfully right, especially since I'm still crashing down from my blissful high.

I don't even know when he unfastened his breeches.

"You feel," he manages between haggard breaths, sliding himself out before driving back in, "unbelievable."

My only response is a moan as he grabs my breast and rolls my hard nipple between his fingers. His other hand stays on my lower back, keeping me pressed firmly down on my knees. The entire sensation of him is so overwhelming I think I will shatter inside out.

My gaze snags on the full-length mirror in the corner of the room. The moonlight filtering in through the curtains offers enough illumination for me to glimpse our silhouettes. In its reflection, I watch his free hand trailing across my breasts, exploring every inch of my skin, and I do my best to commit the image, the feeling, the sound—all of it—to my memory. Capturing it as perfectly as only the most talented of painters could.

"I would do this all day, every day, to you," he breathes into my ear, "my queen."

"Elaric . . . "

He groans, and then his next stroke is so terribly out of rhythm that I think he is already crashing down from his peak. But then his tempo steadies, and he murmurs against the back of my neck, "Watch yourself in the mirror. Watch yourself come around me."

My core clenches at his words, and they seem to have ensnared me into some spell, since there's nothing I can do but stare at the mirror, watching as he thrusts into me. His hand is at my center, tracing lavish circles over and over. And through the mirror, I see him watching us too. Hear the desire in his every breath.

"I don't think I will last," I choke out, overwhelmed by the sheer intensity of this moment.

Though it's been mere minutes since I just came, it's all I can do to grip the sheets and prevent myself from climaxing again so soon.

In the end, it's Elaric who breaks first.

"Adara . . . " he rasps.

The raw passion in his voice slams me over the edge. The waves of pleasure which wash over me are so much more potent than the ones from before.

His body relaxes as the tension seeps from him. Then the two of us fall still, ragged breaths filling the otherwise silent room. My knees ache, but I can't move, as if I am caught in a trance.

Elaric is the one who stirs first, sweeping aside my sweaty hair and kissing my neck in such an achingly sweet gesture. "You are so beautiful," he says, every syllable filled with as much reverence as a prayer.

All I can do is close my eyes and lean back against him, savoring all his warmth.

We stay like that for another minute before Elaric slides out of me, wrapping his arm around me and pulling me beside him onto the bed.

In the darkness, he stares at me, bright eyes trailing over my features. I watch him before reaching out, tentatively at first, and trace his face with my fingertips. The gentleness of it is a stark contrast to the uncontrollable passion we shared moments ago.

And when at long last I'm done, he captures my hand and kisses the top of my head. "Sleep well, my queen."

Chapter 30

I spend the entire night cradled in Elaric's arms, sleeping more peacefully than I have in years. Not since Dalia vanished have I rested this well. All those nights after her disappearance were filled with so much grief, and when the sharp, raw pain faded, it became a burning hatred which consumed my soul for three long years. Even after entering the Crystal Palace, my sleep remained uneasy, the weight of my scheming taking its toll on my mind. And then, ever since our wedding night, my heart has been warring against the regret which threatened to devour it.

Maybe tomorrow night, when we've left behind this village and return our focus to finding Isidore and ending the curse, my unconscious mind will be once more engulfed by the fear of our failure. But tonight, nestled against Elaric, my mind is untroubled. His presence eclipses all my worries and doubts.

The serenity doesn't exist in my sleep alone. It lingers even as I wake, my eyes fluttering open and adjusting to the gentle dawn light filtering through the curtains.

Elaric is already awake, a hint of a smile on his lips as he watches me shed the fogginess of slumber. I stay encircled in his arms, which are more comforting than any blanket.

"Have you been awake long?" I ask.

"A while, I suppose."

My attention slides over to the curtain, trying to decide how late into the morning it must be. With them drawn shut, it's impossible to know if it's closer to dawn or midday. "You should have awoken me."

"It's still early," he says, "and you were sleeping."

I yawn. "What time is it?"

"Around eight. Or perhaps nine. I awoke just after sunrise, and it has been an hour or so since then."

"You've been lying here that long?" I ask in disbelief. "Weren't you bored?"

"Not at all," he says, fingers trailing my temple and tucking a stray lock of hair behind my ear. "I can think of nothing better than watching you sleep."

I lower my eyes, cheeks flushing.

His fingers settle on my chin, and he tugs my face up, forcing me to look at him. "Well, perhaps that's a lie," he says, lips pulling into a smirk. "I do much prefer this."

"Prefer wha—" I begin, but my question is answered when he lowers his lips to my breast. He glances back up at me with a glint in his eyes.

"And this," he murmurs, his lips leaving my breast to deposit a trail of kisses down my side, brushing across my hips and my outer thigh until he reaches my knee.

"Elaric," I breathe.

"Yes, Adara?" he asks, arching a silver brow at me.

"We . . . " I swallow, doing my best to temper my own rising desire and prevent it from igniting into an inferno. Or else we will end up spending the whole day in bed.

But with the way his gaze is greedily roaming over me, extinguishing the building heat is a great challenge.

Exhaling deeply, I say, "We need to head to the harbor and find a boat, and then we also need to find fresh supplies and—"

"It can wait," he says. "All of it can wait until I've finished with you." His hand skims the inside of my thigh, tracing my hip bones.

In that moment I know I've already lost.

By the time we're ready to leave, it's much closer to midday than I prefer. The blame lies entirely with Elaric. I'm forced to get dressed twice, since the first time, I didn't make it to the door before being intercepted by a kiss. Which, despite my fleeting protests, soon landed us back in bed. However, it's difficult to be annoyed by it, even when the barkeep informs us that we owe him more money for the room since we've stayed the whole morning.

After we eat a late breakfast, our first destination is the harbor, which proves to be busier than I expect. Though it means people almost walk into us many times, it also means plenty of vessels are anchored along the pier. With luck, one will be suitable for our voyage.

Elaric pauses at the edge of the pier, scanning across all the boats and ships. Some vessels are enormous, filling most of the harbor with their impressive hulls. While others look slightly larger than rowboats, their small sails barely more than flags.

Before I finish scrutinizing all the vessels myself, Elaric signals to one near the far left of the harbor. "There. That one should suffice."

And before I can say anything—not that my opinion bears much merit on such matters—he sets off toward the boat in question.

I'm forced into an ungraceful trot in order to match his lengthy strides.

The boat possesses a single mast fitted with two sails, and a third sail is rigged across the stern. As we draw nearer, I notice a man standing on the pier, issuing orders to several other men who are occupied with transferring barrels of fresh fish from this boat over to the larger one docked beside it.

"Good day," Elaric calls as we approach.

The man's eyes sweep over Elaric, cautious though he offers a friendly: "Good day to you too, sir." He doesn't spare a glance for me, however. I may as well be invisible.

Elaric skips pleasantries, cutting to the point. "How much for your boat?"

"I beg your pardon?"

I can't help from cringing at the exchange. I don't think the man notices my expression, since he's too busy staring at Elaric in bewilderment.

Perhaps we should have discussed how exactly we will negotiate buying a boat, as it seems Elaric has decided to handle it with kingly assertiveness. I suppose at least, his blunt approach will allow us to quickly determine those who are open to selling.

"This boat," Elaric gestures to the smaller vessel, unfazed. "I would like to purchase it."

"It isn't for sale," the man blurts.

"What a shame," Elaric says, rolling back his shoulders. "We'll have to find someone more willing to part ways with their boat. Thank you for your time."

He turns to leave and I follow, the man standing dumbfounded on the pier behind us.

As I tug Elaric's arm to discuss an alternative approach, the man calls, "Wait!"

Elaric doesn't miss a beat before swiveling back around to face him. "Yes?"

He reassesses Elaric, this time scrutinizing him more carefully, and I'm certain he must notice the regal grace beneath his plain tunic. "I might be willing to sell the boat . . . for the right price." Surprise ripples through the workers, but the man's eyes stay on Elaric.

Elaric examines the boat. "How about two hundred gold?"

The man scratches his chin. "I don't know. Two hundred seems fair but hardly covers my costs, let alone the income lost until I find a replacement. That could take weeks."

"I understand," Elaric says. "Shall we make it two hundred and fifty?"

"Three hundred and fifty," the man counters.

Elaric winces. "That does seem rather high for this size of boat. Let my wife and me first discuss it, and then I shall return shortly with our offer."

He goes to leave again, but the man stops him. "All right. Two hundred and fifty gold then."

Elaric smiles broadly. "It seems we have a deal."

Heading back into the village for supplies, Elaric and I find a butcher where we purchase salted meat, and at some fruit stands, we buy apples and grapes. We also visit a tailor and purchase a fresh change of clothes, as what we're both wearing is dirty and tattered. Unsurprisingly, the tailor gives me a curious look when I request breeches instead of skirts.

When we return to the harbor, the boat's deck is clear of crates and other belongings. Elaric thanks the man for his willingness to sell the vessel so suddenly, and pays him the agreed amount.

We set our fresh supplies on the deck. Once the man leaves, Elaric turns to me. "We'll sail out the harbor first, then use the pendant to navigate toward Eruweth." He heads over to the ropes running from the hull up to the sails.

I suppose we would receive suspicious looks if we held up a levitating pendant. "Is magic frowned upon in this part of the world?"

"In nearly every part," Elaric says, loosening a knot. "Few witches use their gifts benevolently." He tugs a rope to adjust the sail before securing it in place. I watch him work, but the complicated loops of the knot blur together.

When Elaric moves on to the next rope, I ask, "Can you show me how to tie the knots?"

He nods and beckons me over. Slowly, he demonstrates tying the knot, though still too quick for me to grasp everything. With a sharp tug, the finished knot comes undone despite the complicated process. "Here," he says, offering me the rope, "you try."

I make my best attempt, though it takes a long while, and Elaric has to correct me several times. Once I succeed, I grin widely at my knot. The next one will definitely take less time.

"Which should we adjust next?" I ask, eyeing the other ropes.

Elaric chuckles. "It's all right, Adara. I'll handle the rest."

"But I want to help," I protest.

"You can be the helmsman."

I press my lips together. "Helmsman? What do they do?"

"Steer the ship."

I glance between the rope he's adjusting and the boat's wheel. Steering seems easier than tying knots. "All right," I say, heading to the wheel before he changes his mind. "Which way do I turn?"

"Neither way yet. The anchor is still lowered, so we can't go anywhere. I'll tell you which way to turn the wheel once we start sailing."

I wait as Elaric finishes with the sails, and then he strides to the capstan and begins cranking it. Unlike the knots, operating the capstan requires little instruction, so I hurry over as well. It spins much faster with both of us.

With the anchor raised, the boat sways to the sea's rhythm. Wind billows into the sails, propelling us from the harbor. But we're veering left, on course to collide with a large ship anchored at the pier's end.

"Starboard, Adara!" Elaric calls, returning to adjust the sails. "The wind is stronger than I anticipated!"

I rush for the wheel without hesitation. Ocean spray splatters my cheeks, red curls galloping behind. I grip a wooden spoke but pause. "Starboard means right, yes?"

"Unless you want to crash," he shouts back.

I clutch a second spoke and turn the wheel. It offers more resistance than expected, and I end up overcompensating, sending us too far right. If I don't correct course again, we'll slam into the opposite pier instead.

Just as I reverse direction, Elaric calls, "Not so far right!"

Carefully, I straighten our path, though waves still drift us left. With cautious adjustments, we sail out the harbor without crashing into anything.

Chapter 31

We sail all afternoon, intermittently checking our course with the enchanted pendant. Every sudden lurch of the waves has me scanning across the endless blue of the horizon for any sign of the frozen kingdom. But even by the time night falls and the clouds surrender themselves to the stars, Eruweth remains absent. The anticipation of knowing we could arrive any moment fills my stomach with dread.

"You should rest," Elaric says, hours after dusk. "We may not reach Eruweth for days. You can't stay awake that long and still battle Isidore."

"But if it takes a week, will not sleeping affect your magic? One of us will need to keep watch for the island at all times."

"Since my magic is currently suppressed, it doesn't need replenishing," he simply says.

With no prior experience of consuming Irremisa, I wonder how he can be so certain. If he's wrong, facing Isidore with weakened power will prove disastrous.

But arguing now is pointless. He'll just insist I sleep and not worry. If we do sail for days, I'll have to keep persuading him to let me take the night watch.

I pull out the small blanket from our sack and fold it over as a makeshift pillow.

For a while, I lie there on the hard deck, staring up at the glittering stars, listening to the splashing waves. I close my eyes, but thoughts of reaching Eruweth and facing Isidore plague my mind.

I roll onto my side, gaze falling on the Sword of Veliantis several paces away. Its luminous jewels glow amid the darkness. After a violent wave earlier, I thought we'd arrived and unbundled the sword, fearing Isidore might ambush us. Though the alarm proved false, having it close seems sensible.

I exhale gently, the sound of my breath faint over the waves. Instead of trying to sleep again, I end up staring at the sword.

Even with this weapon, what chance do we stand of defeating Isidore in her own domain? What if magical wards block Elaric's power like in Belinda's woods?

Though since his magic originates from her own, any such wards are unlikely to affect him. Nonetheless, the thought of battling her without his magic fills me with terror. Our already impossible odds would be a thousand times more impossible.

Yet killing Isidore wasn't part of the incantation used to curse Elaric. No, it involved me. His Summer Queen.

When Belinda first confirmed this, true love between us seemed foolish. But after last night, after our earnest honesty and shared desire, it seems quite possible after all.

Elaric's confession echoes through me—those three powerful words.

I love you.

If he can love me despite my past betrayal, doesn't that prove the strength of his affection? And while I'm not yet ready to profess the same, I've never felt this way for anyone. Every glance, every touch, fills me with such emotion I may burst.

However, there's no guarantee what we share is true and powerful enough. We could turn back, avoid all danger, but I don't know how long it'll take to break Elaric's curse. If ever.

I suppose we could have a happy life, even with the curse. Me aging while he does not would be difficult, and I know how miserable he is chained in this frozen prison, but perhaps my presence would ease his pain somewhat.

But as deeply as I care for Elaric, I cannot abandon my sister to an eternity bound in ice.

Nor can I leave Elaric to endure the same fate.

I've pondered this much already. There is no alternative. We must face Isidore.

I sigh into the darkness.

"Struggling to sleep?" Elaric calls from the wheel.

I sit up to meet his eyes. "A little."

At once, he abandons the wheel to join me. He pulls me into his arms as he lies beside me on the deck. I rest my head against his chest.

"What bothers you?" he asks gently.

"Just thinking we could arrive any second," I mumble. Not an outright lie, but not the full extent of my worries either. Voicing the unrestrained truth may spur him to haul me into a carriage and fly me back to the Crystal Palace.

"I'll wake you at the first sign of Eruweth," he promises, squeezing my hand. I return the gesture, clasping his fingers.

We fall quiet then, staring at the sky as the waves sway us back and forth.

"Do you know much of the stars?" he says.

I lift my head to study his contemplative expression before settling back against him. "Only a little. I doubt I could name many constellations."

"Sailors often rely on them for navigation. When surrounded by nothing but waves, it is difficult to determine your position and direction of travel."

"Would you consider yourself a sailor then?"

"No," he says with a laugh, "certainly not. But during my travels, I worked as a sailor for a few months and learned much of what I know then."

"Didn't the sailors find your proper manner of speech peculiar?"

"I claimed to be a lord's unwanted bastard son. That usually halted all further questions." He takes my hand, using it to point at the sky. "That's the North Star. It always holds the same position, allowing sailors to navigate when all else is lost." He traces a shape with my finger. "The Archer."

"Where's the Ox?"

"It isn't visible this season."

"Oh," I say.

"Is that your birth sign?"

I nod.

His lips twist in barely contained laughter.

"What?" I demand.

"I suppose that explains everything."

I narrow my eyes. "Explains what?"

"Well, you're certainly stubborn as an ox."

I shove his shoulder. "What about yours, anyway? You were born on the sixth of December so your sign is the Tower, isn't it? Is that constellation out tonight?"

"It is," he says, taking my hand to trace a line far right. "Just there. Do you see it?"

"I think so."

"How did you know the Tower is my sign?" he asks, releasing me.

"I may not know much about star gazing, but I know birth signs."

"I meant more about knowing my birthday. I don't recall telling you, and there is no one alive to remember it."

"I read it in your father's journal. He wrote an entry about your birth and the date was recorded there."

"I am surprised you remembered."

"Your birthday seemed an important thing to remember," I say, "especially as your wife."

He presses his lips to my forehead. My heart flutters.

"I suppose with no one knowing, you haven't celebrated a birthday in centuries?"

"That's true. I have not."

"This year we will celebrate it together," I promise.

He smiles softly. "I can think of no better way to spend it."

I return his smile, but then it falters at the thought of facing Isidore. How we might not return to the palace together. Just imagining a life without him causes tears to prick my eyes. "I want to be with you always, Elaric. I can't bear to lose you."

"I could not bear to lose you, either," he mutters into my hair.

I press my lips to his, kissing him desperately. As if for the last time. I don't know how many more chances we will have before Eruweth appears on the horizon like a death sentence, shattering this joy.

When we reach its shores, we will be solely focused on finding and slaying Isidore, and may never return from our quest. This blissful moment together may be our final one. My whole being is consumed by the need to show him exactly how I feel.

"Adara," he says, caressing my cheeks.

I trace his face, across his brows, down his temple and his jaw. He closes his eyes, allowing me to paint this eternal image in my mind. Does he too realize this may be our last chance?

My fingers become lips, trailing his neck, savoring each of his strained responses. But it's not enough. I must capture all of him.

I tug the hem of his tunic. He requires little convincing to pull it over his head.

My hands roam across his chest, testing the solidness of every muscle. Gradually delving lower until they skim across his abdomen, finding the stays of his breeches.

With a sharp breath, he catches my wrist. "I'm not sure this is wise." The only pleasing thing about his protest is the sheer unsteadiness of his voice. "Eruweth could appear and—"

"Forget Eruweth," I interrupt. "I *need* you, Elaric."

While the rational part of me knows he's right to take caution, all I want is to forget everything else and enjoy this moment together, lest it be the last we share.

Perhaps sensing my urgency, he tangles both hands in my hair, pulling me closer. "I'm here," he breathes. "I'm here."

Our lips crash together in a maelstrom of fear and desire, drinking in each other as if dying of thirst. When his teeth graze my lower lip, a deep moan shudders through me.

The sound spurs him on, all resistance long banished. He strips away my tunic as frantically as I did his. My breeches soon follow, and within seconds, the two of us are lying there naked upon the deck, basked in starlight.

He watches me briefly before his hands return to me, exploring my skin. As he trails down my lower back, I lean into him, yearning for more.

"I can't get enough of you," he murmurs, breath hot against my ears. "Even if I have you like this, every day for the rest of my life, it would never be enough."

I press his palm flat against my pounding chest, at the very center of my breast, hoping through it he will understand that which I cannot express with words. That he possesses such an enormous part of my heart. As his gaze meets mine, I tighten my grip around his hand, willing the gesture alone to convey my silent message.

Elaric lifts my hand from my chest, all the way to his mouth, and kisses the back. Though the gesture itself is innocent, my skin scorches.

Then his lips glide up, following a burning path from my arm to my shoulder. He continues onward, skimming over my collarbone and then across the sensitive flesh of my neck. His touch leaves me gasping as I fist his hair, unwilling to let go of him.

"Elaric," I say.

"Yes, my queen?"

"You're . . . " I swallow down the emotion clogging my throat. "You're perfect."

He smiles against my skin, hands roaming over my body, traipsing over every swell and curve. His pace is leisurely, entirely unhurried, as if we have all the time in the world.

If only we did.

His hands run down my body, reaching ever lower, gliding across my stomach. With the back of his hand, he caresses the soft skin of my inner thighs, each brushstroke coiling the tension within me even tighter. Heightening the burning need swelling in my core.

Then his fingers sink into me, parting the wet folds, and a cry escapes me. Deeper, he bears into me, and I oblige, legs spreading wider.

But though the sensation is delightful, it is him I want. Not his fingers.

I push him aside, and at first he looks surprised—worried, even—but then, realizing my intentions, he settles down onto the deck, allowing me to straddle him.

I don't hesitate before taking exactly that which I seek, lowering myself onto him as deeply as I can, burying the full length of his hardness inside me.

Then I roll my hips. A slow, devastating movement which has him hissing my name, his nails biting into my rear.

I can't decide which I like best: the way he feels inside me, or the way he reacts so readily to my body.

He reaches up, cupping my breast and kneading it beneath his fingers. His other hand stays on my waist, steadying me. Together, we move to the same rhythm of the waves crashing around us. Sea spray splatters across my back. Wind rips through my hair. But all those sensations are insignificant to Elaric and the molten fire coursing through my veins.

And in that moment, I realize the truth in his words. Even spending every day like this would never be enough—

A wave slams into our boat, interrupting this bliss. The two of us are torn apart, tumbling onto the deck.

The stars spin overhead.

Then sense pierces my daze, and Elaric is scrambling upright, rushing to the wheel.

I scan the surrounding waves but nothing seems unusual. Nor do I see a frozen island on the horizon. All I notice is the waves are choppier than earlier, the wind having picked up considerably.

"Are we still on course to Eruweth?" Elaric calls.

I tear open the sack and grab the pendant, holding it out until it springs to life. It points further left than before.

Elaric turns the wheel left, and our boat soon shifts direction.

Maybe it's the shock from the sudden wave, or perhaps the desire still smoldering within, but a laugh escapes me.

Elaric glances back, casting me a curious look.

"I never imagined I'd be sailing the sea naked."

His lips quirk. "I suppose we've just demonstrated why doing so isn't wise."

I roll my shoulders back in a shrug. "It isn't as if anything bad happened. We just had to alter our course slightly."

"This time," he says, voice growing stern. "There might be a storm brewing ahead, and should we be hit by a larger wave, we risk our boat capsizing. It's far from the sturdiest vessel I've ever sailed upon."

I heave out a sigh. What he says sounds sensible, but it's hard to think about anything other than the desire still aching between my thighs. And how the moonlight is silvering his every muscle, emphasizing their hard lines, isn't helping matters either. If he's going to insist on staying by the helm, then he really needs to put back on his clothes since this is just torturous.

"Aren't you joining me?" I ask as casually as I can, patting the damp deck beside me.

"You should try to sleep, Adara."

I clench my jaw as I bear the sting of the rejection. The waves already seemed to have calmed down again, and we may have no more such opportunities. Why must he insist on being such a bore?

But as much as I want him right now, I have no wish to beg and demolish the little dignity I have left.

"Fine," I huff, getting to my feet. "If you won't join me, then I'll have to continue without you."

I walk past him toward the mast at the center of our boat, his gaze burning into me with every step. As I turn, I notice his frown but I don't hesitate before standing flush against the mast, back arched into its solidness. My position lies directly in his line of sight, meaning that if he wishes to see where we're sailing then he has no choice but to look at all of my naked body.

And the bold display I'm about to provide.

I slide up my leg, foot flat against the mast behind, and angle my hips just right so he has the perfect view.

Even over the rolling waves, I hear his sharp intake of breath.

"You can be the boring one," I say, hands skimming over my breasts, "but I intend to stand here all night until you come and finish what we started."

I don't wait for his response before rolling my nipples between my fingers and pinching so hard they sting as the briny wind washes over them.

He clenches the wheel's spokes so tightly his knuckles turn ivory. He could look anywhere else, yet his focus remains on me as my hands glide down my body. As they trace up my inner thighs. Even so, he makes no sign of moving, staying as rigid as a statue. From here, I can glimpse enough of him to know he's as hard as he was when he was inside me.

Time to double my efforts then.

I drag my index finger higher until I reach my swollen core. There, I trace lavish circles over the taut peak, a fresh wave of overwhelming pleasure surging through me.

"Elaric," I say again, "won't you join me?"

He does not.

Determined, I sink two fingers inside me, spreading my legs as wide as I can with the mast supporting my weight. Grinding my rear against it, I slide my fingers slowly out before pushing them back in. "It seems I'll just have to imagine you pressing me up against this mast, burying yourself deep inside me—"

In the next instant, his hands tear from the wheel's spokes, and he's at my side faster than I can blink.

"You're going to be the death of me," he says, capturing my mouth in a kiss. Our tongues clash together, each fighting for dominance, and I moan into him, my fingers still driving in and out of myself.

Elaric doesn't allow that to continue for much longer. He snatches my hand from my thighs and brings it to his mouth. Then he licks my soaked fingers, his tongue swirling over them entirely.

Blood pounds through me as I watch him, heat rushing across my lower stomach. My whole body trembles.

But I've no chance to recover. His hands are on my waist and he's lifting me, my rear firmly pressing into the mast behind. He offers no warning' before driving himself into me.

A cry tears through me, lost to the briny wind. Nothing can compare to the sheer feel of him. Not even watching him lick my fingers.

Elaric isn't slow, and he certainly isn't gentle, but I'd be lying if I said I deserved either with how I just taunted him.

His every forceful stroke causes my back to dig in deeper to the mast, and I swear I hear it creak, straining against our weight as we lose ourselves in each other. I knock my head against it at least twice, but register no pain. Just the heady desire pounding through me. I wrap my legs around him, forcing him even deeper.

"I love you," he mutters against my ear. "I love every single part of you." Each word is enunciated with a powerful thrust.

I gasp his name, and though the sound is hardly coherent to my own ears, it drives him to his peak, his body stiffening before he crashes back down.

Between watching him come undone inside me and the wildness of doing this out here in the open sea—the crashing waves and glimmering stars bearing witness to our unbridled passion—I quickly find myself thrown over the edge.

I dig my fingers into the firm muscles of his back, desperately seeking purchase, but the current slamming into me is too violent to avoid. And I'm also thrown into that oblivion of pleasure, tremors wracking through me.

Once all falls still, we remain fixed in place, both gasping for breath as exertion catches up on us. Then Elaric slides out of me, and though I feel emptier, warm waves of contentment still wash over me.

His hands stay on my waist, and he carries me back over to where our heap of clothes lies beside my makeshift pillow.

Kissing my brow, he lowers me to the deck. As he regards me, his soft expression grows firmer. "Now you really must try to sleep."

I cast him a coy smile. "I suppose I can try."

He just shakes his head at me and grabs his clothes.

I lie there, admiring the sight of him. Only when he's fully dressed and returned to the wheel do I pull my tunic and breeches back on. Even with the biting wind, I feel as if I'm on fire.

Once covered up, I settle down onto the deck, resting my head on the folded blanket. I watch Elaric as he turns the wheel, the pendant clenched in his other hand.

My eyes drift shut, and now all of my concerns for Eruweth and Isidore seem so very far away compared to Elaric and the bliss of him upon my skin. The lull of the waves drags me into a deep slumber.

That night, I dream of the Crystal Palace, all the frost thawed and replaced by colorful mosaics and gilded ceilings. I dream of Elaric and me dancing at a grand ball held in honor of his birthday. Not a trace of worry lingers upon his features, though hundreds of nobles swarm around us, for we have long broken the curse and freed him from Isidore's icy chains.

And my favorite part of all is watching as our two children tackle him over within the royal gardens, surrounded by vivid roses.

But the sweetness of these dreams doesn't endure for long. Soon, I'm torn from their tranquility and dragged back onto the hard deck of our boat.

"Adara," comes Elaric's voice. He's shaking my shoulder, banishing the remnants of sleep.

"What is it?" I ask, pushing myself upright and rubbing my eyes.

"Eruweth," he breathes. "We're here."

Chapter 32

An enormous mass of ice lies upon the horizon, its white surface a stark contrast to the dark waves surrounding it. The towering peaks glint like steel blades in the cold moon-light.

I cease breathing, overwhelmed by the sight looming ahead. I'm so fixated on the island that I barely feel the boat's sway beneath my feet.

After enduring every trial thus far, we now stand before our final reckoning. Either we will emerge triumphant or perish here within these frozen wastes.

Elaric is as solemn and silent as I am for several minutes. Then he gestures toward the undulating sea before us, where great shards of ice float upon the black waves. "We need to slow our approach," he says, wrenching me from my trance, "or else we risk colliding with those icebergs."

I give a quick nod. "I'll help you adjust the sails."

He casts me a dubious look. "It would be wiser for you to keep watch. If we are approaching any icebergs, alert me at once so we may steer clear of them."

Given the sobriety of our current situation, I swallow back my protest and take my position at the vessel's bow, having no desire to meet my demise on the jagged ice.

Clutching the edge of the boat, I scan the waves for any sign of danger. We soon pass a lone iceberg, but it's far away enough not to pose a threat. Though it appears deceptively small above the surface, I'm certain it plunges much deeper than one would think at first glance.

Minutes later, another emerges from the darkness, this time closer but not yet a cause for concern. Meanwhile, as we sail on, the island grows larger, reflecting more moonlight off its snow-covered surface. I avert my vision to avoid being blinded by the brightness.

The icebergs surrounding us steadily become more frequent and greater in size. I swallow back a spike of unease as we maneuver past a sinister looking one, and I have little doubt it's even more formidable under the lapping waves.

When my focus returns to the churning sea ahead, I notice a huge iceberg lying there. Our current course is guaranteed to plow straight into its flanks. While a fair stretch of waves still separates us, we'll need ample time and space to alter our direction without colliding into any of the others floating nearby.

I turn to warn Elaric of the obstacle ahead, but my words morph into a gasp as the boat violently lurches starboard.

The abrupt movement hurls me off balance, and I barely grab hold of the nearby rail in time to avoid crashing onto the deck. Splinters bite into my palm, but the adrenaline now rushing through my veins dulls the pain.

I quickly straighten, pulse hammering as I scan the surrounding waves for answers. While I took great care in tracking the icebergs, maybe we collided with a smaller one which I somehow missed?

How severely has the blow damaged our hull? I strain my ears for the telltale rush of water filling the lower compartments.

Hastily, Elaric finishes knotting his final adjustments to the mainsail's rigging. "I will check the hold for any damage," he calls, heading toward the hatch.

But before he's made it even halfway across the deck, another force suddenly rocks our small vessel—this time from the left rather than the right. When I righten myself, I meet Elaric's stony gaze, my stomach dipping. No iceberg could explain two hits from opposing directions.

It must be something else entirely . . .

We both hasten toward the edge of the boat and look down at the inky waters now whirring at a frenzied rhythm. I squint against the shadows and sea-spray.

A twisting form emerges—a serpentine figure thrashing just under the surface. Though the creature resembles an eel's wiry shape, it's colossal compared to those I faced in the lake.

"A sea serpent," I choke.

In immediate answer, a terrifying hiss sounds behind us, vibrating through the very timbers beneath our feet.

I whirl around, praying another explanation waits there.

All my futile hopes are crushed as the monster's head raises from the sea, sheets of water cascading from its horns.

Glowing blue eyes, mirroring Elaric's magic, rake over our vessel. Each impenetrable scale is just translucent enough to glimpse the black veins pulsing beneath. Fangs like towering glaciers line its jaws, hungry to devour wood and flesh alike.

The sight drives the very air from my lungs. I gasp it back in a panicked rush, heartbeat thundering.

The sea serpent coils above us. With its formidable size, it could easily crush our boat like kindling. Even great warships would hardly slow its assault.

I swivel to Elaric, shouts lodged in my throat. But no magic resides within him now to battle this monster. The vial of Ruposley hanging at his neck will restore his power, yet doing so risks alerting Isidore. Perhaps she glimpses us even now through the beast's eyes. But we need his magic. Without it, we stand no chance of surviving this fight.

"Your magic!" I cry, though my voice is lost to the blood pounding in my ears.

I lunge toward the sack still lying beside the boat's wheel. My fingers scramble over the worn material until they close around the hilt of the Sword of Veliantis.

The serpent rushes toward us with terrifying momentum, its monstrous jaws gaping wide to engulf our small vessel. Such an assault would be so devastating it'd obliterate us instantly.

Sword first, I charge.

The creature's fangs bear down, eager to tear through timber and flesh. With all my strength, I swing my sword, the determination to survive coursing through my body like lightning.

Despite the serpent's scales appearing as thick as steel, my blade carves through them as though they're fragile parchment.

A shriek slices through the night.

The serpent withdraws, its fangs snapping closed less than an arm's length from our boat.

Black blood splatters across my face, stinging my eyes. While the burning is so intense it's as if my eyes are melting in their sockets, I have no choice but to keep them wide open.

If I lose sight of the enemy for even a second, I will be dead.

I pray that Elaric has already swallowed the potion and that it won't be long before his magic returns. Then he can conjure a harpoon and drive it through the serpent's chest.

That is, if his magic works against it. Both his magic and the monster's scales are borne of Isidore's power, and so there's a chance it may not work. Even with his magic restored, we may be unable to prevent our inevitable defeat.

The serpent doesn't cower for long. It soon swirls around, letting out a far angrier hiss than the first, and the sea shudders in response. Blood rolls off its translucent scales, dripping into the roiling waves.

Then it lurches forth. But this time, its attention isn't fixed on our hull.

It's fixed on me.

Fangs crash down in retaliation.

There isn't time to roll away. Not without risking being impaled.

So, I do the only thing I can do.

I dive away from the fangs, toward the center of the serpent's mouth. Then I leap up and drive my sword into the beast, muscles screaming with the effort.

"Adara!" Elaric yells, just as the serpent's maw closes.

Darkness encases me.

The splintering of wood echoes from somewhere beyond.

A force barrels into me, but I cling to the hilt of my sword with both hands, the rubies glowing like fire in the all-consuming blackness. I hope my blade is lodged deeply enough into the roof of the serpent's mouth to hold my weight. Should it come loose, I'll be lost to the void below.

My fingers start to slip. I grip the sword so tightly my bones ache. But I'm dragged down, as if an anchor shackles my boots.

And just when I'm about to lose hold of my sword, I'm flipped over.

My back slams into a solid surface—the roof of the serpent's mouth. The impact rattles through my bones and wrenches my sword free. I quickly steady my blade before it crashes into my skull.

Heart pounding, I sit there for several long minutes, my rasping breaths echoing through the darkness. Adrenaline thrums through my veins. My brain struggles to make sense of what just happened.

When my pulse settles, I swallow hard and rise. I must escape. Except finding a way out of here is another matter entirely.

I douse the rising panic before it can spiral into unhelpful thoughts and begin walking, sword extended to probe the surrounding oblivion.

After counting perhaps a hundred blind, shuffling paces, I smack into a spongy barrier. My blade meets little resistance, sinking hilt-deep, and blood spurts out.

Since there's no responding roar, the creature must be dead.

But my relief is short-lived as I realize the implications of its defeat. Right now, I am likely plummeting to the bottom of the ocean, caged in the serpent's maw.

I force aside the churning in my gut before it seizes all my senses.

I wander left, trailing my sword along the spongy walls. My blade taps upward, clinking against gigantic fangs. They mark the exit of the creature's mouth. My path to freedom.

But the fangs span over an arm's width each, with less than half that gap between them.

The gums form a steep, satiny slope up to its fangs. I have just one hand to use for climbing, since I need my other hand to carry the sword. I can't leave our only weapon to slay Isidore in the serpent's remains.

Regardless, this plan is far too risky. The fangs are razor sharp and possibly laced with poison.

I step back, gritting my teeth. My other option is to carve a tunnel through the monster's body. Given how easily my sword sliced through the beast's thick scales, I'm sure it would fare as well against its bones. Yet if I create an opening in its remains, seawater will be free to gush in. And I will drown.

At least it would mean a quicker end than dying from starvation, caged at the bottom of the ocean—

An echo interrupts my thoughts.

Crouching, I press my ear to smooth gum. There's a rubble from somewhere beyond, growing louder every second.

A crack erupts, and when I remove my ear from the serpent's gums, I realize they are no longer made of flesh but are translucent all the way through. Though thick enough to distort my view, I can discern the rippling of water beyond.

My heart skips a beat.

Elaric.

It seems I needn't fear drowning or starving after all.

HOLLY ROSE

The dark splits apart to reveal twinkling stars.

"Adara!" comes Elaric's shout.

I crane my neck until I spot his worried face through the opening.

"I'm here!" I call, waving both hands high for him to see.

A tendril of ice wraps around my waist, plucking me from the serpent's mouth.

Elaric uses his magic to place me next to him, my feet settling upon the frozen scales of the serpent's underside. These are much thinner than the ones on its back.

He pulls me into a forceful hug. "Are you hurt?" he demands.

I shake my head, though he holds me so tightly it's a struggle.

"Good," he says, attention darting up. On both sides, solid cliffs now soar where ocean swelled before. "Freezing the serpent took much of my power, and Isidore will have undoubtedly felt it. We must hurry."

264

Chapter 33

Elaric conjures a winged steed, and together we take flight, bursting up through the frozen waves to land on our boat's deck. Fanged gashes mar the hull where the serpent tried to devour me, but we don't seem to have any leaks, and Elaric is certain they won't impact the vessel's performance.

Once we're on our boat, he dismisses his steed and starts toward our supply sack still lying near the wheel. Recalling his magic hasn't yet retreated, I grab his arm to stop him before he reaches it.

Frantically, I sift through the sack for the blue vial of Irremisa and shove it into his hands. "Drink," I blurt.

He pops the cork, but pauses. "Isidore may already be on her way. Without my power, we will be defenseless against her."

My thoughts race back to the battle we just experienced. While Elaric drank the Ruposley potion in seconds, there was a delay before his magic was restored. A delay long enough for the sea serpent to devour me. Fighting Isidore will be far more dangerous. And if she ambushes us, our loss will be certain.

Sword or not, we'd have no chance of defeating her.

"Then what do you suggest?" I ask.

"Abandon this vessel and fly to shore," he says. "It shouldn't take us long. If we try to sail there, we'll need to pick our way around all the icebergs and they're more clustered together nearer the shore."

Both flying and sailing come with plenty of risks, and I can't decide which is worse. "If you fly us there, she'll be able to sense exactly where we land."

"Indeed," Elaric says with a sigh, "but at any rate, we must decide quickly. Hesitating much longer may cost us dearly."

"We could swim to Eruweth," I say as the idea appears in my mind.

"The waves are too strong, and you won't be able to dry off afterward. The magic surrounding Eruweth is more powerful than it is inside the Crystal Palace, and there would be no way for us to light a fire."

"What if you freeze the water and create a path to shore? You could take Irremisa right after to hide your presence again."

"Like with flying, she would know our location," he counters. "Except it would take much longer for us to reach shore, giving her more time to intercept us."

"Flying it is then."

Elaric pushes the stopper back into the cork, not drinking a single drop, and returns it to hang around his neck.

I swiftly gather our belongings, shoving as many of our fresh supplies into the sack as I can. Elaric conjures his winged steed once more and then pulls me up onto it to sit behind him.

We soar into the sky, our battered vessel dwindling fast below. Given our vast speed and the huge clusters of icebergs beneath, it becomes quickly apparent that flying was the wisest option.

While we're in the air for just a minute, it lasts much too long. I nearly sob in relief when we land and my boots sink into snow at last.

Elaric grabs the Irremisa potion and gulps down a large mouthful.

Then the two of us sprint toward the trees. But as I run, I realize we don't have a way to tell whether the Irremisa is working amid all the snow. I can only hope it'll be as swift and effective as the first time.

Our footsteps form a frantic rhythm as we hurry to the safety of the forest ahead, accompanied by our ragged gasps. We're almost upon the trees when our tempo is broken by an unfamiliar beat.

I stop to listen, holding my breath so it doesn't drown out the faint sound.

It's more than a beat—a flurry. Far in the distance, but growing louder.

And rapidly approaching.

"Elaric!" I shout, running to close the distance between us.

He skids to a stop, gaze jerking to the sky. Whatever he sees must be grave, since he grabs my arm and yanks me into the trees.

Twigs rip the sleeves of my tunic, gouging my skin so deeply they draw blood. I vaguely register the pain. Everything is a blur.

"Get down!" he roars.

In the next instant his arms lock around me, dragging me to the ground. He leans into the frozen bark of the tree behind us.

The sky explodes with the thundering of wings.

A murder of crows, each with icy feathers, storms across the stars. Dread coils through my stomach. I press into Elaric as far as I can, seeking to make us as small a target as possible.

Looking up, I watch as the crows search the sky, glimpsing their forms between the leaves high above us. I pray the shadows cover us. That the creatures don't delve into the trees . . .

They circle back, flying over us. But then they continue onward, out to sea. The beating of wings fades into the distance.

"Do you think they've gone?" I whisper to Elaric once the sky empties. Our meager hiding place is far too exposed. Yet moving now risks being spotted if they return.

But before Elaric can respond, a caw rings from behind us—much too loud and near.

I risk leaning out just far enough to glimpse a lone crow perched on a branch several yards away. Its head swivels as it inspects the crystalline forest.

Its glare rakes toward us. I jerk back.

"Don't move," Elaric whispers, breath tickling my hair.

I turn rigid in his arms, not even twitching.

If that crow swoops near enough to notice our forms, Isidore will know precisely where we are. For all we know, she could be seconds behind her scouts.

Then we'll be forced to confront her without a plan.

I squeeze my eyes shut. Right now, we can only rely on luck.

Elaric must sense the fear pounding through my veins since his arms tighten around me. Or maybe it's just his own trepidation.

Wings beat.

The crow whirs toward us.

I clutch Elaric's tunic so tightly the fabric's coarseness burns my palms.

The crow flies past us without slowing. Its cry fades into the woods.

Chapter 34

We bolt through the trees, though neither of us is certain which direction we should take. We're too lost in the trees' depths to make out the contours of the land. And yet, we dare not stop moving, in case Isidore is scouring Eruweth for us this very moment, her crows having returned fruitless from their search.

The terrain veers sharply uphill. My strides falter, thighs burning in protest. Elaric is forced to slow his pace lest he lose me in this glimmering maze. I try quickening my steps, but the stabbing in my muscles intensifies.

"I can carry you," Elaric offers.

"I doubt that would be wise," I say, letting out a ragged breath. Talking and walking uphill is no easy feat, especially when one has fought a sea serpent barely an hour ago. "If Isidore finds us while I'm in your arms, how will you take the Ruposley quickly enough to restore your magic and fight her?"

"It would be fine if I carried you on my back."

"Even so," I say, "it would leave us vulnerable."

He dips his head, reluctantly conceding.

We walk for perhaps half an hour more until the sharp incline levels, allowing me to better match Elaric's tireless strides. But my relief fades as the trees begin to thin, leaving us exposed should Isidore's spies return.

Yet we have no choice but to continue on. Isidore knows precisely where we landed thanks to Elaric's magic, so turning back isn't an option.

With every step, the trees seem to offer less and less shelter until I start to consider whether we should retrace our path to find a more concealed route. But just as I slow, an edge catches my eye—one far too straight to be natural.

"Elaric," I call. "What's that over there?"

He follows my gesture, frowning. Curiosity piqued, he starts over to where I'm pointing. I scramble after him through the sparse trees, grass crunching underfoot.

When we approach, the strange structure reveals itself as a modest hut. Completely frozen like everything else across this accursed isle. The roof looks as if it was once made of thatch and the walls from crude rocks.

Elaric halts before we draw too close, scrutinizing the building ahead. The sparse trees around us offer little cover from the hut's windows.

"Do you think this is Isidore's home?" I whisper.

"It is doubtful," he says after a moment. "Given her arrogance, she would likely choose somewhere much more lavish. Even Belinda's cottage is more impressive than this. The castle would be my guess."

"There's a castle?"

He nods. "In the mountains. I glimpsed its spires in the distance when we flew here."

Without another word, Elaric stalks toward the hut. I hastily rummage through our sack, seeking the sword. If this place does prove to be Isidore's lair, it's best we stand prepared rather than be left weaponless.

My fingers close around the hilt, and I unsheathe the blade, bolstered by its weight. Only then do I follow him through the trees.

Elaric stops before the door, waiting until I stand beside him. Then he extends a cautious palm to push it aside.

The door creaks open. I wait for our demise to rush forth, but the door stops. Everything remains still.

Elaric's eyes narrow as he peers into the cottage. It's too dark for me to see anything, and with how he offers no remark, I suspect he doesn't notice much either. With only Isidore living here in Eruweth, it's likely this cottage is vacant.

He pushes the door open wider and strides through, each step slow and cautious. I keep close behind him, gripping my sword. Its jewels gleam in the shadows, but they're no substitute for a torch. All they do is act as a beacon for whatever lurks in the darkness.

We descend deeper into the abandoned dwelling, floorboards groaning beneath us. All around sits humble furniture and wares immobilized in frost, remnants of lives now extinguished. My gaze lingers on a ceramic vase where a bouquet remains captured forever, delicate petals transformed into fragile crystal.

"I wonder what happened to the people who lived here," I muse aloud, "whether they had enough time to escape?"

As we step into the next room, I find my answer.

A family surrounds the long-dead hearth at the center. My stomach flips at the sight.

The people of this kingdom had no warning before Isidore laid siege to it.

A woman is frozen mid-motion in her knitting, while the man in the armchair beside her is leaning back, a broad smile eternally carved onto his face.

And the children . . .

Nausea washes over me as I look upon them.

Two brothers are locked mid-play, fingers inches from each other. The younger boy rushes ahead, giggling as he glances back. A pastry lies in his hands, the elder brother's eyes ever fixed on it.

"Elaric . . ."

He reaches out, clasping my hand. For long moments we stand there in solemness, mourning the tragic fate of this innocent family.

Then anger burns within me. So fierce it scalds my heart.

"They did nothing wrong," I seethe, "and yet here they stand in icy graves. For three hundred years."

Elaric lets out a sigh, a note of regret tinging the sound. As if it's his fault. But Isidore is the one responsible for the fate of this family.

Unless perhaps he is thinking of the Crystal Palace, where over three hundred girls dwell in similar prisons. I want to tell him that his situation is completely different, that he was seeking his Summer Queen to break the curse. Whereas Isidore had no noble reasons to freeze this kingdom. This is just senseless cruelty.

I grit my teeth and turn to Elaric, determination flooding through me. "We have to succeed. For them, for Dalia. And for you."

"I know," Elaric mutters back, his attention remaining on the frozen family.

"We need a plan." I peel my fingers from his and pace across the creaking floorboards as I think. "A way to gain the upper hand."

"An ambush," Elaric says. "Though that will be difficult now she's alerted to our presence. Our best choice would be to wait long enough for her to think we've left, that perhaps our courage has run out and—"

"*Your* courage," I say quietly, the realization striking me.

Elaric frowns in confusion.

"She knows you are here, but not that I am. Perhaps she doesn't even know you've found your Summer Queen. Maybe she believes after three centuries of misery, of being unable to break your curse, you've come to beg for mercy."

Elaric scratches his chin. "If you remain hidden, I could openly approach Isidore, feigning defeat. With her guard lowered, believing I came alone, you could strike her with the sword before she detects you."

I nod, scanning our surroundings. "We need to choose somewhere with enough cover for me to hide, or else we'll lose the element of surprise."

"If we make our stand here, she may refuse to enter and force me to confront her outside."

"And if you won't leave the hut," I say, "she might decide to collapse the roof on us and force us out."

"For that reason, it would be best to avoid battling her indoors. We'll have to find somewhere outside."

My eyes shift over to the window, and the shadowy trees beyond. Though a part of me is tempted to stay here and recover from the exhaustion of tonight, this is the only building for miles. If Isidore knows of its existence, she is certain to search here—making all our plans redundant. We can't linger.

With a heavy sigh, I turn back to Elaric. "Then it seems we've no choice but to keep moving until we find somewhere suitable to lure her out. And pray she doesn't find us first."

Chapter 35

We depart from the cottage, continuing through the rest of the forest. With the trees already thinning, I'm far from surprised when they soon end, exposing us to frozen plains.

Now freed from the forest, the impressive mountain range towers before us, its peaks scraping the clouds. And there, tracing the soaring ridges, I spy the castle Elaric glimpsed during our flight here. The castle Isidore has likely claimed as her stronghold.

"We should stick to the shadows as best we can," I say, seizing Elaric's arm and steering us into the shelter of the cliffs. Though the moonlight still finds us, the rocks provide some cover. With the bare land surrounding us, I see no other option to mask our approach.

As we venture upward, the wind intensifies, slamming into us with violent gusts that threaten to throw us off our feet. The snow deepens until it climbs halfway up my calves, crusting thick around my legs. It swirls so dense it obscures the path ahead.

We squint against the blinding terrain, struggling to watch our step as we trudge on.

I tilt back my head, examining the brightening sky. How many hours remain before the sun breaches the peaks and strips all cover of darkness? We need to secure our position before then, somewhere suitable for me to ambush Isidore. But miles of endless snow and sheer mountains offer nowhere promising.

"Adara," Elaric says, stopping abruptly and pointing in the distance. "There seems to be buildings ahead."

I shift my focus toward where he's gesturing. At first, a blur of white disrupts my vision, sleet whirling in the gale. I blink hard, waiting for my eyes to adjust.

Then forms materialize: faint silhouettes of buildings etched into the horizon.

"There are so many roofs," I whisper back, partly in fear that speaking too loudly will cause Isidore to hear us through the flakes blowing around us. "Could it be a town? A city?"

"Perhaps," Elaric says. "Let's take a closer look."

We press on, clinging to the shadows at the mountain's base. Though the city glimmers closer with each step, it stays wrapped in haze.

I scan the sprawling plains, searching for somewhere to grant us cover while we survey the settlement ahead.

Finally, my gaze snags on an enormous rock half-buried in the tundra.

"Over there," I say, pointing toward it. "We can examine the city from behind the boulder."

We abandon the cliffs' dwindling shelter, slogging across the open terrain as we make our way toward the rock.

Snow snatches at our limbs as if to delay us. Wind pummels us relentlessly. Still, we strain against the forces, even as my lungs burn with effort.

At last we collapse behind the boulder. The translucent surface provides meager shelter but out here, it's the only shield we have from the castle high above.

Holding my breath, I peer around the boulder to scan across the city.

Formidable walls hem the city on all sides, melding with the mountain itself. A grand archway stands sentry at the front, marking the main gate, while a smaller entrance lies along the left wall. I suspect there's another on the right as well, though our current vantage denies us even a glimpse of it.

Paths perhaps once approached all three gates but are now long buried. The only traces left of their existence are the rows of scattered lanterns leading up to the city.

"It would be better if we confront Isidore inside the city," I say, "rather than out here in the open."

"Indeed," Elaric replies, "though entering it may prove problematic. We're still a fair distance from the city and traveling through either the main or left gates risks exposing us."

Grimly, I nod my agreement. Entering via the main gate will force us through open snow. While the left gate is closer to the cliffs and offers slightly more cover, there's still a fair portion of the journey uncovered.

Neither path looks ideal. Though I try to get a better look at the right side, nothing suggests it'll be any less exposed than the other two gates.

"Maybe we could follow the cliffs all the way to the walls," I suggest, "and avoid the gates altogether. We could use the sword to carve our own entrance into the city."

"Through the walls?" Elaric asks, a brow rising.

"The blade sliced through the sea serpent's scales with ease. Icy walls shouldn't prove much more of a challenge for it."

Elaric considers my suggestion briefly before shaking his head. "The walls are bound with Isidore's power. She would sense the sword the instant it breached her magic."

I examine the city again, but I can see no way through other than the gates. The walls are too tall to climb, and while snow blankets the city's exterior, it's impossible to know what lies beneath on the other side. Should we fall, we may slam into solid ground.

"Then it'll have to be the left entrance," I say. "Let's hope Isidore's attention lies elsewhere for now."

Without further delay, Elaric seizes the sack and bolts from behind the boulder into the gaping white maw. I scramble after him, the brief yet harrowing sprint back toward the cliffs leaving us dangerously revealed.

Despite his longer strides, Elaric is careful to maintain his pace so as not to abandon me as I flounder through the deep snow. Still, the effort of hurrying after him soon overwhelms me.

Finally, we reach the cliffs once more.

My chest heaves as I double over, bracing my palms on my knees and fighting to regain breath. Elaric pauses beside me, face creased in concern as he surveys my ragged state.

Trepidation sinks into my gut as I envision the longer, more hazardous journey toward the city gates. One glance from the stronghold above, and we'll lose the element of surprise.

"Are you all right?" Elaric asks.

"I'm fine now," I rasp.

Elaric's dubious scrutiny sears into me. But he says nothing more before turning to press on.

We continue beneath the precarious shade of the cliffs, making haste toward the walls glittering in the distance. The waning moon creeps ever closer to the horizon. Before long, dawn will arrive, and then finding cover will be an even greater challenge beneath its brilliant rays.

I double my pace, and Elaric matches it without question. Snow sprays around us as we force our way through the heavy layers.

By the time we near the city walls, the darkness sheltering us has withered to slight wisps. A great expanse lies between where we stand beneath the cliffs and the gate ahead. We'll need to race across as quickly as we can.

Elaric halts. "Ready?"

"Ready," I gasp through the fire in my lungs.

He hurries out without further warning. I lurch after him into the dazzling moonlight, feeling dangerously exposed against the snow's glare.

As I trail his swift strides along the walls' perimeter, I try to align my footprints with his. If Isidore glances down and notices two paths, she'll realize Elaric didn't come here alone.

With every step, tension winds my shoulders tighter, fearing may Isidore appear any second. But as we reach the gate's imposing arch, only stillness greets us.

The street ahead is morphed into a graveyard of ice, people shackled in their last moments. Guards stand with weapons drawn, faces tilted to the sky in warning shouts. Townsfolk are suspended mid-flight toward the gates, their features distorted with fear, aware until the end of their horrifying fate.

Bile scalds my throat. At least the family we found in the forest seemed to be entirely ignorant of their impending doom. Not like these people.

"We must move quickly," Elaric says. His voice is low, as if to avoid disturbing the frozen statues around us. When I drive this sword through Isidore's chest, they will all become flesh and blood again.

I clench my fists. No matter what, I will free them.

Faint lines etch Elaric's brow as he continues, "While we're less visible here in the city than outside, we'll stand out amid all the frost."

"Then it'll be best to keep to the alleyways as much as we can."

We plunge past the gates into the city, and the knot in my stomach twists more with every face we pass. At first, I keep my eyes on my feet, unable to bear their anguish. But with the carts, horses, and people obstructing our path, I'm soon forced to lift my gaze. The only way I can endure looking at them all is by uttering silent promises as I weave past, vowing to release them from Isidore's spell.

Failure is not an option. Too many lives depend on our success.

Elaric turns a corner, leading us into a narrow side street. Here, with the buildings pressed so close together, the risk of being discovered from above is greatly reduced. But our pace slows considerably as we pick our way through a cluster of statues, their limbs outstretched toward escape.

The alleyway opens to a large market square, stalls laden with crystal wares: glistening meats, breads, fruits. More citizens are stuck in eternal hysteria, some pointing at the towering castle, others cowering behind the barrels and cart which failed to save them.

Elaric stops before leaving the safety of the alleyway. His gaze drifts over the square, assessing the frozen chaos beyond. "Perhaps we should make our stand here?"

While the market square is more exposed than the alleys, these narrow streets are too cramped to battle Isidore.

"So far, I haven't seen anywhere better," I say. "And there should be places for me to hide."

Elaric gives a tight nod. "Here it is then."

With that, he marches on, shoulders tensed as if already readying himself for the confrontation ahead.

He makes for a tavern, its open doorway swathed in darkness. A disheveled stall lies a few yards away, along with an overturned cart and heaps of crates. With plenty of cover provided here, no other spot in the whole square is more perfect.

Once we both stand in the tavern's doorway, I turn to Elaric and say, "I'll wait here for you to draw her out. Keep her talking, preferably with her back to the tavern, and when I'm within striking distance—"

"Adara." He cups my face with both hands. While the gesture is sudden, his thumbs are gentle as they trace my cheeks. "It isn't too late to change your mind."

I drop my eyes, afraid meeting his will cause me to agree. "We're already here."

"I can fly us back."

"Isidore will see us."

"We would be in the clouds long before she realizes."

I shake my head. "We can't."

"I can't bear to lose you." Upon hearing the agony in his voice, a part of me longs to concede.

"This is bigger than you and me," I say, gathering my strength. "It's bigger than Dalia, and all the other girls in your palace. Yes, we could return home and there's a chance we could break the curse as it was meant to be broken, even if it takes years. But look at this city. True love might save you—it might save Dalia—but it won't save these people. How can I turn my back on them, knowing that they'll stay like this for eternity? Knowing that driving this sword through Isidore will save everyone?"

He sighs and presses his lips to my forehead. "Though I wish so dearly for you to reconsider," he murmurs, "you wouldn't possess my heart if you were not my maddeningly stubborn Adara."

"I'm sorry," I whisper.

"Don't be." He releases my face, thumb trailing across my lower lip.

Then his mouth is on mine and he's kissing me with such desperation it hurts. I can't help but kiss him back with the same fervor.

Even when he pulls away and stares down at me, I still feel his lips burning against mine.

"I love you, Adara," he says, knitting his fingers through mine and pressing my hand to his chest. "And though this is not the path I would choose for you, I will not stand in the way of what you believe."

I know it is not his intention to break me, but he comes so remarkably close that I'm forced to bite back the tears which threaten to fall.

I refuse to believe we will be anything but victorious. Nor will I invite fear by uttering a farewell.

Over and over, I repeat that mantra, until those tears release their cruel hold on me.

Then I raise my chin, mustering every shred of courage as I declare, "We will return to the palace together."

He gives the slightest of nods before releasing my hand. As he withdraws, his eyes darken.

I don't let his expression shake me. Fear will only prove a liability in the battle to come.

With a deep breath, he strides down the tavern's steps. Every step echoes across the deathly silent market square, chipping away at my resolve.

How tempting it is to call him back, to return to Avella and abandon all we have strived for. Even if it means never freeing Dalia and all these people here.

But I have lived a selfish life for too many years, concerning myself with hatred and revenge, and it is time I made amends. I will face this danger head-on. If we fail, at least I will die with bravery rather than cowardice in my heart.

Elaric reaches the square's center several yards away. There he turns, eyes finding mine, though shadows shroud his view. His longing gaze implores me to reconsider one last time.

Yet I stand fast as he pulls the glass vial from his tunic. As he pops the cork and lets it clatter to the street. As he tips the liquid down his throat in one smooth motion, eyes clenching tight. He waits, hopes, even now that I will call this off.

Only when certain of my unspoken response does he open his eyes. They linger on my hidden form a breath longer before wrenching away.

Jaw hardening, he looks up at the distant castle. Then swallows hard and shouts, "Isidore, I demand an audience at once!"

Chapter 36

Elaric's shout reverberates through the market square.

My pulse hammers, and I sink deeper into the shadows, spine rigid against the wall behind me.

Spotting a slight gap in the masonry, I press my eye to it. Beyond, I glimpse Elaric standing alone among the hordes of glittering statues.

While the thunderous pounding of my heart steadies, the fire coursing through my veins burns fiercer.

I turn my eyes upward, though my restricted viewpoint prevents me from glimpsing the stronghold's distant spires.

When Isidore shows no sign of emerging, Elaric raises his hands and conjures a gust of ice.

The blast slams into a building across the square, ringing through the city. The structure trembles so violently I fear the roof will collapse, smashing anyone within into tiny crystalline fragments. But the quaking ceases, leaving an uneasy stillness in its wake.

Isidore could not have missed such a powerful display of magic. No matter where she may be, whether she lurks in her castle or is currently searching the isle for us, the blast is certain to have seized her attention.

Dread rolls through me.

"Isidore," Elaric shouts again. "I demand to speak—"

He cuts off, looking up.

My limited view doesn't allow me to see much of the sky, and I don't dare leave my hiding place to look. Yet I know what he must be witnessing right now. Only one thing would have caused him to cut off.

Isidore herself.

Though I press further into the wall, it does little to improve my vision. My palms dig in harder, skin blanching as the blood drains from them.

In the next instant, I hear the beating of wings. But not from any crow. This rhythm is akin to one of Elaric's own winged steeds.

I clutch the hilt of my sword, every muscle in my body stiffening.

At long last, Isidore becomes visible through the gap in the wall. Air shudders around her as her steed descends to the square. Silken robes billow around her like a storm, as does her mane of silver hair.

As she lands, she pays no heed to the folk around her, disturbing two statues. One trembles, barely righting itself. The other topples to the ground, shattering against the cobblestones with the macabre sound of death.

I didn't get a good look of the statue before they fell. I don't know whether they were a man or a woman, whether they were young or old. But I do know that even if we slay Isidore, their heart will never beat again. They are lost to this world, and when the curse surrounding Eruweth fades, they will be dearly missed by whomever they have left behind.

Regret wracks through me. This is the consequence of choosing such a busy part of the city. I squeeze my eyes shut, reminding myself that we had limited choices on where to confront Isidore. This is the only way we can save this kingdom and the thousands of people ensnared in this wicked spell.

All concern for the shattered statue vanishes as Isidore dismounts, and I get a closer look at her. While I imagined her to be ancient like Belinda, her flawless features suggest she must be in her mid-thirties.

Though this witch appears breathtakingly beautiful, she is also terrifying, especially as her gaze finds Elaric and her lips curl into an ugly smirk. No amount of beauty can compensate for the cruelty carved into her expression. Nor does it dampen the frightening power which effuses from her. Even tucked away behind the tavern's door, I can't help but shiver.

"You," Isidore hisses. Every hair on the nape of my neck bristles. "You dare trespass in my domain?" Her whisper is faint against the brewing storm.

While I flinch inwardly, Elaric remains composed before her glare. "It has been three centuries."

"Three centuries do not erase what you stole from me," she snarls, bitterness laced within. I know the pain coursing through her too well—the same agony which festered within me for three long years.

But while I may understand her pain, we are not the same. All this started because her sister sought to destroy Avella with her flames, whereas Dalia was innocent. I pursued Elaric's blood, never the citizens of our kingdom. This cycle of hatred originates from Isidore's magic, from her seeking to lessen her own pain by inflicting it upon Elaric.

Now only her death can end it.

"You are a fool if you came here to beg me to release you from your curse," Isidore says, sneering. "The magic binding you is tied to the land itself, and even I do not possess the ability to release you from it. Although there is nothing in this world which could convince me to do that."

"I did not come here for myself," Elaric says, "but for my people. They too suffer from this power. How can I rule a kingdom when I can scarcely meet my council without freezing them all in their seats?"

A grating laugh escapes Isidore, like the scrape of a blade over glass. "Then renounce your crown and allow another to rule in your stead. Have these centuries failed to instruct you in the lesson of humility?"

My attention flickers between Elaric and Isidore. I must move as soon as I can, or else when an opportunity to strike arises, I won't be close enough. But right now, it's far too risky. Isidore is partly turned away from me, and there's a chance she will notice my movement. One wrong move will doom our entire plan. I must wait until she's more distracted.

"Humility?" Elaric repeats, arms sweeping around the market square. "You dare lecture me on the virtue of humility when you have seized this kingdom as your own?"

"The two of us are not alike." She raises her head, nose creasing as she looks down at him. "Humility is the place of a human, not a witch."

Silence falls. Their gazes lock, neither yielding an inch of ground.

Finally, Elaric says, "I will not continue like this."

"You speak as if you have a choice." She scoffs, shaking her head. "Your only salvation from this curse is death. But perhaps that is why you came here."

Elaric clenches his fists.

A cruel smile carves onto her lips. "After spending all these years searching for your Summer Queen, you could not find her, no matter how many young women you stole away. Perhaps your palace has turned into the streets of Eruweth City, serving as a permanent reminder of the curse flowing through your veins. Of the monster you have become."

Blood roars louder in my ears. Isidore is utterly without remorse for those she hurts. She relishes in their misery. This woman embodies wickedness through and through, and it's all I can do not to rush from my hiding place and drive my sword through her chest. To wipe her existence from this world.

But I can't act on my hatred. Doing so will unravel all our plans. I must control my emotions and use them as a source of strength rather than a weakness.

"I see the self-loathing behind your eyes," Isidore says, her musical voice dripping with malice, "and the longing to end this nightmare. Fate may tarry three centuries more before she deigns to send your precious Summer Queen. Such a bleak reality must burden you day after day."

I exhale slowly, smothering my fury with a blanket of calm.

Isidore tilts her head, studying Elaric's stoic expression with amusement. "Have you perhaps put a blade to your heart before,

I wonder? Desperate for the respite which has escaped you for so long?"

Revulsion almost shatters my resolve. Yet Elaric reveals nothing, steadfast as granite beneath her relentless taunts.

"Though I wish to prolong your torment for centuries more," Isidore muses, "I fear you may seek some tender-hearted witch and beg her to release you swiftly from your curse."

Still, Elaric does not respond. He cannot deny her words. Doing so risks her suspecting his true motives in coming here.

"Have you nothing to say?" Isidore rolls back her delicate shoulders and sighs. "Very well. Death it shall be."

Chapter 37

Isidore raises her hand, and the earth shudders as razor-sharp icicles burst from the ground, their deadly points glinting in the moonlight.

Elaric leaps back just in time to avoid being impaled. No sooner than he lands does a quick blast surge from his palm, which Isidore deflects with a bolt of her own.

I need to move. Now. The two of them exchanging blows is the greatest distraction I'll get. And I must act before Elaric is hurt. Isidore wields far greater power, and I don't know how long his magic can withstand hers.

As Isidore summons a swarm of blades to rain upon Elaric, I bolt from my hiding place, rushing down the stairs in a low crouch. Hoping the surrounding chaos cloaks my movements. Though centered on Elaric, a few shards detonate farther out, one narrowly missing me.

I twist my shoulder away. The bolt skims so close I feel its deadly kiss.

Just as I'm sliding underneath the nearby stall, another shard plummets toward me. This time I'm a second too slow.

I fail to yank my arm to safety before the shard slices through cotton and flesh alike. It clatters onto the cobblestones, leaving my forearm oozing blood.

Pain blazes through my arm, and I clench my teeth to bite back a cry. The blood coating that shard could alert Isidore. And I can only hope she doesn't spot it before I strike.

The blizzard rages on. Elaric maintains his shield while shards pile around him. Several slam against my stall with such force I fear it'll collapse and expose me. I grip my sword, angling the hilt away from Isidore's sight to hide its gleam amid the darkness.

The storm ceases.

Elaric releases his shield, and the square descends into an uneasy quiet.

It doesn't last long before Isidore shatters it. "You still resist me? Perhaps death is not what you seek after all."

"The only death I seek is yours," Elaric says, tone glacial.

A shrill laugh escapes her lips. "Through what means? Your magic is but a fraction of mine. You may wield winter, but I *am* winter." With effortless grace, she flicks her wrist, loosing a volley of conjured arrows.

Though Isidore's expression remains impassive, the shield Elaric conjures requires more effort than before, evident from his furrowed brow and strained temples. His spell also forms slower than hers. When it finally manifests, it does so a second too late.

An arrow slams into his shoulder just before his shield can cover it. The blow causes him to stagger, but his shield stays intact.

With wicked delight twisting her lips, Isidore unleashes a second, far stronger volley. Elaric struggles to hold his shield, jaw straining against effort and pain. It just manages to stand until her assault stops. Then he forces himself upright and flings the shield's remnants at her—a hasty attack.

Though it comes quick enough to surprise me, Isidore blocks it easily with her power, barely sparing a thought.

She stalks toward Elaric, closing the distance between them. Her eyes shine brighter with every step, fixing upon the wound in his shoulder.

Ice writhes up from the ground at Isidore's command, slithering toward Elaric.

He conjures a blade to parry the first chain, fracturing off a few shards before it recoils. A second chain rises, attacking from the other side. The clash and clatter echoes through the markets square as he fends off both.

I slide from under the stall's drape and scramble to a cart ahead, pressing low against its planked side. After a moment, I dare to glimpse around the edge.

Isidore is focused on Elaric, seeking to ensnare him with her serpentine chains. He's summoned a globe now, and it seems to provide better protection than a blade. Fortunately for me, his efforts make Isidore concentrate harder on overcoming him.

At last she halts her assault, realizing Elaric isn't yet weakened enough for capture. She lets the chains dissolve into glittering dust, and then with a flick of her wrist, unleashes another volley at Elaric.

I seize my chance to strike.

Sword raised, I charge from behind the cart, praying the clash of Isidore's attack against Elaric's shield will mask my footsteps.

As I race toward her, I become wind and rain rather than flesh and bone. For those heartbeats I am no longer merely mortal but transformed into something far greater—something without a trace of fear flowing through her veins.

My blade bears down on Isidore. I'm certain it will strike its mark, piercing her back.

But the city falls silent, and she turns. Shock transforms her ethereal face to something far more human. My sword sinks in—

Into ice.

It slices through as if parting sand, gliding effortlessly. Yet the shield has granted Isidore an extra instant between herself and the blade, allowing her to twist away so it doesn't pierce her chest.

Instead, my sword slashes through her arm, spilling blood. But no crimson stains the ground. Her blood gleams indigo, so deep a shade it resembles polished onyx within the shadows.

Isidore's pained hiss brings no satisfaction, just sinking dread. The transcendent strength rapidly draining from my limbs reminds me how mortal I really am. Fear coils through my veins, constricts my thundering heart.

I have failed.

Isidore's bright eyes narrow, flicking between me and the sword I clutch. "The Sword of Veliantis," she seethes, eyeing the ruby-laden hilt. Her gaze shifts to Elaric, burning with a molten fury so unlike her power. "The weapon you used to murder my sister."

"Your sister murdered my father and people," Elaric says evenly. "Her death was deserved, and I would choose the same again."

A snarl twists Isidore's face. "A thousand mortal lives cannot equal one witch's."

She throws her arms wide. A whirlwind of hail spins around her, driving Elaric and me back.

I shield my face from the shards.

The storm swirls faster, obscuring Isidore's form. If she directs such power toward us, we'll be doomed.

"Elaric!" I shout.

He stretches a wall around us, thickening into a globe. The shield completes just as Isidore's blizzard erupts.

I brace for impact, fearing Elaric's magic won't withstand her attack. But my worry proves unfounded. While hail glances off our shelter, the blows lack significant force.

From the whirling snow a formidable shape rises—a silhouette akin to the sea serpent we battled on Eruweth's shore, but thrice the size. Twisted horns and sprawling wings adorn the creature.

A dragon.

My lungs empty. Defeating Isidore in her mortal form seemed impossible. But battling a dragon . . .

I turn to Elaric, unable to hide my fear.

"Her sister also assumed a dragon form when I fought her." He straightens, voice hardening with resolve. "I had to drive the blade through the beast's heart."

I glance between the jeweled sword and the hulking beast looming over us. My gaze trails down to its talons which gouge craters in the cobblestones.

"How did you get close enough?" I ask, mouth drying with trepidation.

"I had a thousand men at my side. And still, it was through sheer luck that the beast didn't incinerate me during the attempt."

Since we have no army, I'll have to draw near and pray fortune graces me as it did Elaric centuries ago.

I tighten my grip on the hilt.

The dragon beats her mighty wings. If not for Elaric's shield, we'd be flung to the ground. Statues topple, smashing into thousands of shards. As does the stall behind us.

Though the dragon's maw doesn't move, Isidore's voice bellows across the square: "Allow me to show you the true difference in our power."

Her nostrils flare, inhaling deeply. Readying her attack.

Elaric shuts his eyes, reinforcing our shield. Through it, I glimpse the dragon's jaw unhinging, hurling a barrage of frost at us.

The volley slams into the barrier. One punctures through, and I duck just in time to avoid it. The rest of our shield shatters apart.

Elaric seizes my arm, towing us behind a nearby cart scant seconds before another blast devours our former position. We double over, sheltering heads and necks lest any needles pierce our new cover.

An irritated snort rumbles through the square. The earth trembles as the dragon stalks toward us.

We bolt up and sprint for the inn ahead.

Seeking shelter in a building that those jaws could crush might be foolish, but what choice do we have? Right now, we can't fight her or flee quickly enough. Even if Elaric conjured a winged steed, we'd never outrace her through the sky.

Isidore lunges, seizing the cart in her massive claws. Another instant, and we'd have been caught with it.

Boards crack and splinter beneath her might, raining on us as we run.

A large plank crashes onto the tavern's steps, blocking our escape. With Isidore mere paces behind, we've no time to clear it or find another path.

"Elaric!" I shout, seizing one end with my free hand. Together, we heave aside the frozen wood.

I glance back, expecting to see fangs snapping for us. Instead, tremendous wings beat, their force nearly toppling us off the stairs.

Isidore takes to the air, her terrifying form eclipsing the moon. But she soars only briefly before angling back, plummeting toward the inn itself.

We scramble clear mere yards away from the collision.

The entire building collapses beneath the dragon's might. We sprint on through the barrage of debris now pelting our backs.

Ahead lies a gap between the buildings, leading to an alley. Perhaps we can lose Isidore in the side streets? Even if she searches from above, the cluster of roofs should hide us. And with Irremisa masking Elaric's presence, we could run halfway across the city before she spots us. Granting us enough time to summon a steed for our escape.

But my blooming hope is crushed as Isidore's tail lashes across the street. It pulverizes the cobblestones, cutting off our path.

The ground heaves with a quake so fierce it splits open in a yawning crevice.

I stumble. As does Elaric. The hilt of my blade slips through my fingers, just as the ground tilts downward.

I lunge, trying to catch it before it's lost.

But the sword slides too quickly.

I dive forward. My fingers close around the sword, right before it tumbles into the chasm. So much momentum propels me that stopping is impossible. I narrowly slow in time, but then my foot slips over the edge.

And I fall.

Chapter 38

"Adara!" Elaric shouts. Through the wind's deafening roar, his voice sounds distant.

I glance up, suspended on a ledge jutting out from the smooth chasm wall. My fingers ache from supporting my full weight. I grit my teeth, unsure how long I can hold on.

"Adara!" he calls again. This time his face appears above, gaze frantically scanning the darkness until he spots me clinging halfway down the abyss.

My hand starts to slip, jolting my heart. I tighten my grip with a pained hiss. But no matter how hard I try, exhaustion seeps through me. My strength is swiftly waning.

Elaric takes in my precarious position. He stretches down, leaning out over the edge. Even with his considerable reach, his fingertips hover inches shy of my own.

As he meets my eyes, his jaw sets. "I've got you," he vows.

I stare up at his hand, which is so close yet infinitely far. My only chance at reaching him is releasing my hold on the sword.

But without it, how will we defeat Isidore? Or perhaps that no longer matters. Perhaps only fleeing matters now.

Before I can decide my next move, a violent gust slams into Elaric.

Crouched dangerously over the ledge, the blast catches him off guard. He disappears from my view, without so much as a cry. I wince at the resounding crash from above. It's only a slight relief he didn't plummet into the chasm with me.

"Elaric!" My shout is drowned out by the echoing debris. I pray the chaos comes from the gale's aftermath and from not his body smashing into a solid wall.

With only numb fingers clinging to the ledge, I should worry about my own predicament. Yet Elaric consumes my thoughts.

"Elaric!" I try again.

Silence falls.

Then comes the beating of wings, sweeping overhead toward the direction Elaric disappeared.

Isidore.

I glance at the sword in my hand. Without it, Elaric doesn't stand a chance against her. I have to pull myself out of this pit before it's too late.

I scan the wall above, looking for any grip. Most of the surface is smooth, but jagged edges protrude in some places. If I had a free hand, I might manage to reach one. But if I release the Sword of Veliantis and Isidore captures Elaric . . .

My gut twists at the impossible choice. I clutch harder to the wall, racking my mind for a solution.

There has to be another way.

I examine my body, searching for somewhere to secure the sword. But with no belt or sheath, my only option is wedging it between my knees and praying it doesn't slip free.

Carefully, I reach down, moving slowly as to not disrupt my delicate balance. I tilt my legs up and wedge the sword's flat edge firmly between my knees. I squeeze with all my might, clenching every muscle. The sword must not fall.

I stare up at the smooth wall rising before me. I'm still countless yards from the top. Scaling it would prove a great challenge even with both feet to support me. Yet to save Elaric, to end this nightmare, I have no choice but to haul myself up with my arms alone.

I spot a jagged outcrop above which offers grip. I reach up and pause as my hand closes around it, allowing my other arm a brief respite.

But I mustn't delay. Right now, Elaric may be at Isidore's mercy.

Bracing myself, I resume climbing. Every muscle—arms, back, shoulders—burns. I dare not make any jerky movements that could dislodge the sword. I squeeze my knees tighter together and pull myself up another precious inch.

Bit by agonizing bit, I scale the cliff with my hands alone, summoning every scrap of strength.

When I near the top, I shove the sword onto the ledge above. And then, with both hands, I shakily haul myself over.

Once on solid ground, I collapse onto my back, chest heaving as delayed exhaustion crashes into me.

I push myself to a sitting position, scanning across the square. Isidore stands on the other side of the chasm, surrounded by a dissipating flurry of hail.

Her wings and horns fade away as she shrinks back into her mortal form.

A few paces before her lies Elaric. Icy debris pins his legs. From here, I can just make out the crimson streak trailing from his temple. He barely stirs. I'm not sure if he's conscious.

Isidore must assume the sword and I plunged into the depths. An opportunity—if I can cross this chasm and catch her unaware again. Last time I failed, but with Elaric so gravely injured, surprise is his only chance of survival.

Swaying, I stagger to my feet. I need to reach him before Isidore can hurt him any more.

I quickly survey the area, searching for a way across. About two yards from where I sit, the chasm narrows. If I get a running start, I could leap far enough to make it.

This plan will have to do. I can see no better option.

Isidore stalks toward Elaric's unmoving form.

Clutching the sword, I rush toward the narrower part. Isidore hisses something to Elaric, but I'm too distant to hear.

With a deep breath, I break into a sprint and hurl myself over the gap with everything I have.

For a heart-stopping moment, I fear that I haven't jumped with enough power. That I'll land inches short of the ledge.

But then my feet hit solid ground. I release my held breath.

The relief lasts just a split second. I look up to see Isidore raising her hands, magic coalescing. The murderous glint in her eyes chills every bone within me.

She means to strike the final blow.

Rage clouds my vision. Subtlety and stealth vanish. All I see is a fatal blast hurtling toward Elaric's lifeless form.

There isn't an ounce of hesitation within me as I charge, sword first.

I'm only a yard away as a spear launches from Isidore's hands. Oblivious in her murderous rage, her focus stays solely on Elaric.

I lunge forward.

My blade sinks deep into her back before she realizes I'm there.

This time, she does not turn. Does not defend herself. My sword sinks through all the way.

Inky blood spills everywhere. On my blade, on my hands. It even splatters onto my cheeks.

Only when my sword has found its mark, the crystals in the hilt thrumming with power, does Isidore whirl with an agonized shriek.

The force of her movement wrenches the blade from my slick, bloodied grip.

She lunges, talons swiping. I dodge left, but unneeded. She crashes to her knees, white satin dress flooding with dark blood.

My strike pierced her heart. The sword now protrudes hideously from her chest.

"You—" She chokes, struggling to speak.

A hacking cough of blood cuts her off. She opens her mouth, and I brace myself, waiting for her to launch another blast at me.

But then her body pitches forward. The tip of my blade clinks against the cobblestones. Her fingers twitch, grasping at nothing.

I stand tense, panting, waiting for her to rise.

She does not.

My pulse hammers as realization sinks in.

It's over.

Isidore is dead.

I stand there stunned, hardly believing Isidore lies dead at my feet. Part of me expects her to rise again and shatter the illusion.

But ice recedes, the tree opposite me returning to bark and leaf. The color in the market stall banners slowly reappears, and the clothes of those gathered around me also brighten.

Isidore's curse upon this land is fading.

Elaric . . .

I swivel around, remembering the blood tracing his forehead, the attack hurtling for him.

My worst fear is realized. I succeeded in killing Isidore, but it was already too late.

"Elaric!"

As I reach him I crash to my knees, heedless of pain. My hands grip his shoulders, vision blurring.

Isidore's spear has left a horrifying wound in his chest. Crimson stains his tunic.

"Elaric!" A ragged sob chokes from my throat. I want to shake him conscious but fear I'll cause further injury.

To my relief, he stirs with a mumble. "Adara . . .?"

"I'm here," I breathe, tremors shuddering through my body as I cradle his head in my lap. "I'm here."

I trace the blood trailing from his temple, reassuring myself that at least for now, he remains with me.

"I've got you," I vow.

His hand finds mine, grip feeble. "Adara . . . "

My name on his lips sounds terribly faint. I tell myself it's my pounding pulse which distorts his voice. He sounds weaker only in my imagination, not reality.

I weave my fingers through his hair, clinging desperately to him. "You're going to be all right."

"Of course . . . " he wheezes. Yet then he chokes, blood bubbling on his lips.

My futile hope dies at the sight.

When he continues, his voice echoes as if from the bottom of a deep well. "How could I not . . . when with you?"

Pain crashes into me, blinding in its intensity. I want to deny it, but the truth is unavoidable: the fatal gash in his chest, the growing limpness of his hand in mine.

I clutch him tighter, irrationally trying to tether him here through my will alone. But with each faltering breath, he slips further away.

I vaguely register the stirring kingdom around me, the people fleeing or gazing around in confusion as they stir from their three-hundred-year sleep.

"Please!" I cry out to the scattering crowd.

But no one stops to listen, and I can't bear to release Elaric to catch their attention.

"Healer!" I gasp. "He needs a healer!"

This time, my pleas are met with a response.

Behind me, a hoarse voice calls out, "No healer can save him now, my dear."

Chapter 39

I glance up to see Belinda emerging from the tree on the square's perimeter. Emerald magic envelops the thawed trunk behind her. In the chaotic square, no one else notices her arrival.

"Please," I beg, not caring how pathetic I sound. I'll do anything to save Elaric. No price is too steep. "You must have a potion or spell. Anything!"

Agony tears through me as Belinda shakes her head. "It is too late."

"It's not!" I press my fingers to Elaric's neck, seeking a pulse. It flutters under my touch. "He lives! You can save him. I'll give you anything—name your price!"

Belinda paces to Isidore's corpse, eyeing the golden sword protruding from her back. "You have nothing left to offer, girl. And no potion can save one so close to death." With a nauseating squelch, she withdraws the blood-slicked blade.

"Why?" I grip Elaric's hand. "The curse is lifting. Why isn't he freed?"

Dread constricts around my heart. Is it because her blow struck first?

With a cackle, Belinda raises the sword. Indigo drops splatter across the ground, the jeweled hilt blazing.

"Foolish girl," she sneers. "Eruweth's curse is lifting because the spell was tied to her life. Such an incantation is appropriate for enchanting a place, not a person."

"Then—"

Belinda's grin sharpens. "Killing a witch only breaks the curses linked to her life. Your kingling's curse was never tied to Isidore, but to you."

Her words land like a crushing blow.

We should have returned to the Crystal Palace. We shouldn't have faced Isidore. Maybe the curse would never have lifted, but at least we'd be together.

Now he's dying, and there's nothing I can do to save him.

"You tricked us!" I snarl, fury bursting from my grief. "You lied that her death would free him!"

"I never lied," Belinda retorts, eyes glinting. "I did not state slaying her would break his curse. You merely assumed such a thing."

Fury, so much fury, pounds through me—at Belinda, at myself. Without thinking, I lunge for her. Weaponless, magicless, driven only by blind rage and pain.

I make it only two steps before magic erupts around the witch. Cries sound from the townspeople, but Belinda ignores them.

She raises the Sword of Veliantis higher, a ribbon of blue spilling from its rubies. She inhales deeply, eyes alight with ravenous hunger. The stream rushes into her nostrils, disappearing entirely.

The cloud surrounding her flares blue—the same shade as Elaric and Isidore's magic.

Frost spirals across the cobblestones, eliciting renewed panic from the crowd.

Belinda throws back her head with a screeching caw. She flicks her wrist, and a barrage of ice crashes into a fallen stall. The wood explodes into useless splinters.

"You used us," I hiss. "Used us for your own gain."

"You seemed more than happy to be used at the time," Belinda retorts. She raises her hand, letting green magic bloom. "Wood." She snaps her fingers, and the magic turns red. "Fire." Then it becomes blue. "And now ice, thanks to you."

Rage reignites, and I lunge, determined to exact my wrath. She manipulated us as puppets for her own ends.

Yet she raises her hands and conjures a wall of fire. I leap back to avoid being incinerated.

Screams sound as a man nearby is engulfed.

Through the writhing flames, Belinda grins. "Until next time, my dear."

I scream after her retreating form. But there's nothing I can do to quench her flames.

The tree from which she emerged reopens in a vortex of magic, and I watch in horror as Elaric's final chance vanishes.

My stomach turns to lead.

With Belinda now gone, her fire soon burns out, leaving swirling ash in its place. The creeping frost also melts away, erasing all evidence of her presence.

I race back to Elaric and pull him into my arms, gripping his face in shaking hands. "Elaric," I rasp, but no response comes.

I hold my hand under his nose, feeling just the slightest wisp of breath.

"We'll go home together," I gasp out. "Just hold on!" Even as I make such promises, I know he hangs by only a thin thread of life. I must find a healer.

His fingers twitch, seeking mine. The strength behind his grip is frighteningly feeble, but the small gesture kindles a fragile spark of hope.

"Adara," he murmurs.

"I'm here," I whisper. "I'm here."

But then his fingers slacken around mine, and I'm losing him.

I cling to him with all my might, yet I can't stop him from falling.

"Elaric!" I scream when he stops twitching. My whole world is awash with pain. Devoid of light. "Elaric!"

I cradle his head to my chest and rock back and forth, wishing I could stir him from this dream. But he doesn't move. No matter how many times I scream his name, he doesn't move.

"Don't leave me," I choke. "Please don't leave me. I can't lose you."

Everything around me ceases to exist until there's just me and Elaric's lifeless body.

He's gone.

Just as Belinda said, it was too late.

My hands tremble uncontrollably. My body quakes so violently it's as if my flesh itself will split apart.

"Please," I wail to the heavens, begging any god who will listen. "Please don't take him away!"

But only silence answers my prayers.

"Elaric," I rasp, white hot grief spilling down my cheeks. Wrenching through my soul. "I love you, Elaric. I love you so much. Come back. Please. Don't make me live this life without you."

A tear trickles from my cheek and lands upon his forehead. Then another. They hiss and fizz, spreading across all of him.

Before my very eyes, Elaric disintegrates.

"No!" I yell, clasping his shoulders. Refusing to let him go.

I press my fingers to his forehead, trying to prevent my tears from harming him any more than they already have.

But I can't contain the damage. The tears spread across his face, warping his features until they become unrecognizable. "No!"

A force rips him from my arms. I scream into the roaring wind, but it doesn't return him.

Thunder cracks.

I stumble back, slamming into the ground.

A gale rips through my hair, billowing around me so wildly I struggle to see what is happening.

Blue light bursts from Elaric, shattering and dissipating into dust. The surrounding maelstrom quickens, and then a feminine voice pierces the howling wind.

Wherever you go shall forever snow,
And all you hold will grow cold.
For eternity this spell will be,
'Less your Summer Queen thaws you free.

The chanting voice drones on, each syllable a deafening drumbeat.

Magic flows from Elaric's dissolving form, swirling around him as he's suspended in the vortex. I watch half in awe, half in dread.

Color floods his cheeks, more than I've ever seen on his alabaster face. Golden strands weave through his hair, consuming all silver.

And when he opens his eyes, it isn't blue eyes which look at me, but green.

As the strange magic lowers him down, I scramble up and race over on shaky legs, almost tripping over my own feet.

"Elaric! Elaric!" I cry.

I crash into him, wrapping my arms around him in the tightest embrace my arms can muster.

When my arms finally yield, numb from having squeezed him so hard, I place my palm against his chest and gaze up at him in disbelief. Though his tunic is torn and stained with blood, not a scratch lies upon his skin. "You're alive," I whisper, and clutch his tattered tunic, barely believing that he's here with me.

He takes my hand in his and threads his fingers through mine. Then he presses his lips to my forehead, and warmth rushes through me at his touch.

"Of course," he says, breath caressing the top of my hair. "Never will I leave you, my queen."

Chapter 40

Dawn pierces the sky with its crimson rays, as if the heavens have conjured flames to melt away all remnants of Isidore's magic from Eruweth.

With no sign of witchcraft remaining on the streets, the panic raging through the crowds dies down. Of course, there's still the deep chasm running through the market square and the countless demolished stalls and buildings, but the people begin to calm and instead question what has happened. I can only imagine what it must feel like to be fleeing from fatal danger in one moment and then in the next, awakening from a daze three hundred years later. How will they feel when they discover three centuries have passed in the blink of an eye?

His curse now broken, Elaric stands before me as flesh and blood, as entirely mortal as I am, and that means the magic imprisoning my sister must have also lifted.

"Home," I whisper. The word is quiet compared to the bustle of the confused city around us. "Let's go home."

Elaric exhales deeply and then is silent for a moment, scanning across the market square. "We'll need a ship," he says. "Since Eruweth is an island kingdom, there's bound to be a harbor nearby. If we're lucky, perhaps we'll find a ship there."

If Isidore left a vessel intact during her sacking of Eruweth, that is.

I keep my doubts to myself as I say, "Perhaps if we ask around, we might find someone who can tell us where the harbor is?"

We don't hesitate before swiveling around and hurrying toward the city gates, though the countless people flocking through the streets makes reaching them difficult.

We pass some citizens who are fleeing, fear plastered across their faces, while others stroll aimlessly down the streets, confusion glazing across their eyes, as if they are not yet entirely awake from their centuries-long sleep.

Elaric and I call out to several people, but neither the panicked nor the confused so much as look in our direction. It's as if the busyness of the city has rendered us invisible.

It isn't until we've almost reached the gates that an elderly woman stops at our shout.

Wrinkles weather her face, and her silver hair is scraped back into a green bonnet. She clutches the hand of a young girl who is drowned in heavy layers of petticoats and can be no older than six.

"Excuse me!" I call. "Can you help us?" I step forward, closing the distance between us. Elaric follows.

Her attention flickers between us and the street ahead, as if weighing up whether her business—whatever it is—can wait long enough to stop and talk to us. Finally she relents and says, "What is it?" The words are clipped, thinly veiling her impatience.

"The harbor," I blurt before she can change her mind. "Do you know where it is?"

She eyes us curiously, glancing across at our torn and dirty clothes. "You're not from around here, are you?"

I shake my head.

"And yet, you don't know where the harbor is?"

I squeeze my fists, hoping she won't ask how we arrived at an island kingdom without entering its harbor. We can't afford to linger and for people to ask questions. We must return home as soon as we can. Dalia will already be awakening, as will the three hundred other Summer Brides. I dread to think of the chaos which will be erupting through the Crystal Palace this very second.

Thankfully, the woman doesn't press us any further.

"The harbor is on the southern side of the island," she says, pointing to the city gates behind us. "Follow the main road out the city and through the forest. Before long, you'll reach cliffs, and the harbor lies at their base."

Elaric dips his head. "Thank you."

"If you seek to escape Eruweth," the old woman says, "every ship will already be full. I doubt they'll have space left for the two of you."

I press my lips together. Perhaps the woman is right. All ships may have long departed Eruweth or be too full to accommodate us. But we have few other options. Now Elaric has no magic, the only way for us to return to Avella is to sail home.

The old woman doesn't spare us another second before gripping the girl's hand and turning on her heel. She hurries down the street until they both disappear into the frenzied crowd.

When I look over at Elaric, his expression is as grim as I feel. Though we planned in great lengths how we would defeat Isidore, we hardly considered what would come after and how we'd return home. If we can't find a ship, I don't know what else we can do.

"Come on," he says, tearing me from my thoughts. "Standing around will do us no good."

I give him a quick nod, and we hasten toward the gates. But the closer we draw, the denser the crowd grows, and advancing further becomes a great struggle.

Since there are no guards by the city gates, the masses are free to spill into the thawed fields like water gushing out a broken dam.

We push past people and weave around them, cutting ahead, but it only gets us elbowed in the side several times. We have no choice but to proceed with everyone else, waiting until our turn to reach the gates.

"There they are!" a shout bursts from behind us.

I glance back, squinting at the crest of the hill which overlooks the gates.

Horror lances through my gut. It's a guard who shouted, pointing in our direction. Several more are gathered around him.

A muscle feathers in Elaric's jaw as he too whirls around and surveys the scene.

More guards cry out in alarm, their ranks quickly bolstering as others rally toward them.

My heart seizes. There are so many of them, and we're still so far from the gates. There's no chance of us reaching them before the guards descend upon us. And the citizens of Eruweth are more likely to part way for guards than they would for two disheveled strangers.

I hold my breath, praying I'm somehow mistaken. That the guards aren't really after us.

But then my foolish wish shatters as the guards charge forth, pushing through the crowd. They're solely focused on the two of us.

There's no time to talk, to devise a plan.

We just run.

We squeeze past everyone in our way, not caring who we are pushing and shoving, and this earns us countless annoyed shouts and ferocious glares. Blood rushes in my ears. The guards' shouts seem ever closer.

We break free from the crowd, and I stagger. Elaric steadies me before I fall.

"This way," he says, grabbing my wrist and pulling me down a side street. It's a slight relief there are fewer people than on the main roads.

Just before we turn the corner and disappear into the shadows, I dare to look over my shoulder.

By now, more guards have gathered. There's at least two dozen in total.

Throat tightening, I sprint after Elaric as hard as I can, narrowly avoiding the barrels and crates strewn across the street. Our footsteps bounce off the tall walls either side of us.

Why are the guards chasing us? Do they somehow think we're in league with Isidore?

Right now, there's no time to stop to consider what's going on. As I run, I'm only conscious of my burning lungs and aching legs, trying to match Elaric's furious pace. None of his physical prowess seems to have been lost with his magic.

We reach the end of the side street, skidding to a stop as it opens to a main road. Shouts echo to the left as the steel mass of guards race after us.

We turn the opposite way but are cut off as another patrol rushes over to investigate the commotion.

I glance around, searching for an escape route. But these houses are terraced, and the only other path I spot is an alley a few paces from the guards. There's no chance we'll reach it in time.

My shoulders tighten, as if to brace for a fight. Not that fighting will be any use. We're unarmed and severely outnumbered. We stand no chance of defeating them.

"Seize them!" shouts the captain.

There's little we can do as the guards surround us and grab our arms. I thrash out, frantically trying to pry myself free, but they clutch me tighter.

I meet Elaric's gaze, noticing the worry in his eyes. His rigid posture. Yet unlike me, he doesn't struggle in their grasp. It seems he recognizes the futility of our situation.

But I refuse to surrender. All I can think of is returning home, reuniting with Dalia. And these damned guards are standing in the way of that.

Despite my efforts to fend them off, they grip my arms so firmly behind my back I can't move even an inch.

With their hold on us secured, the guard captain turns to the rest of his men and declares, "Take them to the castle."

Chapter 41

The guards lead us out the city and up the steep road carved into the castle's cliffs, the streets vanishing below. We mostly walk in silence, aside from my attempts to demand an explanation for our arrest. Though I ask multiple times, none of the guards responds.

In the end, I opt to keep my mouth clamped shut, not bothering to waste any more breath. It's clear they're unwilling to yield, no matter how frequently I ask or how carefully I phrase my questions.

Since they're taking us to the castle, the king must wish to speak to us. I can only hope we're being summoned for an audience in his halls rather than in his dungeons. If he lets us first explain everything, maybe he'll believe the truth: that we have liberated Eruweth from Isidore's curse.

Then again, I'm not sure how well he'll take the news of three hundred years having passed. I doubt anyone has yet realized this, and unless we inform them, they likely won't know for weeks since Eruweth is so isolated from the rest of the world.

Perhaps it's best not to lead with this, lest it overshadow everything else we say. It is, after all, difficult to believe. Not so long ago, I too would have been dubious such a thing could be true. It's strange to think how I've grown accustomed to the extraordinary during these past few months.

The path to the castle is as long as it is steep. The higher we climb, the farther the castle seems. By the time we're halfway up, agony already scorches through my legs.

Gritting my teeth, I force myself to walk and ignore the pain as best I can.

Though resolve blooms in my chest, ascending these cliffs in my current fatigued state is near impossible. The sun has mostly risen from the horizon by now and its rays brush over me. They aren't even blisteringly hot, but sweat drips down my neck in rivulets.

With each stride, my legs grow sorer and stiffer. Until at long last, they cease to function.

If not for the guards' iron grip on me, my knees would give way, and I would collapse onto the gravelly road. Thanks to them, I'm kept suspended on the spot, unable to take another step forward.

"Keep moving," the captain hisses.

Shame brands itself across my cheeks. I urge my feet to move but they only manage half a step.

All in one day, I have battled a sea serpent, slain a witch, and almost lost the man I love. It seems my body is finally yielding to the claws of exhaustion tearing through me.

"Are you blind?" Elaric growls. "Can you not see she is too exhausted to walk?"

"We mustn't keep the king waiting," the captain snaps back.

The glacial fury in Elaric's glare is so cold it burns. "Then I will carry her," he seethes.

The captain flinches but meets his stare. "You will not."

Elaric edges toward me, but the guards block his path. Those escorting him grip him tighter.

"If she can't walk," the captain says, "then my men will carry her."

Mortifying as it would be for Elaric to carry me, at least he's my husband. I will not let a stranger haul me onto their shoulder, march me into the castle, and set me down before the king like an oversized bag of grain.

No. I am the Queen of Avella, and no matter how much my legs protest, I will walk into that throne room with my head held high.

I just need to tackle the rest of the road, step into the castle and talk to the king. Then I can collapse and succumb to sleep, granting my body the rest it desires.

I can do this.

Before any guards can lift me, I tip my chin upward. "I can walk perfectly well on my own, thank you."

The captain bristles at the sharpness in my voice but only replies with a curt grunt, jabbing his fingers toward the road and silently spurring our escort back into motion.

Elaric's eyes linger on me, clearly doubting my strength. I don't turn to look at him. Meeting his gaze risks him glimpsing the heaviness in my eyes and protesting to the guards again.

Pushing against taxed muscles, I concentrate on putting one foot in front of the other. I craft a portrait of Dalia in my mind, my brushstrokes so vivid that I can all but see her face reflecting upon the guards' gleaming steel armor.

Determination floods through my limbs, shaking away the numbness which has sunk into them and granting them renewed vigor.

I will return home. I will be reunited with my sister.

It feels like an age passes before we arrive at the summit. A deep sigh of relief shudders through my lips as I step beneath the enormous iron portcullis and into the castle's outer courtyard.

I pause, scanning over our surroundings and marveling at the intricately detailed statues of great birds and beasts. Scores of bright flowers flourish here in the courtyard, adding plenty more color to all the greenery.

The only castles I've ever stepped inside have been frozen or ruined, ghosts of their former selves, and so it's little wonder Eruweth's castle ensnares my attention. As I peer around, I can't help but wonder what the Crystal Palace will look like now the curse has lifted. Given how its size dwarfs Eruweth's castle, I imagine it must look even grander. And if the gardens aren't as colorful once thawed, I will persuade Elaric to plant countless rows of flowers. Having lived amid snow for three hundred years, I doubt he will need much convincing.

My examination of the courtyard is interrupted as the guards shove me forth, leading us further into the castle.

They escort us beneath ornate archways and up towering stone stairs toward the innermost part of the castle. As we pass, the servants stop to stare. I'm not sure what they must think of us. Do they take one look at our tattered clothing and believe us to be criminals? Or do they fear us, believing us to be involved in witchcraft?

I don't stand still for long enough to identify whether it is fear or disgust etched into their faces.

We reach the castle's great hall, and the guards heave open the doors, ushering us inside.

Our footsteps ring through the high, vaulted ceiling. Morning rays spill in through the mosaic windows, painting the gray stone walls with a tapestry of color.

Countless pillars line our path, leading the way to the dais at the far end of the hall. There, the king sits upon his throne. A gleaming crown perches atop his head, auburn waves framing his face. Several gray strands weave through his hair, and judging by both them and the lines creasing around his eyes, I wager he must be in his fifties.

The king doesn't look up as we approach. His attention stays on the mass huddled before his throne. It isn't until we stop that I realize what it is: Isidore's body.

While I know the witch is already dead, I can't stop my gut from clenching. Nor can I stop my hand from twitching toward the sword no longer in my possession.

"Your Majesty," the guard captain says, dropping to a deep bow. The others follow suit. Aside from the ones securing us, that is. They just bow their heads. Once the captain and the rest rise, he continues, "We've brought you those suspected to be involved with the witch."

Involved with Isidore? It's hard to repress my snort.

Our only involvement with her is her death, and it's ridiculous they think otherwise. Do our ragged clothes not provide enough evidence of our struggle?

At the captain's words, the king stirs from his vigil. His gaze drags across to us, though his expression remains carefully masked, neutrality veiling his thoughts. Somehow this proves more nerve-wracking than if he were to curl his lips at the sight of us. At least then we would understand precisely where we stood.

The king gestures for his guards to release us, and though they retreat a pace, their hands still hover near the hilts of their swords. As if fearing we may strike their king at any second.

As the king speaks, his voice echoes through the cavernous hall like the rumbling of thunder. "Witnesses report you were sighted at the center of the chaos engulfing this city."

I chew on my lip. I suppose there's no arguing that first point.

"There are also claims that another witch was present, besides this one." The king's focus drifts back to Isidore's lifeless body, her white robes bloodstained. "Reports state you were seen conversing with this unknown sorceress."

Again, neither I nor Elaric attempts to deny the king's statements. We cannot argue against the truth, even one so poorly understood.

"In one instant, Isidore threatens my city with endless winter," the king says, "and then the next, disorder erupts through our streets as frost recedes from our lands. Tell me the role you both played in this and tell me swiftly. With the hysteria spreading through Eruweth, I find my patience quickly waning."

"We killed her," I simply state. Steel edges my words as I meet his eyes. "Isidore cursed your kingdom, and then she cursed my husband, the King of Avella."

"The King of Avella," he repeats, leaning forth. His hands tighten on the throne's gilded arms as he examines Elaric. "That cannot be. I know King Theron of Avella well, yet you are not him."

"I am his son," Elaric says, unfazed. "My father has been dead for over three centuries."

At this, the king nearly tumbles from his throne but swiftly regains himself. A strangled sound escapes him, one somewhere between a scoff and a laugh. "Three centuries you claim? What a ridiculous tale!"

Elaric regards him steadily. "It is no tale but the truth. I am Elaric, Theron's second son. My elder brother, Caltain, died from disease many years before Isidore cursed me for killing her sister."

"If Theron died centuries ago," the king says, knuckles bleaching around his throne's arms, "then my kingdom . . . "

"Has slumbered under her spell all this time," I finish gently.

He slumps back in his throne, horror dawning in his eyes. "It has been mere moments since Isidore froze us . . . How can three whole centuries be lost?" He clasps his head in his hands as if battling inwardly with our words.

In that tense silence, unease ripples between the guards. But none dares to speak, to intrude upon our audience with their king.

At long last the king sighs, heavy as the truth now weighing upon him, and regards us once more. "If your words hold merit, then how did you defeat the witch? How did you arrive here? And what role does this other witch play?" His brow creases. "Might we fear her return?"

As I meet Elaric's eyes, he gives me a tight nod. Bracing myself, I return my attention to the king.

Then I tell him of our quest to break Elaric's curse, how Belinda demanded an elusive herb in exchange for the mythic Sword of Veliantis. I recount crossing kingdoms and sailing the seas to reach Eruweth, and battling Isidore against impossible odds.

As I speak, astonishment overtakes the suspicion upon the king's face. And when I finish, he releases a strained breath and sinks deeper into his throne, as if the weight of all we've endured presses down upon his shoulders.

When the king next meets my gaze, his voice is a murmur. "It seems I must offer my sincerest apologies for how you were brought before me."

"It is understandable," Elaric says. "Your kingdom was plunged into chaos, and the two of us were reported as being involved. It's natural you sought answers to restore order to your city."

"Nonetheless, Eruweth owes you an enormous debt, one we can never repay."

"No repayment is necessary," Elaric replies. "We pursued our own interests in coming here."

The king lowers his head. "From this day, Avella will have a loyal friend in Eruweth."

"And Eruweth will have our enduring friendship in return," Elaric vows.

The king studies us again and then says, "Though you waive repayment, I cannot in good conscience allow you to depart empty-handed."

Elaric goes to say something, probably to refuse him again, but I speak first.

"A ship," I blurt. "A ship is all we desire, and then you may consider all debts cleared between our kingdoms."

The king smiles. "Very well. A ship it shall be."

Chapter 42

Elaric spends the rest of the afternoon with the King of Eruweth, explaining all which has happened over the last three centuries.

As for me, I sleep.

The king bestows us his finest chambers, treating us as his most esteemed guests, and provides a change of clothes far more splendid than our tattered rags. He wastes little time in making our standing as the King and Queen of Avella known to his court.

And that means later in the evening, when he holds a banquet in our honor, there's no end to the countless nobles who approach us, offering earnest expressions of gratitude. Our only respite comes while dancing together at the hall's center. I keep Elaric there with me for as long as propriety allows.

When at long last the music and revelry fade, as well as our energy, we retire upstairs to our guest chamber, which comes equipped with the fluffiest pillows I've ever seen.

That night, before succumbing to sleep, I study Elaric's face while wrapped in his arms. Just yesterday I feared losing him forever. Now, having glimpsed such anguish, I will always cherish even simple moments like this: lying together with moonlight bathing us from the open windows, both of us too weary to get up to close the curtains and shut out the night's splendor.

"What is it?" Elaric murmurs. His fingers trace a meandering path from my shoulder to my hand.

"Just . . . " I falter, searching for a distraction from my true thoughts. Too many emotions swell within me, and I have no wish to burden this peaceful moment. "Still adjusting to your hair and eyes."

"Does it bother you?" Concern shadows his features.

I quickly shake my head. "Of course not. It'll just take me a while to adjust."

He hesitates before saying, "If I no longer please you, I shall understand."

"Don't be ridiculous!" I exclaim. "I married you for more than your hair color."

"Yes, to kill me."

I smack his shoulder.

His lips pull upward. "Too soon?"

"Much too soon."

"A pity," he says. "But I shall have my revenge by tormenting you throughout all our years together."

I arch a brow. "What was that about annulment?"

He meets my threat with far too much laughter.

"Oh, you think I'm joking?"

Elaric tackles me, pinning my wrists to the mattress. His eyes rake across me. "I know you're joking."

"If you insist," I say, struggling to restrain my smile.

"Then say it. Tell me you wish for our marriage to be dissolved." He twirls a lock of my hair, awaiting my response.

Despite my teasing, the pain of almost losing him is too raw. I can't voice such words, not even in pretense. Instead, I free my arms and embrace him fiercely.

Elaric stills, surprised by the sudden fervor, but then returns my desperate grasp.

"I love you," I whisper into his shoulder.

"I heard you before," he says softly, "when you thought me gone."

I squeeze my eyes shut. "I'm sorry it took this long for me to say."

"Don't be sorry," he whispers. "For so long, your heart harbored such hatred. And I too am at fault for concealing the truth about your sister, causing you great confusion." He pauses, his hold around me tightening. "But the past is in the past. I'm merely grateful to have earned your forgiveness and claimed even a fragment of your heart."

"All of it," I say, pressing his palm to my racing heart. "All of it belongs to you."

Elaric lifts my hand to his lips, grazing my knuckles in the softest kiss. "As is all of mine forever yours."

True to the king's word, a ship awaits us the following day.

By late morning, we board the vessel, and then Elaric and I stand side by side along the railing, his arm wrapped around my shoulders. Together, we watch as Eruweth's cliffs dwindle into the horizon.

While the voyage spans three pleasant days, each hour drags past like an anchor scraping the seabed. My heart yearns to see Avella's shores, to look upon my sister's face once more.

Day after day, I stand sentry at the bow, eyes scouring the horizon, willing the line between sea and sky to morph into familiar lands. Yet the endless wait persists, my patience constantly tested.

Until at long last, land emerges from the rolling waves.

I brace myself, wary of wishful thinking. But as we draw nearer, certainty stirs within. These shores can be none other than home.

The harbor in which we anchor is situated to the north-east of Avella. There, Elaric and I acquire a horse, and we ride onward together, leaving behind our ship and its crew.

My pulse pounds to the swift rhythm of our horse's hooves, and I cling to Elaric as we ride, burying my head against the back of his silken tunic. Every step closer to the palace feels a step farther away, until finally its mountain swells before us.

Elaric pulls our horse to a stop.

The fields surrounding the palace's mountain have always been starved of color but now wildflowers burst through the sea of green, petals of every hue under the sun. We stay there for a while, staring out at the landscape as the wind wisps through flowers and grass alike.

Enraptured by the tranquility ahead, I barely notice that Elaric is trembling.

"Are you all right?" I twist awkwardly to glimpse his face, but our angle restricts my view.

Elaric is slow to respond, transfixed by the mountain before us. Terrain once so bleak and foreboding now shines so bright and beckoning.

Eventually he says, "I never imagined . . . " He trails off, heaving a deep sigh. "Never did I dream of seeing the Summer Palace restored to its glory."

"It's a title well deserved."

"You ought to see these slopes in late spring," he says, nostalgia warming his voice, "when the wildflowers are even more abundant."

We linger a moment more before Elaric spurs our horse on. We climb the winding mountain road which leads to the palace at the very top.

As we ascend, the wind grows fiercer, causing the temperature to drop. Yet it's nowhere near as cold as the night Father and I traveled up here for the Midsummer Ball. Though it's been mere months, it feels a lifetime ago compared to all I've endured since.

I dig my nails into my palms at the thought of Father. After I reunite with Dalia, we will seek his whereabouts. Maybe Elaric can advise on how best to locate him. And perhaps curiosity alone will lure Father here when news spreads of Summer returning to the Crystal Palace, all traces of winter banished forevermore.

Summer Palace.

I suppose adjusting to that change will take as long as adjusting to Elaric's golden hair.

When we reach the palace's walls, I almost weep at the sight. Gone is all the ice, replaced with gleaming white stone that's so smooth and flawless it appears to be marble. Vibrant color now infuses everything: the verdant leaves adorning nearby trees, the flowers blooming from perfectly trimmed bushes.

As we stop before the gates, a guard calls down, "Who goes there?"

"The King of Avella," Elaric says, "and his queen."

There's a brief pause, and then a great rumbling as the gates swing open.

We ride into the courtyard, and Elaric dismounts. He holds out his hand, helping me down beside him.

Barely have our feet met the ground before guards swarm around us, their captain exclaiming: "Your Majesty! You have returned!"

Elaric surveys the men. "What have I missed during my absence?"

"Everything," the captain says, shaking his head in disbelief. "First the palace turned from frost to stone, and then hundreds of girls appeared from nowhere, flooding through the halls. But"—he eyes Elaric's golden hair—"I suspect Your Majesty may understand these mysteries more than any of us do."

"What of the girls?" Elaric asks. "Where are they now?"

"Confined to all the guests' and servants' chambers," the captain says. "We were unsure what to do and thought it best to detain them here until we received your orders."

"Release them immediately," Elaric commands. "And inform them that those who have no place else to go may stay here as our honored guests."

"I will see to it immediately," the captain says, gesturing to the other guards.

"Wait!" I call before they leave. "Were there any men among them as well?"

"There were." His brows pinch together. "They protested so greatly to being detained that we had to physically restrain them. We later recognized them as the men who broke into the palace several months ago and captured you, Your Majesty."

My heart skips a beat.

"Where are they now?" Elaric demands.

"We locked them in the dungeons for the time being."

"They are also to be freed," Elaric says. "Is that understood?"

"Yes, Your Majesty."

The guards hurry off as Elaric passes our horse to a servant. Then we start across the sunny courtyard to the steps leading into the rest of the palace.

But before we reach them, two voices cry out, "Milady! Milady!"

Kassia and Elona rush down the steps, throwing their arms around me.

"We knew you'd be back soon!" Kassia exclaims. "When the ice vanished, we knew you'd broken the king's curse and it'd be a matter of time before you returned."

"How are you feeling, milady?" Elona asks, examining me with great care. "You must be exhausted from traveling for so long. Were you at all hurt along the way?"

Grateful though I am for their warm welcome, I can't stop myself from rasping: "Dalia?"

"Your sister was one of the first to awaken," Kassia says.

I inhale sharply. My sister—awake!

"Where is she now?" My voice is the slightest of whispers, hesitant to breathe lest this dream dissolve.

"We placed her in your chamber for now," Elona explains, "as all the other rooms were full."

I turn to Elaric.

He gives me a nod and squeezes my hand. "Go to your sister. I will ensure Orlan and his men are freed."

Needing no further encouragement, I race up the steps, taking two at a time. My maids follow close behind.

When I reach the double doors leading to the inner palace, I shove them open with such force they tremble, earning me several startled gasps from the servants inside.

Though I've traipsed the palace's halls countless times, they're such a stark contrast to what I remember that I temporarily lose my bearings.

Numerous portraits of both people and landscapes offer far more color than I've ever seen here. Mosaic floor tiles form geometric patterns down the corridor, and the pillars lying along the walls sweep up into arched ceilings. Everything is gilded with lavish filigree detailing.

The palace's transformation is even greater than I imagined and glimpsing it steals my breath. Later, I plan to inspect every room and discover how everywhere has changed, but right now my curiosity is overshadowed by my burning need to see Dalia.

I hurry to my chamber, taking one or two wrong turns along the way in my confusion, but my maids are quick to correct my path.

Servants swarm the passageways, and the palace is busier than I've ever witnessed. Though it's little wonder with three hundred unexpected guests to accommodate. Every servant must have been running around non-stop since the Summer Brides awakened.

Even in the heart of the palace, where it is the busiest, I don't slow. The servants must all see the urgency upon my face, in my every stride, since they all wordlessly step out of my path.

By the time I reach my room, my palms are clammy and my breaths are so ragged they burn my chest. Hands shaking, I reach for the doors, but then pause.

Despite all my haste until now, I just end up standing there, staring at the doors. My mind reels with a thousand thoughts all at once.

For so long I've dreamed of this day, and now it's finally here, I fear I'll push open the doors and be greeted by an empty room. Or perhaps by a Dalia who is as frozen as the last time I saw her.

Three years is such a long time, and she may not recognize me. Maybe she will be furious I entered the Crystal Palace to avenge her. Maybe—

My chaotic thoughts are interrupted by Kassia squeezing my shoulder, warmth blossoming through me. Elona raps on the door, the sound so deafeningly loud it almost eclipses my relentless heartbeat.

If there's a response to Elona's knocking, I don't hear it.

In the next instant, she's shoving aside the door and Kassia is ushering me in.

I stumble inside, half in hope and half in fear of what I will find.

My gaze sweeps across the room, slowly processing the spectrum of color which transforms everything.

All air empties my lungs as my attention snags on the figure settled at the end of my bed, skirts pooled across the bright damask sheets.

Silken dark waves cascade down her back. Her delicate face fills with surprise as she turns to me.

"Adara," Dalia breathes.

Hearing the voice I thought forever lost pierces my heart, shattering the trance which has engulfed me. My lifeless limbs stir. Sense floods back.

I dart forth, desperate to prove she's real and not a figment of my imagination soon to be snatched away again. The rest of the world fades around us.

Dalia bolts from the bed, crossing the chamber to meet me at the center. Her fingers lace through mine, warm and solid.

And she is real.

I can only stare at her, hundreds of words crowding my tongue yet none forming.

I tremble as her slender arms wrap around me, as she pulls me into a forceful hug. My whole body is so weightless, I'm certain I'd crash to the floor if not for her firm embrace.

"Oh, Adara," she murmurs, stroking my hair with aching familiarity. "My brave and ferocious sister."

"I missed you," I choke. Tears flood my cheeks, dampen her hair. "Every second, every day, I missed you so much."

"I'm here now," she says, squeezing me tighter.

When at last Dalia releases me, I wipe away my tears with the back of my hand, struggling to believe this moment is real.

Linking her arm through mine, she guides us to sit cross-legged upon the bed, where we're surrounded by countless embroidered blankets.

"How much you've grown since I last saw you!" Dalia exclaims with a laugh. "And your maids tell me you're now our queen? Imagine that, my little sister, the Queen of Avella!"

I just shake my head, overwhelmed by her really being here. By us really having this conversation.

"They told me fragments of what happened," Dalia says, smile growing, "but I've waited to hear the full tale straight from you. So, tell me every last detail of your adventures, dear sister. All of it, from the beginning."

Swallowing hard against welling emotion, I lean closer.

And then I tell her everything, right from the very start.

Epilogue

The trees blazed with the vivid hues of fall. As the carriage rattled down the winding forest road, crimson leaves broke free and blew past the window. Elaric couldn't help but watch as they drifted by. Seeing how Adara didn't stare out even half as much as he did, he supposed such a thing would look unremarkable to anyone else. But not to him. He had been gazing out the entire morning since leaving the palace. It was a sight he hadn't seen for an eternity, and he'd almost forgotten the season existed.

Intending to make the journey to Netham and back in one day, the carriage they'd chosen was on the smaller side, and so there was barely enough room for them both on the cushioned bench. Shortly after departing, he'd risen and offered to sit on the other one, but she'd grabbed his arm and insisted for him to remain where he was. As Elaric had only suggested shifting seats for her benefit, he'd made no protest. Besides, he preferred staying close beside her, cramped though it was.

In the weeks since returning home, Elaric regretted they hadn't been able to spend more time together. The palace had been in a state of chaos when he'd arrived, with those hundreds of recently awakened girls. Soon after resolving that matter, his schedule had filled with a steady stream of visitors—mostly elderly lords who hadn't set foot in the Crystal Palace for years, due to their fears of its chill on their ailing health. But it seemed the palace's transformation and the truth of his curse had lured some even from their deathbeds.

So, it was only the nights which Adara and him had to themselves. And those hours usually passed by in a blissful flurry. Not that he minded.

Still, there was much to be said for simply sitting quietly in each other's company, and he dearly hoped that when the novelty of recent events wore off, they'd share more of these peaceful moments.

With that thought, Elaric reached for her hand, lacing his fingers through hers. His gaze lingered on her for some time before she noticed and met his eyes.

"What is it?" she asked.

"Just looking at you," he murmured.

Heat rose in Adara's cheeks at his words. How he loved it when she blushed.

The carriage rolled on through the forest, and he didn't release her hand. After a while, his attention shifted to the bouquet which perched on the bench opposite them. The reminder of what was to come caused the tension within him to coil ever tighter. He instead tried to focus on Adara beside him—the delicate warmth of her fingers around his. The triumphant grin she'd worn that morning, bursting into his chambers and clutching the same bouquet now across from them. She hadn't arranged it alone. Her sister had also woken early to help select the roses, the two of them accompanied by a flock of maids. Elaric was surprised such a simple task had required so many. But he hadn't dampened Adara's enthusiasm by saying so.

Yet the closer they drew to Netham, the harder it became for him to ignore the trepidation churning within his gut. His nerves grew tauter with every passing moment.

And then, when the city's stone walls finally came into view, nothing could distract from the nightmarish images which echoed through his mind. Though they belonged to centuries past, they played out before him as if they'd happened mere hours ago.

Releasing her hand, Elaric leaned forth to shut the curtain on his side. Then he reached over Adara, closing the one beside her as well.

With both drawn, the carriage dimmed, faint light penetrating the silk. A golden glow rimmed the fabric's edges, where it didn't fully cover the window.

Frowning, Adara turned to him. To his surprise, she made no comment. Perhaps she would assume he wanted more privacy during their ride through the crowded streets.

Elaric inhaled slowly, forcing his body to relax into the bench. He listened to the clatter of hooves, the scrape of wheels on stone, the mutters of the guards escorting them.

And for the briefest of moments, his uneasiness began to retreat.

Then the cries erupted.

Every muscle in his body seized tight once more, his hand twitching toward his sword.

The shouts were so chaotic that they were almost indecipherable. He could only just make out fragments such as "king!" and "queen!"

His stomach lurched.

All he could think of was the bloodshed during his last visit here. The demands for his head. One woman claiming the cold which had seized her son last winter was his fault.

Adara's eyes seared into him.

He didn't turn, barely daring to breathe.

Perhaps the dimness would disguise the tension in his shoulders.

But then she said, "Are you all right?"

"Yes." He didn't intend to say it through clenched teeth. He swallowed, banishing the strain in his voice as best he could. "I'm fine."

He could still feel her gaze on him and knew she was far from convinced, but she didn't press him further.

After that, Elaric forced his body to ease lest she question him again.

Yet that attempt lasted only minutes. The carriage slowed to a crawl, while the shouts roared louder outside.

If the people demanded his life, a dozen guards wouldn't stop them.

As much as he'd hated his curse, there was something to be said for the power—the invincibility—it had provided. With a mere thought he'd frozen hundreds of soldiers, arrows useless against his power. That rebellion had been instantly crushed.

Now mortal, he was powerless, and he loathed it. What use was steel against these masses? How would he protect Adara?

What if she perished because of him?

Despair washed over him. Magic had flowed through him that wretched day, yet he'd still failed to save Cerise . . .

His throat tightened at the memory.

Clearly his discomfort showed more than he realized, since Adara was already reaching for the curtain near her and pulling it open, flooding the carriage with light.

She gestured to the clustered, shouting crowd around their carriage. "They're only curious. Many here have never seen you, and even those who have will know of your changed appearance and be desperate for a glimpse themselves."

At the mention of his appearance, Elaric studied her face carefully. Since leaving Eruweth, this was the first time she'd mentioned it. Like then, he worried that her opinion of him had shifted. After all, the transformation of his appearance was so stark. If he couldn't adjust to his own reflection, how could he expect others to?

Granted, he did now look more like the noble lord she might have married if not for him. But he no longer looked like the man she'd wed—the man she'd somehow fallen in love with—and he couldn't decide whether it was a good or bad thing. Day and night, it burdened him.

Steeling himself as best he could, Elaric said, "I know."

Adara narrowed her eyes. "Remember our conversation?"

Somehow the screaming citizens seemed less terrifying than his wife.

"There is nothing to talk about," he said.

Adara sighed so heavily that her disappointment speared his heart.

Only a week ago, he'd made a promise. Hiding the truth had nearly cost them their marriage once and so, from now on, they'd vowed to always lay everything bare before each other. No more lies, no more secrets.

Yet he couldn't have this conversation right now. Not mere minutes before facing Cerise's grave and the memories which haunted him to this day.

So, he took her hand in his and looked deeply into her eyes, hoping she could see the sincerity within them. "Later," he vowed.

Her expression softened, and she leaned up, kissing his cheek. Her warmth helped mend the fractures in his resolve.

"Don't shoulder everything alone," Adara said, her voice low. She gave his shoulder a gentle squeeze to emphasize her point, and Elaric had little doubt she'd feel the tension within it. "Whatever you're feeling, I'm here to share it with you—always."

Perhaps she had a point. Already he could feel the weight clinging to his chest lifting.

He tilted her head back and kissed her the way he knew she liked, the way which always had her moaning and arching into him. And as he did it now, in a slow, deep kiss, with his teeth grazing her bottom lip, he heard that telltale sound from the back of her throat. It turned his blood molten.

It took great restraint not to pull the curtain closed and take her right there and then, inside this carriage. How easily she ignited him. As he gazed down at her, with her glimmering eyes and swollen lips, his troubles retreated far into the distance.

Tempting though it was, he decided not to cause all of Netham to witness him claiming his queen. If only for Adara's dignity.

Elaric wasn't sure how he made it all the way through Netham without making some very questionable decisions. And while his mood had lifted from when they'd first entered the city, it fell again the moment their carriage drew to a halt.

A knock sounded on the door.

"We have arrived, Your Majesties," a guard called.

Elaric didn't move. It was as if he was chained in place, his gaze fixed on the bouquet opposite him.

Adara's fingers brushed over his cheek and then nudged his head toward her, so he had no choice but to look at her. She cradled his face in her hands as she murmured, "I'll be with you. Every step of the way."

Rising slowly, she retrieved the flowers. Her hand clasped his as she waited for him to stir.

How long he remained shackled there, Elaric did not know. But at last he slid from the bench, following her out the carriage. She kept hold of his hand, even when they were outside.

His first steps across the grass were hesitant, half-expecting frost to emerge underfoot. Since his curse had lifted, he'd hardly left the palace, only venturing into the gardens briefly.

Yet no ice came. He expected that would remain startling for the foreseeable future.

His gaze slid across to the crumbling castle walls before them. All he could see were the spears which had lined the castle's gates and what had lain upon them.

His breath faltered, limbs turning to stone.

Adara squeezed his hand, tugging him back to the present. Though she didn't push him onward, it was enough to dispel the shadows for now.

Elaric managed a step forth, then another, until they passed beneath the portcullis, forever drawn open.

The castle was even more decayed than reported. Stone was eroded to grit, and weeds swallowed fallen archways whole. Despite the war raging here on his last visit, at least it had resembled a castle.

Elaric quickened his pace, praying the gravestones hadn't met the same fate. That they wouldn't be toppling over in worn fragments, engravings lost to wind and rain.

Adara matched his urgent strides, her hand still clasping his.

Finally, they reached the gardens, which were so terribly overgrown they should instead be called a forest. Elaric's pulse raced as he climbed the tiers leading to the pond.

When the headstones appeared before him, the relief which shuddered through him was so forceful it nearly drove him to his knees.

All stood upright, and while some edges had chipped, each inscription was still legible.

The grass was also more tamed here, with wildflowers providing some color to temper the gloom.

While it wasn't the resting place his sister deserved, he was grateful it wasn't the wreck he'd envisioned.

For a long while, they stood in solemn silence. Distant birdcalls rang through the trees as wind rippled through the grass surrounding his boots.

Though he'd longed to say farewell to Cerise and her family for so many years, right now he didn't quite know what to say. Such eloquent sentiments didn't flow naturally for him. Adara, on the other hand, likely would have fallen to her knees and unleashed every shred of heartache within.

He didn't know if it was the lingering effects of his frozen curse or if he'd always been this way. Either way, he wished there was something he could say to Cerise, rather than staring numbly at her grave.

Adara offered him the bouquet, and gratitude swelled within as he accepted it. This gesture had been her idea entirely, and he was thankful to have an offering instead of mere silence.

Elaric laid the flowers on Cerise's grave, placing a hand atop the cool stone.

When he closed his eyes, her face appeared amid the shadows.

If only he'd arrived sooner that day. If only she and her family had been spared.

Elaric was no fool. He knew that with his curse, he'd have been forced to say goodbye to her one day, but he wished more than anything that one of her children had survived to continue her line. He'd have treated every descendant as his own. What he would give for some trace of her to live on in this world.

Opening his eyes, he stared at the sky, at the clouds sailing through it.

For three hundred years, these regrets had tormented him, but he knew he could cling to them no longer. The past could not be changed. He could only focus on the future Adara and him would share, and cherish every single moment.

Because the one thing he'd learned throughout these long years was that life was much too short, merely a fleeting candle. So easily and so quickly extinguished.

The graves before him now were tangible proof of that.

He released the stone and stepped back, though his attention didn't leave the graves.

Cerise had never been one to wallow, and she'd have no patience were she here now. So instead, he thought of something which would have made her smile.

"What do you think of the name 'Cerise?'"

He must have spoken softly, for it took Adara a moment to realize he addressed her.

Closing the distance between them, she gripped his hand tightly. "If we have a girl, we'll call her Cerise." The promise burned in her eyes.

The corners of his lips rose. "Do you hear that?" he said to the stone. "You had best hope we have a girl."

Adara wrinkled her nose. "I hope so too. I'd hate to have only boys."

With a chuckle, Elaric said, "My sister often bemoaned having three. Each pregnancy, she hoped the next would be a girl."

"I wish I could have met her."

"It's for the best. The two of you would have proven a dangerous pair."

Her eyes glinted. "I take it she didn't dote on her baby brother then?"

"Not at all. She and Caltain took turns pulling the worst tricks on me."

"What kinds of tricks?"

"I'll tell you a few on the way home."

Adara nodded. Then after a moment said, "Before I forget, my father will expect a son named after him."

"Will a middle name suffice?"

She shook her head.

"It's not a problem," he said.

It couldn't be. He was already on such shaky ground with her father. While the Duke held his tongue out of respect for Elaric's station, distrust lingered in his eyes. And Elaric couldn't blame him. He'd stolen both daughters, one for three long years, and the Duke had nearly frozen inside the palace's dungeons. He was thankful Adara had stopped him through her stubbornness that day.

Elaric wasn't sure how long it would take for him to earn the Duke's forgiveness, if ever. Earlier in the week, Elaric had suggested gifting him with gold or land, but Adara had only said her father cared far more for family than he did for power, and such gifts would risk causing further insult.

Her suggestion had instead been for them to visit her father regularly in Brindale, starting as soon as possible. Dalia would be returning home in a few days, and so it made sense for the two of them to escort her home.

He held no illusions that it would take countless visits over the years. But for Adara, he would do all he could to mend these fractures.

Elaric wrapped his arms around her, drawing her close as he stared at the gravestones. The wind tugged on the bouquet, causing a few petals to loosen, and they scattered into the pond ahead. He watched them drift across the rippling surface, their bright colors a stark contrast to the murky water.

And then, at long last, he kissed her cheek and whispered, "Let's go home."

ABOUT THE AUTHOR

Holly Rose has been obsessed with high fantasy since the age of 5, when she first watched The Fellowship of the Ring (her parents raised her right). After realizing she couldn't become an elf, she decided to start writing about them instead. She also grew up on World of Warcraft and copious amounts of anime.

She was born and bred in Wales, United Kingdom, where she currently spends her days terrorizing teenagers with mathematical equations (and sometimes teaching them useful things). When she gets home from school, her real work with writing about magic and mayhem can begin.

You can find her online at:
http://hollyrosebooks.com/
https://www.instagram.com/hollyrosebooks
https://www.facebook.com/hollyrosebooks

Milton Keynes UK
Ingram Content Group UK Ltd.
UKHW040825250224
438359UK00004B/149